# The Hiding Game

Also by Naomi Wood

*The Godless Boys*
*Mrs. Hemingway*

Naomi Wood

# The Hiding Game

PICADOR

First published 2019 by Picador
an imprint of Pan Macmillan
20 New Wharf Road, London N1 9RR
Associated companies throughout the world
www.panmacmillan.com

ISBN 978-1-5098-9278-5

9 8 7 6 5 4 3 2

A CIP catalogue record for this book is available from the British Library.

Typeset by Palimpsest Book Production Ltd, Falkirk, Stirlingshire
Printed and bound by CPI Group (UK) Ltd, Croydon, CR0 4YY

Visit **www.picador.com** to read more about all our books
and to buy them. You will also find features, author interviews and
news of any author events, and you can sign up for e-newsletters
so that you're always first to hear about our new releases.

for Joan, Ari and Ed

'Again it is astonishing how defencelessly
everything collapses.'
Victor Klemperer, *I Shall Bear Witness:
The Diaries, 1933–41*

# 1

## England

So: Walter König is dead. Irmi called with the news in the middle of the night: she sounded upset, and couldn't understand why I wasn't. 'He was your friend, Paul,' she said. 'How can you feel nothing?'

I said I didn't know.

Tricksy Walter, unlovely Walter: he was no more a friend to me than Jenö, really, who had disappeared decades ago in London. What should I care that Walter was dead? His life was no more than easy treacheries and lazy spite, and I'd washed my hands of him when I'd left Berlin for good.

I felt nothing; it was hardly a surprise.

Half of our group are gone now: Walter, from stroke; Kaspar, his plane shot down over Alexandria, and then there is Charlotte, dead in the beech forest, not five miles north of Weimar, where this story begins.

I think of Charlotte every day. Memories of her are all electricity. I can be sitting at a canvas, brush poised, ready to paint, when I am strung with a pain I do not know what to do with, even after all this time: nearly thirty years have passed since her death; forty, since we lived together in Berlin. Now she comes to me in dreams, over lunch, when I'm in the bath; I see her at the loom, strolling the Tiergarten in her men's clothes, and finally, before the Bauhaus raid, saying she would not leave Germany.

I would rather Walter dead three times over than to have lost her, but there; that's a dreamt-up notion. The truth is, I hold Walter accountable for her death. He could have asked Ernst Steiner to spring her from the camp; he could have talked to the right people. It was within his power. Perhaps it was even the last move in his stratagem: to let her die, in the clearing before the forest began again, where we had camped during so many summers, before we'd cycle down to the city, watching the blinking negative of the rushing forest take us back to Weimar, when all six of us were together in our first golden years at the Bauhaus.

My friends would all have different accounts of what happened to us, and I can't deny my subjectivity. I know the story is lit now by later sorrow: my happiness glows stronger, and grief has perhaps given more depth to the harder times. Sometimes, I envy my younger self, at others, the past is a dereliction.

This is my account of what happened to us in the 1920s: a decade of resplendence and tragedy. But if I am to tell this story, then I can't tell it slant. Now that Walter is dead, I will give an account of him; but I must also give an account of myself. This is my confession. A confession I haven't yet made to anyone, and one I haven't even really admitted to myself. For all those years I blamed

Walter, there have been as many – more – when I have put aside my knowledge of what I did, and didn't do, to save Charlotte.

A friend of mine once said that a secret is truly abject when it can never be voiced; its shame buys its silence. All this time, I have kept my silence, but here it is. There was a moment when Charlotte and I were living together in Berlin, when I, too, could have saved her. It was Walter who gave me the choice, and I looked at all the evidence, and then – methodically, carefully – I chose not to act. It was not a fleeting decision over the course of minutes or even hours. I came to my decision over two weeks.

If Walter killed her, then I killed Charlotte too.

# WEIMAR, 1922

# 2

## Weimar

Sparkling year! Our first year at the Bauhaus was one to envy. Back then, there were six of us: Walter and Jenö; Kaspar and Irmi; me and Charlotte. Right from the beginning, those were always the pairings. We were eighteen, and Jenö (a Hungarian diminutive of 'Eugene' he had won from a favourite uncle) was twenty when we began our preliminary studies, and it was at the Bauhaus that we learnt everything we were later to rely on: about colour and form, texture and materiality. It was here we learnt about an object's very nature: the paper-essence of paper; the timbery-ness of wood; the strength of rope and string. But most importantly, perhaps, it was here that we learnt to fast, and where we learnt how our fasts might trick from our hungry selves a world of shimmer; havoc; pleasure.

From the first day of the new semester Charlotte was fascinating to me. I met her in the school canteen over lunch. September light tumbled the shadows of the trees onto the long tables and so her skin too was a canvas where the day leapt and swayed. I thought it was a trick

7

of the day's turbulence that made her gaze so impossible to read; it was reserved but also flamboyant.

I sat at one end of the table with Walter and Jenö: I'd met them in the Director's introductory class, and immediately liked both of their unabashed desires to be my friend. Charlotte was at the other end with Irmi and Kaspar. Here we were: stalled in light; friendship on the brink of things.

Walter and Jenö were talking about where their siblings had been during the war. I didn't really want to talk about my brother Peter – it was too painful and too complicated – and anyway Charlotte was distracting enough. Her bright blonde bob was cut severely along her jaw. Her blink was languorous and slow. She had lovely green eyes that made her look both serene and empty. More boy than woman, she was thin, her bones razorish at wrist and collar. She didn't smile much.

When Walter and Jenö left to visit the city – Walter wanted to see Goethe's house – I stayed at the table where Charlotte sat alone, finishing a green apple, which was all the more vividly coloured in proximity to her eyes.

'You're in Master Itten's class,' I said.

She blushed, but then said, 'Aren't we all?'

I asked if I could sit down; she gestured to the chair.

'What's your name?'

'Charlotte,' she said.

There was a trace of an accent to her German. 'Where are you from, Charlotte?'

'Prague. What's yours?' she asked. 'Your name, I mean.'

'Paul. Paul Beckermann.'

You can sometimes feel such an intensity of happiness that it threatens to shut you down. I wondered if my head was about to smack the table in sleep: if that was the only way to endure this blonde girl's teeth. There is a word in German: *Herzenslust*. Heart's content. I had met mine. 'I'm going for a walk. Do you want to come?'

She smiled. Such loveliness! As I walked with her, I thought: don't tell her you love her. Not within minutes of meeting her.

We walked to the Ilm Park and Charlotte told me of home: she had already been to Charles University in Prague, an institution approved of by her mother. Here, they copied marble busts and made drawings of the musculature of life models – as if, Charlotte said, with throwaway disdain, they were surgeons preparing to cut people open. Her parents were furious when she had transferred to the Bauhaus. They wanted her to paint family portraits; better yet, find someone good to marry. 'My father's still not talking to me,' she said, as we came to the river. 'He's quite angry. He thought he'd already secured my future. He's bitter really; not just angry.'

Grave girl, walking alongside me in the parkland; perhaps I should have left just then: got shot of her, and gulped down the air while I was still, that day, Lotti-less.

'But the Bauhaus!' she said, a touch of panic in her voice. 'And what on earth shall we do here!'

'I don't know,' I said, because in a funny way the question hadn't really occurred to me. All I knew was that ever since I'd seen Kirchner's *Bathers at Moritzburg*, I wanted to be nowhere else but here.

'I live over there.' She pointed to a pink building. 'Up in the rafters. Next to the library. You can just see the Rococo Hall.'

'And the palace.'

'And the palace. It smells of shit from the stables.'

We walked past Goethe's garden house, pale blue, with its roof pitched in an inverted V, and further on some students worked at an allotment. They waved. Somehow they already knew we were part of them. Walter and Jenö came into view at the iron bridge and we followed the river back to them. The Ilm moved slowly; on its top were circling eddies, as if many things had been dropped in there. Up on the bridge Jenö smiled at us; maybe he was already working things out.

'Do you think you could fish in this river?' he said.

'Probably.'

The tops of the trees were cut off in the water's reflection. It was still warm and we bathed our feet in the shallows where the whips grew. Walter didn't join us; he couldn't swim, he said, as he watched the eddies with mistrust. We talked mostly of home; where we had come from, and the small lives we had escaped. None of us had known the war. We knew our good fortune, and in the ripening day our lives felt golden.

We tramped back to school for more introductory classes that afternoon, all of us eager to spot Masters Klee and

Kandinsky, the stars of the department. Many of us had come because of them, but it turned out neither had much to do with first years, or, as we were known, the Bauhaus babies.

Instead, it was Master Itten, a Swiss painter, who took us for our first lesson. He was dressed in a ruby robe and had a shaved head; he wore round spectacles that in certain lights obscured his eyes. When my parents had come to visit the school they had nodded genially along with the Director, dressed in his architect's collar and tie, because they knew this type of man. I wished they could now see Master Itten, who had the look of a monk in whose eyes burned a devout fire. Through the workshop window we could see the beech forest a few miles off: a shimmer of pleasant green.

Master Itten said little by way of introduction. He explained that there wasn't enough money for chairs, and that we were to sit on the floor. He arranged us in groups, and then set up some books and a lemon in each group, and told us to make our first impressions of the still life. Then he left.

At school I had always been adept at verisimilitude, and I was so engrossed in the task that I hadn't realised how much time had gone when Master Itten returned. I showed my sketchbook to Charlotte and she nodded, though she was coy about showing me hers. Itten took a look at everyone's sketches, and he moved so quietly that I wondered whether he was even wearing shoes. Everyone was tense. My books were straight, the lemons plump; but we were at the Bauhaus, we couldn't have got it right.

'No,' he finally said, confirming all our suspicions. He took one of the lemons to the front and opened the fruit with a penknife so that the scent reached us immediately. When he bit into it the room cringed. 'How can you draw a lemon without first tasting its flesh? Your whole *body* is involved in drawing. Your mouth, your gut, your lungs. If you think it's only about the hand and the eyes and the brain, you're dead, and the picture's dead too. A lemon is not just a lemon: it *is* its acidity, its astringency, its pith, its seed chambers and pyramid interior. It's not yellow skin wrapped around air, or pencil strokes on paper. The lemon is an odalisque. You must seduce it. You must *be* seduced by it.'

He threw the fruit and Walter caught it.

Itten began to pace, working up his theme. 'The sketch is not preparatory work. The sketch *is* the end. Vasari knew this: what we do when we sketch is an act of *furor*; a passion. Only when Leonardo had paper, not papyrus, was he able to not just sketch, but freely invent. Renaissance thinkers asked the artist to seek balance between *decorum* and *licenza*. The sketch is all licence, because the sketch allows for all possibilities: that the lemon is a breast, a mouth, a tumour, or that the lemon' – he opened out his hands, palm up – 'that the lemon is not even really there. Begin again. But with *licenza*,' he said, smacking his hand against the table: '*Licenza! Licenza! Licenza!*'

The Master watched as we began feeling up the lemon: smelling it, peeling it, tasting it. Later, he put his hands on Charlotte's shoulders. 'You still have sleep in your neck,' he said. 'You must release it.'

It was dark by the time we arrived for our welcome party. Since lunchtime the cafeteria's windows had been covered with old newsprint. Townspeople tried to see what was going on inside but there wasn't much light from the edges. As Walter and I drew closer, we heard strange music inside. 'This,' he said, 'is it,' though I had no idea what 'it' might mean. I remembered Charlotte's tremulous voice when she had said 'And what on earth shall we do here!' and I wondered if this evening might provide her with an answer.

To get into the cafeteria we had to crawl through a tunnel made from a beer barrel. Inside, the other students had painted motifs on the wallpaper: red squares, blue circles, and yellow triangles; I already knew these as the colours and shapes of the Bauhaus. Scraps of cloth and threads hung from the ceiling. A trumpeter was playing some tuneless *beeps* and *bops*.

We were a few drinks in when Master Itten reappeared. Now he was dressed in what looked like mayoral robes, with a Napoleonic hat and turned-up Turkish shoes. He tapped his glass, and the shuffling of others moved Charlotte over to me.

'The graduates of this year have dressed me in these ridiculous vestments.' There was laughter from the crowd, who were mostly dressed in black slacks and shirts, for the men and women both. 'But there is a point. This morning the Director talked to you about the practicalities of your first year. You will learn about texture, light, colour, temperature, and form. This applies to all things, not just paint and charcoal but wire, stone, paper. From here on in you will only draw and paint when you understand the material. Production is the apex, but we will take a long time to get there.

'Now the reason I am standing here, like this' – there was a whooping from one side of the room, and some uncomfortable shifting from the suited Director – 'and the reason you had to enter crawling, like toddlers, is that you – we – are here to *play*. There are those outside this room who cannot stand the notion of adults playing, but this is the operative approach. Play. Risk. Experimentation. Draughtsmanship. Study. Observation. *Licenza*. Putting your tongue in the lemon; call it what you will. Every day I want you to spend a part of it doing nothing but day-dreaming. To many people that is a maddening thought. Do it. It is a radical act to do nothing.

'What we will do here – and I urge you to learn this early on – is disposable. Indeed, in many of my classes, I will urge you to jettison what you have made. Our animating principle is not originality, it is methodology. Thinking *is* making; and making is thinking. If you abide by this principle, you cannot fail to enjoy yourself. Creativity is, in its babiest incarnation, freely associative, lawless, and chaotic. That is all. My voice sounds like a drum at the best of times. May God save the Bauhaus babies!'

A cheer in the room, and the sentiment was echoed all round, even by the Director, who looked more like an accountant than an architect. Then a student called for all the preliminary students to line up.

'Brilliant, wasn't he?' Charlotte said beside me.

'Yes,' I said, though I knew I hadn't really understood his point, 'quite brilliant.'

We queued and crawled outside. Then we marched in single file toward the Frauenplan, where there was a fountain piping water from a creature – half fish, half man – and cafes lining the perimeter. Each new student was then brought forward, turned around, and had to fall backward into the outstretched arms of two others. With a squeak from the trumpet, another student would then baptise them as a Bauhaus baby with the fountain's 'holy water'. The townspeople watched us as if we were deranged, and the waiters stamped toward us, as they would have to scatter stray dogs.

The organisers took no notice. The Director had long ago disappeared, but then so had Master Itten.

I felt Charlotte shifting as we watched the baptisms of our new friends: Jenö and Walter, then Irmi and Kaspar. When it was nearly her turn she seemed unexpectedly tense, and I watched as she walked to the fountain with some misgiving. Indeed, when she fell her arms shot upward, and she stumbled and stayed upright. In that moment she seemed terribly exposed and I knew the other students noticed too. Then she had to fall again. The priest-student anointed her forehead, the trumpeter played a *toot*, and Charlotte went back to standing. When she was done she walked toward one of the waiters who had stopped at the edge of his cafe, and she got so close to him that eventually, at the last moment, he was forced to step away.

# 3

## Weimar

Weimar froze that winter. Iced over, the city enchanted. When it was dark, you could roam around the cobbled streets looking in at the ancient rooms lit orange, and it was easy to dream up secrets and potions, witches and hobgoblins. The mullioned windows split the warm light like a wedding diamond. The frost made everything glimmer.

Weimar will always be a burnished city to me. North of the Bauhaus, south of the beech forest, it was the prettiest place I'd ever seen. There was hardly a plain building around; hardly a residence which hadn't housed a poet or philosopher. Women, angels and lions adorned the houses so that Weimar (especially when the Christmas lights illuminated the upper tiers) always had an extra set of eyes upon us.

Though its people did not like us, were suspicious of us, sometimes even hated us, I loved the city: the classical houses enamelled in pinks, lemons, limes; the smell of the chestnuts cooking on the coals; the Ginkgo which stank in summer; the greening statues of Goethe and Schiller by the theatre where the republic's constitution had been signed three years before. (Though even in rich Weimar there were men hunched in thin coats, pockets stuffed with meaningless money; soup kitchens, dole queues, begging women, children scavenging. It was just hard to see; I was so spellbound by all the other beauty.)

I don't know how the Bauhaus had ended up here; it didn't really make sense that it would choose as its home such a conservative place. Still, we were far enough from its centre to be mostly ignorable. The school was in a yellow *Jugendstil* building with neither a ribbon nor cherub about it. Mostly the Bauhaus was made up of gridded windows just above eye level, so that you could only see the top of everyone's head, and you had to divine who it was from their haircut alone.

That winter, we were all Master Itten's. We had nothing to do with any other staff: we were his to be confected. Our lessons took place in the big ateliers, and it was where we investigated the nature of our materials. The Master was always challenging us to see more intensively: he was obsessed with the purification of vision. 'The world is only replica until it is truly seen,' he'd say, as he padded around the workshop barefoot. 'Pain will only make you see more beauty.'

I was still waiting to understand what this meant; Charlotte and the others had a quicker grasp of all this. At home in Dresden I had been lauded by all my teachers for my painterly skill, and it was confusing not to be picked out as especially talented. But that, I suppose, was why I had come. Or at least, that's what I told myself.

As a teacher, Itten's composure was occasionally interrupted by strong emotions. One time, for example, we were asked to paint our impression of the Somme. Max, who had been there, drew exhausted men with bayonets. But Willem, who had been nowhere near France, punctured his paper with his pencil six times. The Master had preferred Willem's, and hadn't even really looked at poor Max's figurative display.

Lessons from the lemon continued. We tasted glass with our tongues; arranged textures of leather, furs and cans; scratched each other with steel wool; smelt the difference between lumber shavings and polished driftwood. Only in the last part of the day would we get to drawing. And when we did, we drew standing up, holding our breath, to music, after meditation, with the left hand, with the right, and, our breath puffing in the freezing school, after gymnastics. Just to see what might come out of it.

In the new semester I felt a constant pleasure of preoccupation. How should I please Charlotte? How could I make her smile? How could I help her in her work? And then too I had to be attentive to my own presentation: how could I please her without being servile? I didn't want her yet to know the intensity of my feelings: it might put her off, and there were promising signs that she might think of me as more than a friend. Wrapping a twist of hair behind my ear; leaving notes in my lunchbox scrawled with doodles – sketches of naked women, messages with all the Ps written in red; a possible portrait of a man with kiss curls, which could have been no one else but me. Goodness, the smallest gesture made me happy for weeks.

Our actions around one another were gentle arcs of flirtation: our kisses closing in on the other's lips, hands knocking each other's in the park; it was always, really, a slow chase to the other's skin. When together, it was all loveliness; when apart, the situation was an emergency. It felt as if I were about to flood.

It sounds small, but one morning before Christmas she put my shoes on for me, and it was probably the most erotic moment of my young life. Down on her knees, she lifted each of my feet and stowed them into my brogues. She looked up at me, her green eyes flashing – what was it? Knowledge of what we were? Of what we would become? – and then tied the laces in bows. 'There,' she said. 'Much better.' In class that day she kept on looking over; she too must have known of the morning's grace. I'd smile; she'd half-smile back.

All day the shoes bit. I did nothing to adjust them.

Like this the days passed.

Over the winter I'd had every kind of fantasy about how we'd end up together. We'd go to the forest and roll in the mulch; at the Ilm she'd kiss me and we'd roll in the blond grass; we'd be reading in my room, then we'd roll by the open fire. Always, this rolling. This was all I could conjure, since I knew her boyish body would not be like other women's, which made her nakedness more improbable and exciting. Also: I was a virgin. I wasn't even sure what would happen next.

Discreetly I studied her. I began to predict her expressions, when we were in class, or at the cafeteria – where we always ate, our laughter high in the room, feeling bigger than everyone else. (It was well known that our six could not be separated. I don't think we were resented for being such a tight-knit group, but I do think we were envied. People joined us sometimes for lunch or breakfast, but they didn't come back. Perhaps we were more forbidding than we knew.)

The best was when Charlotte was studying an object very seriously, one of the materials the Master had given us, say, then would catch me looking, and her smile would turn enormous as she blinked the fringe from her eyes. 'Oh, Pauli,' she'd say. 'I didn't know you were there.' Or the opposite: when someone – Walter, probably – had said something off (he was always able to put his foot in it with her) and she'd scowl, her lips almost disappearing.

When she dozed on my bed in the wintry, high attic light, I kept on wondering if our daughter would look like her, and then I couldn't help adding more children to our growing family – *mutti* a sculptor, *papa* a painter; all of us hungry, poor and very happy.

To be in love is to be stricken; distraught, most of the time, but when things are going well there is the gentle rising of the soul to the top of the room. Ours was a slow game. All the best love affairs are. In the new semester, several students referred to her as my girlfriend. I could have purred.

I think Walter fell in love with Jenö about as quickly as I fell for Charlotte. But Walter was a different man to me. At some point, I don't know when, or even whether it was conscious, I thought I'd woo Charlotte with nuance. This was the approach she took with me, and so I mirrored it. Whereas Walter! You couldn't have found a more different man: Walter was all show. When Jenö wasn't paying him enough attention, he would sulk and make his displeasure known, so that Irmi (with her rolling *rs*) would say, 'Oh, do stop frrrrowning, Walter!' But when Jenö was fully attentive, it was as if a thousand lamps had lit the room. And yet Jenö most often looked lost as to how he'd found himself the beloved of this tall Westphalian. I didn't even know whether Jenö liked men or women (but how much I wanted to show my parents the audacity of a queer love affair at the Bauhaus! How much that would tremble their Dresden foundations!).

I suppose Walter couldn't be called classically attractive, but there was something about him. He had a baronial look: you could see him in one of those oil paintings of hounds and Prussian huntsmen, mouths crisped with wealth and displeasure. Indeed, he was some sort of aristocrat – though an impoverished one – and could trace his lineage to Frederick the Great. He had round spectacles, his nostrils kicked, and his lips were plump. His hair was wondrously thick; his skin olive, like an Italian's. In his face there was a handed-down imperialism; he looked at the world in judgement of it, as if on a horse. You could see in his face both the poverty of his childhood and the grandeur of his bloodline. I enjoyed his company enormously, and if I wasn't with Charlotte, then I would inevitably, that winter, be with Walter.

I always did find him alluring, and especially next to Jenö, who, I must admit, was as bland as a bean. Jenö was all breadth. There wasn't a slender part of him, which made it even more surprising that he fashioned kites thin as moth wings, or made delicate sculptures from rubbish; pan lids, washers, a child's shoe. He had a symmetrical face, which gave him a peaceful if bovine aspect. I found a dullness to his gaze that others thought mysterious. I said he was bland, but that's envy talking. Jenö's mind, I admit, was a labyrinth.

No, I'd never seen Jenö's allure, though lots of the Bauhaus *Frauen* liked him very much, but then again lots of Bauhaus *Frauen* liked me very much; a fact which had me baffled. This had never happened to me as a young man. Now I was in the unusual position of having to break off coffee dates when it became evident that our meetings were romantic. Irmi teased me, saying I was the Bauhaus heart-breaker (*Herrrrrrzensbrrrrecher*), but then said this wasn't such a bad reputation to have.

Charlotte and me; Walter and Jenö; Irmi and Kaspar. Only between Kaspar and Irmi could I detect nothing but friendship; though even a friendship in the Bauhaus was made of kisses and caresses. But utopias are frisky places. All of us loved all of us. Had you given me any one of them, man, woman, Czechoslovak, German, blonde or brunette, I would have been a happy sultan.

I frequently had to rub myself against the bedroom furniture; a chair or the bedstead, anything to find a place for the erotic clouds that so often streaked against the sky of my soul.

Goodness, I was happy.

# 4

## Weimar

She was a master craftsman, my Charlotte, an almost perfect Bauhäusler. She could make skyscrapers from paper, concertina the floors, dramatise their depths. She could work any scavenged material: wiring hairnets and pipes into extravagant sculptures. More often than not she tossed them away. Sometimes I'd retrieve them from the rubbish and hang them in my room. She'd always give them a wry look, when she saw them later, hanging above my bed like a witchy totem.

But it was in anything Charlotte produced from the loom that I thought I could detect frustration (it was a relief, to know she wasn't perfect). Charlotte's weaves appeared made not from wool but horsehair and twine. Wool lists from warm fingers; is split by warm hands. In her weaves there were knots and humps; shocked fibres and knolls. 'Women's work,' she had said, tossing aside the weave, 'nothing ever came of stitches in fabric.' It was obviously unreasonable that she'd be so bad at something.

Jenö was a wonderful sculptor; Kaspar and Walter made

fine things in the Metal Workshop, and Irmi, like Charlotte, was good at almost everything. It was frustrating that I couldn't paint at the Bauhaus, since this was my talent, but it was deemed old-fashioned and uninteresting, and in any case something that had to be earned rather than done.

Charlotte told me it didn't matter, after a workshop when she was so productive that even Master Itten had had to tell her to slow down (though he'd looked at her multiplying sculptures with quiet astonishment). The big paper edifices were cathedrals, the miniatures were lanterns with internal chambers and windows. I marvelled at her work; I put mine in the fire.

After school that day we went to the Swan. 'You've got the skill that'll sell,' Charlotte said, as we sat at the bar. She had paper-cuts on her fingers. 'No one actually needs stonemasons and quilters. Painting won't go out of fashion.'

'Don't I need to make an impression now?'

'We all want to be further on than we are.'

There were always a few locals in the Swan, but the students and the citizens manoeuvred around each other tolerably enough. The bar-hall was a dark cave: its tables were engraved with students' initials, the light was dusty from the sinking upholstery, and it always smelled of malt and fruit. It was one of our favourite places.

'But how am I going to show my worth if I'm never allowed to paint? You're fine. Look at you today! I came up with one lantern and you made Manhattan.'

'Maybe the Master doesn't care about being impressed. Have you thought about that? Maybe that's not his priority.'

'He was impressed with Willem.'

'Puncturing holes in the paper? That was just a stunt.' Charlotte turned her glass round in circles then drank her beer. The thing about Charlotte was that she could match you pint for pint. It was always fun to drink with her. 'You want everything to be beautiful. It means you can't fail.'

'Yes, yes, I've heard that before.'

'Doesn't mean you actually listen,' she said, tugging at one of my earlobes. 'How is it,' she said, trying to read my gaze, 'you're eighteen and yet such a tired old dog?'

Outside the trees were thrashing about in the February wind that whistled against the door. A flag of newspaper flew against the mullioned window, then flew off again. Weeks ago, the fountain had iced over, and the wishing coins had been frozen in disorder.

'Can I blame the war?'

'You certainly cannot,' she said.

'Excuse me.' The man's voice made me turn. 'Sorry. I don't want to interrupt.' Sitting behind me at the bar was a bald man, quite fat. The fingers around his glass were so blunt they looked sawn off at the knuckle. He wore a long jacket which came over the seat of his chair, just like the one my father wore at work.

'Yes?'

When he stood his height came as something of a surprise; his frame made me think he'd be a squat man. 'I'm interested in your dilemma. Though I didn't mean to overhear. I run a studio of painters. Up at the beech forest, in an old cabinet studio.'

'That's nice,' I said, because I didn't know what else to say.

'We make big oil paintings on commission. Rural landscapes. Allegorical scenes, and mythological, too. The theme is chosen by the client, then we put them together. Meadows, farmhouses, sheep, girls, that kind of thing.'

'Ah yes. *Blut und Boden*, and all that?' said Charlotte.

'No,' he said, and he gave her a look that said he did not need to solicit the opinion of women. 'It's whatever the client wants. The sacking of Troy, for example, but also the Prussian plains at sunset.' He gave me his card. 'You said there's no chance to paint at the Bauhaus. Well, if you want to paint, and want to be paid to paint, come to the studio. You'd be welcome.' The man assessed me from head to toe, as if sizing me up for a uniform. 'I pay a good wage to a decent painter.'

'What's a good wage?'

'Thousands. Tens of thousands. Whatever the day decides to do with money, I keep up. You could try a night shift; fit it in around school.'

The address on the card showed his studio was in the part of the beech forest nearest the city, on the road west.

'Try it out? If you're interested, that is.' He touched his forehead, as if a cap were there, then he drifted over to a table where other men sat in navy overalls.

'Don't,' said Charlotte, as soon as he had gone. There was warning in her voice. 'It will only be a distraction.'

'Tens of thousands, though. Can you imagine?'

'The sacking of Troy, sunset on the Prussian plains? It would undo everything the Master teaches us at the Bauhaus.'

'It'd be a weekend job.'

'Are you desperate for the money?'

'I would like not to rely on my parents.'

Charlotte twisted her hand into my skull, as if she were trying to screw something into my brain. 'All this begging for clarity, then you go and paint *Völkisch* oils!'

She tutted at me; I grinned.

'It's a bad idea,' she said, 'and you know it.'

While Charlotte bought another round, I knew the man's eyes were on me. I wondered if he was waiting for me to tell him I'd do it. When I finally looked back, I wasn't surprised that I found him staring straight at me. How doglike he looked, with his bald head and big eyes. There was a tattoo of an anchor on his neck. Maybe he'd been away at sea during the war: I could imagine him as a sailor, or a captain of a big ship. I turned the card over. On its reverse was his name written in a heavy Gothic script. His name was Ernst Steiner.

# 5

## Weimar

For a while I forgot about Mr Steiner's invitation. My father had paid March's fees upfront, and the pressing need for money had gone. A few weeks later, though, as I was sorting through old papers and collapsed lanterns at my desk, Ernst Steiner's card turned up again. I held it for some moments: wondering what it meant, and thinking back to what Charlotte had said about *Völkisch* oils. The card was cream, heavy, expensive; and the lettering, though old-fashioned, was embossed. His clientele must be wealthy indeed.

I hadn't much liked the man on first meeting, but I also knew that his money might prove helpful in the long run. If there was a way I could avoid asking my parents for my fees then I had to take it.

If I'm being honest, though, there was also a part of me which craved something else as well as the cash. Wouldn't it be lovely, I thought, to hear someone marvel at my talent, my specialness? (How schoolboyish; this desire to have a man like Ernst Steiner tell me I was good enough!)

The woods were starting to green when we went on our camping trip that first warm day of March. Our six had a favoured spot in the forest: a clearing where the trees were held back. At night it had a spooky feel, but in the days it was our small kingdom: not far from Goethe's Oak, a tree with a crown so big that in the summers it could shade the whole student body of the Bauhaus.

We went to the woods after class. Though it may be a cliché, the sensation, of wheeling our bikes through the city streets and then up to the woods, was of flight. Vistas opened out between the rows of beech just as I'd seen in photographs of Manhattan: roads narrowing from the foreground between skyscrapers. And for a while I could pretend I was a New York taxicab, wheeling my way through the grid, and that the woodland was a cityscape filled with smells of the subway: ventilated air, and frying onion.

It wouldn't be much of a detour, I thought, to turn my bike westward and enquire about the possibility of a shift or two.

On the cycle I caught Walter grinning at me, and Charlotte too. Jenö was already ahead. I loved my friends in that moment, their faces caught in the flickering wood, stained by the shadows, hair lit by sunshine. There were stories of pilgrims going into the woods for spring rites that ended in romping bacchanalia, emotions far outrunning reason. There were six of us in our saintish tribe. A man might hope, of course.

In the beech forest the density of the wood was like a bonfire. All the trees were so tall; cherry, green, and rust, their bark so sensitive you could carve your name with just a coin. In the autumn the forest would be aflame with colour, and in the evenings, with a good sunset, the beech could turn violet or blue or pink. In the winter the wind made the branches moan; but in the summer, with the leaves, there was an electrical sound, as if the woods had charge.

It was a gift. These woods, that place, back then.

When the road split I told them I'd catch them up. Charlotte narrowed her eyes but said nothing.

Steiner's studio was at the edge of the beech forest: not quite town, not quite forest. As I wheeled my bicycle on the gravel path I was surprised to find Mr Steiner on the front porch of the large cabin, cleaning something with an old rag. Again, he wore the foreman's coat. He took a moment to recognise me, but when he did, his look was one of pleasure. 'Ah,' he said, 'it's you!'

It struck me again how blunt his head was, and how hairless he was, like a baby. 'I came about the job.' I felt awkward. I wondered if he wanted to see my sketchpad; I'd made studies of yolky sunsets and fattened sheep. Surely he wouldn't just let me loose without first seeing my work.

'I thought your girlfriend had persuaded you not to come.'

'No. I'd be glad of the money.' I stumbled. I didn't want to seem too mercenary. 'And I'd like to paint.'

Mr Steiner tossed the rag and beckoned me over. The door was unlocked, and we walked up a flight. In the main studio there were men in overalls working on several different canvases: flashy oil paintings which, Mr Steiner explained, sold by the square foot to American collectors and Prussian Junkers. Sawdust was everywhere, gumming the light coming in at the windows. As we walked to his office, a couple of men – there were no women – were busy at a particularly lurid scene: slabs of childish light, crazy dappling; women baptising fat babies in the river's golden waters.

'Good, aren't they?' Mr Steiner said with a broad grin.

I didn't know what to say. It was all broadly awful, but it did have a kitsch appeal. Inside his office there were no signs of any real art either: only files and accountancy ledgers. We might as well have been in my father's shoe factory.

Mr Steiner opened a big notebook: inside was a sketch of a watering hole with a host of robed women getting ready to bathe. It was as tacky as anything in my parents' house.

'Can you come tomorrow? The courier's coming then.'

'But it's not much more than a sketch!'

'Three men overnight, then you can finish it off tomorrow. It'll be done in no time.'

I told him I could come when he wanted, though I doubted his grounds for optimism.

'What's your specialism?' he said, his eyes passing my mouth.

I wasn't sure what to say but then opted for something a teacher had told me. 'I'm good at light.'

'There we are. Remind me of your last name? In fact, I'm not sure I know your Christian name, either.'

'Paul Beckermann.'

In a long, loose hand, he wrote my name across what I already knew would be the golden sky at break of day. 'Then all of this,' he said, expansively, 'is yours.'

It didn't take long to cycle from there to the clearing. Up here I could see for miles the velvet fields of Thuringia, and the city of Weimar was laid out at my feet; the Bauhaus the last building before the city turned back to green.

It was always cooler in the forest than in town, but the trees were filling out and the whips growing. Finally I found my friends around a fire. Walter was picking leaves out of Jenö's soles, and Charlotte was talking to Irmi, who had just moved into rooms opposite hers in the Fürstenplatz square.

The steep cycle had made me feel rather high. The trees were blurred, but the separated flames of the fire were crisp. I steadied my gaze on the fire but saw inside it a swarm of crows, billowing out, and then being sucked in. I could smell my own scent, and it was sharp and animal.

'Where's Kaspar?' I asked.

'He tailed back,' said Walter, patting his stomach. 'Poor Kas couldn't make the climb. Where'd you go?'

'I had an errand to run.'

Three tents had already been pitched around the fire. I wondered with whom I was going to bunk. Probably Walter; Jenö in a tent by himself; the two women, together.

'Very mysterious,' said Irmi.

'Not really,' said Charlotte, unable to help herself.

I took out Mr Steiner's card and threw it in the fire. Charlotte smiled, but we both knew the gesture meant nothing.

'Did you enjoy the river glades?' asked Walter, and the rest of the group laughed.

So everyone had already been well informed. 'All right, all right. You all already know I'm a dyed-in-the-wool Romantic.'

'Charlotte says you might be overcome by the "imitation impulse".'

'It sounds contagious,' said Jenö. 'Like the flu.'

'It's just oil paints, and tons of money. You'll be envious when I start driving my own automobile about town.'

'I don't think it's a bad thing,' said Irmi. 'Why not? Especially doing something as easy as painting.'

'He'll be able to paint our portraits soon,' said Charlotte. 'I can just imagine it. Set up like a Caspar Friedrich in an ancient castle.'

'First one to be nice to me gets the first gift.'

'Which is?' said Jenö.

'I'll be nice to you,' said Irmi.

'Then you, Irmi, shall have the best of what Steiner will pay for. Champagne. Italian truffles. New dresses and shoes.'

Irmi laughed. As we talked she scooted closer. Twisted around one side her hair was pulled into a complicated plait. Irmi had a wide smile with small teeth, slightly dirty on their edges. Her grey eyes showed all the weather, their changeability nothing like Charlotte's flat stare. 'Granite and crystal,' Walter had once uncharitably described them together; though I'd never learnt which one he'd thought which.

As the dark came, Jenö told a ghost story. It was a child's tale, and hardly frightening at all, about a kid who lived on his own in the forest, and who let in any man who knocked and called him son, even the man with the axe in his bag. I watched Charlotte as he told it: her face blank as she listened. I imagined her concentrating like this, at the State Opera in Prague, or studying the life models at Charles University. Had anyone else ever loved her as I loved her? Surely that was an impossibility.

'Did you know,' Walter said, taking over from where Jenö had left off, 'that Charlotte von Stein haunts these woods?'

'Nonsense,' said Irmi.

'It's true,' Walter said, 'she and Goethe used to walk this forest. She was married, but her husband was so often away that she saw as much of Goethe as she liked. They met in the Ilm Park. He fell in love with her on the spot.'

I knew the feeling: Charlotte and Charlotte, me and Goethe, all of us in love by the River Ilm.

'Charlotte used to read his poetry, and offer him suggestions. He prized her as the best editor he'd ever had. They were great friends. Lovers, maybe. She certainly loved him far more than she loved her husband. None of her four daughters had survived, and she said walking these woods with him was a balm. Goethe couldn't have been a more sincere, more faithful friend, and he said she was his soul. To read their letters . . . Well, they are so full of affection that you can't help but feel the force of it.'

Walter cleaned his glasses with a handkerchief, squinting before putting them back on. He caught my eye, and smiled, but went on in a solemn tone: 'Then, one day, Goethe simply left. He didn't tell Charlotte where he was going. He wrote to her from Venice. He said he'd be gone a year or two. Charlotte was bereft. How could he have left her here? Without even saying goodbye? His heartlessness was incomprehensible; unthinkable. All that time she roamed these woods, waiting for him to return. That year she wrote an opera about Dido, who cursed Aeneas for leaving her in Carthage, and vowed revenge.

'Goethe thought of his Italian journey as the happiest of his life, in the land where the lemon trees blossom. And yet Charlotte was here, miserable among the beech trees, while he was in Italy, sighing about lemons. When he returned they became friends again, but it was nothing like how it had been. How can a man be so sensitive to the human condition, and yet be so cruel as to leave her behind, without even saying goodbye?'

Our group was quiet, not used to Walter's mood, which was usually sardonic and powerful. But then he flipped the solemnity to something else. 'If you listen carefully to the trees, it sounds just like a woman's voice – Charlotte's, some might say – moaning, *von Goethe, von Goethe, von Goethe!*'

And at this he pulled himself up to a tree in a passionate embrace, and started rubbing his crotch against it.

Jenö shook his head. 'You're mad!'

'Sounds like an oil painting for you, Paul,' said Charlotte. 'Dido and Aeneas. Or Goethe and Charlotte, under his Oak.'

I ignored her. Walter, anyway, wasn't happy that the attention had been diverted. '"Beware," Charlotte continues to moan, even to this day,' – and his voice was high-pitched and witchy, as he humped the tree, '"Beware ye men of fickle hearts! The woods will have their revenge!"'

He unclasped himself and lay on the forest floor, showering mulch on his face in a strange kind of burial. Was it my tiredness that pricked the thought I could see his excitement tenting his trousers? Or it could have been nothing; in memory I seem to catch them all in the erotic net of a dream – and Walter, surely, wouldn't have been titillated by a beech tree.

In any case he scrambled to his feet when we heard the distant spray of gunfire. Clubs often used the woods for target practice and we heard the *pop, pop, pop* of a rifle. The fire lit Walter demonically. 'You see! Blood comes to the woods again!'

Charlotte threw a conker at him. 'Oh, do shut up, Walter.'

And the rest of us laughed.

# 6

## Weimar

Ernst Steiner was right. After the oasis scene (women bathing their breasts in the aquamarine waters) what followed on my first shift at the studio was a scene of rural German life. Meadows; mountains; sheep; peasants; et cetera. Swans flew with heavy throats and alarming wingspans. Children frolicked in the river's spray. It was for a rich lady in Zurich with big tits, Ernst said, and she'd be paying in Swiss francs. *Valuta*: hard currency.

The paintings were all hectic and overlit, and, I must say, I loved the work almost immediately. 'Good job,' Ernst said to me at four in the morning, once I'd lit the kindergarten of kids. 'They don't look like they do anything but eat.' I didn't have the opportunity to worry before it was taken away; in truth I didn't even know whether the paint was dry.

As I worked more shifts – I ended up doing one or two a week – I soon realised the turnover at the Steiner Studio was exceptional. There were new commissions every few days, and Ernst had a group of workers (they were never called artists) operating day and night so that the paintings could be wrapped and boxed for the courier at four in the morning. The courier often appeared in the middle of the night, and no one knew how long he'd been there, nor why Mr Steiner's paintings had to be shipped at the crack of dawn. His name was Leo, and his face was as smooth as a boxing glove.

I have no idea when Ernst Steiner slept, since he was the one constant in the studio between the day and night shifts. He organised everything from his office, barking instructions to the floor, with the telephone rattling the new orders. The mark was inflating like crazy, but there were always more and more Americans who wanted idylls and riverbanks, farmyards and sunsets; girls with their unending plaits and nursing mothers, all bosoms.

The exchange rate, anyway, made our work cheap.

Surprisingly, the other workers took little notice of me, and, give or take a few stares, I had been accepted into the fold as any other worker would be. Soon they became comfortable enough to gently deride my practice at the Bauhaus. In fact, they thought us spectacularly stupid: I had been laughed away when I told them how we privileged process over output. 'That,' said a big man called Daniel, 'is what people say when they have no talent.'

The money began to flow in. Mr Steiner paid me at the close of each shift by filling my bicycle basket with cash. I wrote to my father and told him I could afford my fees on my own: a part-time job had come up, and I was determined to pay my way at the art school he so hated. He neither replied nor sent me more money. I'm sure he thought I'd soon be back, begging for more, and it did cross my mind that I shouldn't be too hasty in rejecting his money outright. But the letter was sent by the time I'd thought of this.

It was nice to have my talent appreciated again. Ernst Steiner thought I was brilliant, and it gave me a glow to think of how highly he held me in his esteem. He said, as my teacher had said, that I had a gift for light. This was about as far from Master Itten's praise as was possible. If I had painted the sky when asked to paint the sky, well, he would have laughed in my face. But here in the woods there was no singularity, no *instress*. Here was only blowzy representation, and I was surprised, and a little ashamed, by how much I loved not just the old-fashioned paintings we made, but how it made me feel. Master Itten didn't favour me, but that didn't matter. I had a different master now.

Besides, the Master so obviously favoured Charlotte it was useless to court his attention. Perhaps it was because they were both foreigners, and they had their outsiders' affinity. He always spent longer with her in class than the rest of us, and sometimes they had private meetings where he'd advise her on what she ate, how much she slept, and how she held her body in space.

It was from one of these meetings that Charlotte emerged one morning preoccupied but also excited. As we went down the school staircase, painted with bright Constructivist murals, she said the Master had proposed a fast. He said being full of rich food only dulled the senses, and a fast would sharpen our perception of colour. The forms of things would emerge. Hunger would open a Jerusalem in our hearts. And besides, he'd said, a fast might do our souls some good.

I watched as Charlotte went into the cafeteria: bent, I knew, on persuading everyone else to follow her plans. As I picked up my meal (vegetarian; heavily infused with garlic) I remembered seeing her at the bandsaw earlier that morning. How rapt she had been by the hot seam between the blade and metal. Maybe this is what she imagined was inside her: a clarified eye; a burning stitch.

'I don't know,' said Irmi, who had listened attentively to the same speech about hunger and Jerusalems. 'It sounds dreadful.'

'We'll get to a new transparency. Master Itten says only then will we know ourselves, and the true form of our desires will emerge. After the fast we'll be better artists.' Charlotte tailed off, slightly losing her mettle. 'That's what he said, anyway.'

'All this with lemon water and bread?' said Kaspar. 'How about absinthe? That'd get us to transparency quicker.' Kaspar loved Charlotte, but he was also doubtful of some parts of Bauhaus life. He didn't buy into the festivals, didn't join in with Itten's vegetarianism, and often smirked during the kinaesthetics.

'He said it was the most important thing he'd done as an artist.'

'Good for him. Doesn't mean I want to do it.'

'What's infuriating about you,' she said to Kaspar, with

a poke, 'is your laziness. I wish you'd try something new.'

'Master Itten's mad!'

'Master Itten's world famous!'

'I think we should do it,' said Jenö, out of the blue.

Charlotte looked at him, surprised, as did Irmi. I don't think Charlotte saw Jenö as an ally as much as me, and I hadn't yet raised a word of support. Actually I thought her plan was a terrible idea, and embarrassing, given people were going hungry across Germany.

'Why?' said Walter. 'Do you need your desires clarifying?'

'I suppose it wouldn't hurt.'

Now that Jenö had consented, Walter would have to as well. 'Well, why not? I suppose it might get us some-where. Certainly, I've got to find some way of livening up my output. Who knows? A fortnight fasting might help.'

Like me, Walter was struggling in Itten's workshops; I think we both found it hard to relinquish the rules learnt at school. And, like me, his devotions were channelled elsewhere.

'Paul?' Charlotte said, looking at me with her frank eyes.

I was the last one to speak, and I didn't want to be a voice of dissent. Charlotte was excited about her plan, and I was sure I could play along, if only for the sake of her pride. 'Sure,' I said, wondering how to play up my enthusiasm. 'Let's start tonight.'

'Good. Irmi, you're in too?'

Irmi nodded.

'Black bread and lemon water for breakfast and dinner,' she said. 'Nothing else.'

Kaspar pouted.

'Agreed?'

He gave a shrug.

'*Bon appétit*,' she said, with a spoonful of stew; 'this might be our last meal for some time.'

Days later we were in Irmi's rooms. We were sitting in a circle doing one of the Master's breathing exercises. We had to take a breath in for ten seconds, then a breath out for five. I felt light-headed. Long ago the air had begun to shimmer.

In the first few days of the fast my limbs had begun to ache. My skin had dulled; the whites of my eyes were grey; my tongue, spongy. Though I had had nothing much to eat there was always the whiff of the eating-house about me. I'd thought of abandoning the fast several times so far: it didn't feel right, and I was exhausted.

But Charlotte was so full of energy, and so obviously excited, that I stuck with it. Maybe she'd be proved right: I really might start seeing things anew – although I hardly needed to clarify my desires. And besides, Master Itten kept on giving us approving looks, which were of course a pleasure, given that he so rarely commended my work. Now, we were all – not just Charlotte – part of his elect.

Though I was meant to close my eyes during the meditation, Kaspar and I kept on locking our sights on each other, and it was hard not to laugh. Kaspar couldn't really stay still: there was always a restless leg, or a finger twirling his curls. Though he liked to quote Nietzsche and wear all black, he was hardly a nihilist; instead he was a sensuous man, full of appetite, and I knew during the past few days he'd taken secret meals to tide him over until the evenings. Fair enough. He was only doing it to go along with the group – and, had I not been Charlotte's devotee, I'm sure I would have cheated too.

When we were finished Jenö opened a window to let some air in. 'Look,' he said to Charlotte. 'You can see your room from here.'

She wandered over. 'Ah, so you can! You'll soon know all my secrets, Irmi. I'll have to keep the shutters closed.'

Walter lay back on the divan: from there he had the best view of Jenö. That pose, one knee hitched, his head in his hand, invited you to think of him naked, and done in oils. 'For how long are we to eat four slices of black bread a day?'

'Master Itten said two weeks would be good; three, ideal.'

'It's useless!' said Kaspar. 'By two o'clock I'm out of my wits.'

'Tell that to the men at the dole office,' said Walter.

'Oh, don't get righteous.'

These two had a funny sort of relationship; they often chipped away at each other, but there was fondness there too. The thing about Kaspar was that he was open to everyone. Me, Walter, Jenö: we were warier men.

'Just wait,' said Irmi, who'd told me she had found the fast more exciting than she'd predicted. 'The world has changed colour a little. Things are clarifying.'

'Are your desires taking on a new shape, Irmi Schüpfer?'
Irmi looked at me and then blushed. 'No.'

Jenö sat down by Walter. He began to sketch in his notebook.

'It says here,' Kaspar read from a dating manual, 'that I should leave a week in between dates.' Kaspar was always taking women out; he always had someone on the go. He could be moody, but he was also very charming when he wanted to be, and it was a combination deemed irresistible by many in the Weaving Workshop. 'I only ever leave a few days.'

Charlotte flipped the book. 'Oh, tie them up like dogs and they'll still let you take them out for ice cream.'

Walter's head was resting on the top of the sofa; how nicely it could have dropped, pat, onto Jenö's shoulder. He watched with interest the development of Jenö's drawing.

'"Be firm in your enthusiasm but not overly passionate,"' Kaspar continued. '"Do not be threatening in your affection. Women can feel menaced by what you may perceive as light flirtation." Good grief. When was this written?' He flipped the book and looked for a date. 'Am I a menace? I always thought they wanted me to carry on. At least I thought they did.'

'You're more a mouse than a menace,' said Irmi. 'Ask Paul what to say.'

'How would I know?'

'I can't remember when you were with the same woman twice on your little coffee trips.'

'They keep on offering to pay,' I said, though I knew the

excuse was laughable. 'That's the only reason I accept.'

'Even with your studio fortune?' Charlotte asked.

I blushed. Charlotte often made jibes about my job. Sometimes it was comic; at other times she was earnest, saying as long as I was *there*, I'd never be *here*. In some part, I knew she was right, but the fee was too good, and the rebuttal to my father's financing too satisfying.

'God, I'm hungry,' Kaspar said, shoving the book away.

'Don't you feel better? More alive?' Charlotte asked.

'No,' he said, 'my stomach hurts.'

'I had a moment yesterday when I saw a blackbird with a yellow beak,' she said. 'In the cemetery by the Russian church. I couldn't keep my eyes off it. All day I'd been wobbling around, wondering what was the point, just like you, but then for ten minutes the bird held my attention and nothing else. It was transfixing: I was watching an opera. It felt like hours, and all that time there were so many images inside my head: what if I had the bird's wings? Or what would happen if I crushed its small bones in my hand?' She cast her eye at Kaspar. 'Really, it was a joy. Such visions wouldn't have happened on a stomach full of food.'

'You sound,' said Kaspar, 'as mad as the Master.'

Jenö dropped the sketchbook and went to the kitchen. Walter looked at the drawing then shot me an alarmed look. 'Handsome Pauli,' Walter said. 'You'd have looked wonderful in uniform.'

I turned the sketch the right way up. Jenö had made my expression look sour. How strange that he should portray me like that. I bore no ill will to any of them; certainly not to Charlotte, who had been speaking the longest, and whom I had been looking at – I would have guessed – for the duration of her speech about the blackbird.

# 7

## Weimar

For the first few days I had wondered where the fast might take her. I knew Charlotte would want to escalate things; that it was not in her nature to keep things still. Privately, I hoped that our empty stomachs might draw us together. We might do our breathing exercises, light candles, and in the magic-lantern of a fasted afternoon, we'd finally, lazily, instinctively, end up in bed, too weak to resist temptation a moment longer. Hours of hunger would tip us together. We'd apex. We'd roll around.

For this fantasy I found auguries everywhere, and perhaps this too was a product of the starved mind. The blackbirds were the first thing I noticed, chirruping so sweetly it was as if Charlotte herself were serenading me. Then there were the things she began to leave in my room: bags and notebooks, and even some clothing: signs of her moving in with me. More notes written with red Ps. Perhaps Master Itten was right: if Jerusalem might spring up in this medieval town, perhaps it might even appear in a corner of my bedroom.

That week I began to vibrate. Even when the fire was lit in my room, there was a tremor in my hands, and my body was shivery and cool. The fast was adrenal. There was a hard ledge in my stomach off which I hung, and I brought that ledge around with me, leaning on it when I was weak. After the meditation I wondered whether there might indeed be a sharpening of my perceptions as promised. All morning I had watched how Charlotte's lantern moved in the room's draughts. It was deliciously warm beneath the blankets on the badly sprung mattress, and I went in and out of dozy sleep, moving from one pleasant dream to the next as the lantern circled above me, lightweight, planetary, perfect. If this dreaminess was an effect of the fast, then it was a sweetness to dream on.

Life, like this; it was no bad thing. Sure, all morning I dreamed of what Kaspar was privately devouring (beignets, blood pudding and dumplings), but I had more focus. It was as if the fast had shut down all the unnecessary parts of my brain. I spent hours preparing for Master Itten's class, and I thought how good I was getting at what it was he wanted us to do: understand the true nature of the material at hand. It seemed plausible that I could be an old master in the beech forest, and a modernist at the Bauhaus.

What I hadn't expected was Charlotte's first escalation to happen elsewhere, and without me.

Though I lived three floors up, I could always hear Mrs

Kramer screaming at me with ease. 'Beckermann! You have a visitor!' I heard Charlotte's voice from the vestibule; famously, my landlady liked her and no one else. As she walked up the flights I thought how today we'd inexorably come together. My skin tingled. How pleasant it is: anticipation.

Nothing, however, could have prepared me for her appearance as I opened the door. Charlotte's hair had been shaved off. Her head was nothing but scalp, and her flat eyes looked stranger still. 'I've just been at Jenö's,' she said, her breath quick from the climb up. 'Now's the time to take the fast further.'

'What do you mean?'

'All this hair,' she said, pulling at one of my curls. 'It's just confection!' She came into my room, looking around, as if expecting to see someone else here. 'Oh,' she said, looking at the hanging lantern with a frown. 'I hadn't realised you'd kept that.'

I touched her bald head. 'Is this because of Master Itten?'

'Does not the very nature of things teach you that if a man has long hair, it is a disgrace to him?'

She registered my confusion.

'Corinthians. You should read your Bible.'

'I didn't know you were such a zealot.'

'My childhood,' she said, 'was full of wonders. What you don't know, Paul, is that I am one of life's obsessives.'

'I did know that, actually. Who did yours?'

'Jenö.'

'This morning?'

'Yes. I told you already. Keep up, Pauli!' She looked excited. Charlotte carried all that in her mouth.

I checked my watch: it was almost noon. I could have sworn it was only nine or so. I lit a fire to take away the smell of mouse; at the mirror she brought out scissors and a razor. Charlotte laid out newspaper by the sink. She snapped the towel like a matador. 'Ready for your appointment, Mr Beckermann?'

I realised I hadn't quite consented before she began cutting at my hair. The curls – which my mother had always adored and called 'my glory' – fell to the newspaper below. Charlotte worked methodically, snapping away with the scissors. 'Did you know that nuns were able to stop menstruating just by controlling their breathing? They were the true masters of the fast. Much better than the monks, who anyway drank stout to offset their hunger. No, it was the nuns who ate nothing during Lent, and it was then there appeared the most visitations of Jesus and the Virgin. The two,' she said, 'cannot be separate phenomena, can they?'

'Has either visited you yet?'

'No. But Jesus once appeared to me in a dream.'

'What did he say?'

'He didn't *say* anything. He just put his hand on my forehead and when I woke I felt a great heat there, a burn.' She placed my hand on her forehead. 'I walked around that day feeling empty but pleasant, like a vessel for religious feeling.' She smiled. 'Afterward I became obsessed with Margaret of Cortona. I decided to enter a convent; become a nun. My father wasn't too happy about that either. But that's the trick. Master Itten says it's not about depriving yourself – of food, of hair, of luxuries. It's simply about making more space to see.'

I didn't tell her that my mother, a few years ago, had had an epiphany too. She'd been fasting for Lent when she'd had a vision of a British shell hitting my brother's trench. For days she kept a vigil, believing that if she ate nothing she would keep him alive. And Peter had survived – but at a different kind of price.

Charlotte picked up the razor, which must have been Jenö's. All the curls were gone so quickly it was as if they had never really been there. 'Do you think Walter's in love with Jenö?'

'Yes,' I said, 'of course.'

'Do you think Jenö knows it?'

'I think he's pretending it's not there,' I said. 'So that they can be friends.'

I saw her expression modify as she pulled the razor around my ear. 'What about Irmi and Kaspar?' I said.

She smiled, concealing something. 'She's too serious for him.'

In the mirror I looked like a half-skinned apple. 'Kaspar's the most serious man I know!'

'Ah, that's what he wants you to think. Really, he's a buffoon.'

Just then the razor nicked, and I felt a drop of blood on my face, then drop down my neck. 'Charlotte, can you—'

'Paul?'

I imagined my chin hitting the sink and my tongue bursting; my mouth filling with blood. I felt a wave of nausea, and I saw a brownish film. I tried to blink it away but it was no good. 'Can you clean that away?'

Charlotte swabbed at it with tissue. 'I forgot. I'm sorry, Paul. Here, look,' she switched on the tap. 'All gone.'

The dizziness felt worse on an empty stomach and I waited for the fur on my sight to go. Again there was the scraping sound of the razor. As she worked I held onto the sink, trying to concentrate on the cold ceramic. I had always been phobic of blood, ever since I'd seen a friend in the playground pull a nail from his foot and a jet of blood spurt everywhere.

Eventually my vision returned, and I saw myself in the mirror, as bald as Master Itten. I touched her scalp, and then mine. 'How strange we look,' I said. 'Like wizards.'

Later, we wandered to the park. I felt the air on my scalp as she must have done on hers. We made a tour of the Ilm then headed back on ourselves. By the cafe there were mothers and children eating sandwiches as pigeons waited for scraps. The breeze moved the toy sailboats on the pond. We watched the kids play then headed to the bridge. 'Are you warm enough?' I asked.

She poked her bald head out from an orange scarf. 'Just about. I hadn't banked on all that hair keeping me warm.'

'You look like a monk.'

'So do you.'

We lay down by the river and watched the clouds pass. I wondered what everyone else was doing. I guessed Jenö would be shaving Walter's head just as Charlotte had done

53

mine. She hadn't mentioned Kaspar and Irmi – maybe they had both exempted themselves. I wouldn't have put it past either of them to be more sensible than us.

'Let's play the hiding game,' she said. 'You're the sleeper.'

This was a ritual we kept. One person closed their eyes and counted to twenty. The other found an object and held it in their palm, describing to the 'sleeper' what they held in three words. I opened my eyes. Her hand was a fist.

'Refractive. Colourless. Very wet,' she said.

'That's four words, so you're cheating.'

'Wet,' she said, 'if I can't have "very wet".'

'It wouldn't be water?'

She opened her palm, some drops fell. 'How did you guess?'

'All right, you be the sleeper.'

She counted with her eyes closed.

I held out my hand to her. 'Encased. Minced. Piggy.'

'Sausages?' she said, her head cocked, confused.

'Wrong.' I opened my fist. '*Imaginary* sausages.'

'Doesn't count. It has to be here. Materially here.'

'How do you know it isn't? The whole river might be atremble with sausages if only you could see its singularity.'

'Even Master Itten would suggest the river is only water.'

'Master Itten can't always see what's in front of him. Just look at his attitude to my painting.'

I regretted this as soon as I said it. I didn't want us to argue about Mr Steiner's studio, not when we had been given a day as divine as this one. And, like a gesture from the gods, without warning the clouds split and the sun poured jewels so that the river heaved and brimmed.

'Charlotte! Look!'

The trees were struck yellow in the hectic blaze, and the grass beyond was as vivid as a painted field, and the Ilm was so bright that I wondered if Jerusalem hadn't indeed discovered itself.

Charlotte herself was spectral; transparent. She beamed!

Just then there was a curl of pleasure in my stomach and an odd sensation that I wanted to turn myself outward to reveal more of my nerves to the world. In that quickening moment I had the feeling that I knew everything quite vigorously. I stood at an apex. I knew, then, that I would continue with the fast as long as I could, to see what it would give me. If it was anything like this, a feeling of omniscience, then I wanted more.

Even when the cloud returned, the sun gone in, it didn't matter, because Charlotte's hand was still in mine for as long as we lay there. Yes, here it was; not Jerusalem, but paradise itself, discovered, in the scrubland, by the River Ilm.

# 8

## England

In the summer the optics here are almost useless. It's as if all the day's light has come through gauze rather than glass. It curves lines meant to be straight, makes pastels of colours intended to chill. The sea air has this softening effect. No more the rinsed light of our apartment in Kreuzberg, where the foundry powdered at the windows. Charlotte always said I was deeply susceptible to the weather, and it's true: a bright day can open a palace in my heart. It's just not so good to paint in.

I've been in England for so long that I should be used to it by now. Some years I simply leave work to a winter's pursuit, and in the summers instead I watch the sea and the fishing boats: men reeling in nets sequinned with water, their catches glimmering, and though I am alone, tramping around in my wellingtons, pretending I am nothing more than Paul Brickman, anonymous as any other Englishman, I imagine myself as happy with all this before me: this seafarer's bounty. It is almost enough.

It's a scenic picture, not unlike a Steiner painting: all

plashing water and oiled sunlight and fattened kids. I have said I am one of the lucky, and I still believe that is true: as a young boy I thought I'd die in French fields; in the thirties, I escaped Germany, because Irmi was able to lend me the money. No, I would not swap my life for any other. Walter, moaning about Goethe, humping a tree; sunshine by the Ilm with Charlotte; drawing lemons with Master Itten. Each memory is a loveliness, and I can't shake it off; this rebounded optimism.

My home here is comfortable and big. There's not much that doesn't have its place. In fact, there's really not much here at all. A simple kitchen and den, my bedroom up a level, then the studio on the top floor, which traps the more useful winter light. On the studio walls there are photos from the Dessau Bauhaus: one of us on a balcony, another from the Metal Ball. There's also one of Charlotte's weaves, damaged during the Berlin raid. It does its bit to brighten the place. Looking at one of her tapestries is like listening to a record. The yarn sings.

Aside from its simplicity, the house does not show my lineage; there are no Breuer chairs or Brandt lamps. With its rounded rocking chairs, pale walls and wooden furniture this house is more Shaker than Bauhaus. There's a print in the living room that I love: a Lucio Fontana, a canvas slashed: *Concetto Spaziale (Bianco)*. I think this is what Charlotte was aiming for when she introduced big holes into her weaves; a technique called openwork she trialled in Dessau. If she had lived, I imagine she might have taken her work in this direction; making space in the weaves. I look at the Fontana often: to think of the life she might have had, and the work she might have done.

●

Irmi calls again. Her voice is rich and mischievous, though we are having to talk carefully. A long time ago we stopped talking of our group because it caused too much tension between us, but now there's nothing else to speak about. Walter's dead, and Irmi has matters to attend to. She asks if I can come to his funeral. It will be held in Mitte, next week.

'I can't.'

I don't want to see him buried. I'd feel compelled to offer him forgiveness, or else St Irmi, good to a fault, would chivvy me to it. Besides, if Jenö were there I don't think I could bear it: our hopeless three watching the softly descending coffin, not knowing how to mourn our friend. 'I can't get a pass,' I say.

'Nonsense. You're a Saxon: you'd be coming home.'

'I'm bourgeois. I'd be a scalp.'

'You don't paint tractors or workers. They're not interested.'

Nothing she can say will persuade me to go.

'It's not his fault that Charlotte died in the camp, Paul,' Irmi says. She always was a straight talker. It's no surprise that she should feel no compunction about saying this outright.

'He could have got her out.'

'It was more complicated than that.'

'All it needed was a quiet word to Ernst.'

'Ernst Steiner was very high up then.'

'Exactly.'

'That's not what I mean. Steiner couldn't be seen meddling in the fate of a single prisoner.'

'Walter managed it for Franz.'

'That was in 1937! So much had changed by the time
she got there.'

'I don't believe the distinction, frankly.'

'It doesn't matter what you *believe*. You weren't there;
you were in England. Both you and Jenö, you don't know
what it was like.'

Pips on the line. I wonder if we are being overheard.
Maybe the conversation is commonplace: about who
was responsible, about who did what; about how much
exiles are allowed to judge. *Richtet nicht, damit ihr nicht
gerichtet werdet. Judge not, lest ye be judged*: this was an
embroidered panel my mother made for her Dresden
drawing room. And yet I can't help it; I do judge Walter; I
hate Walter, and my hatred makes me feel better.

'Charlotte was right. She said he was always strategizing
against her. Trying to rob her of what she had. Leaving her
in the camp: it was his last act. Don't you see? It was his
revenge.'

Irmi sighs. 'He wasn't a monster, Paul.'

'Then why didn't he *do* something?'

'I don't know. Besides—'

I try to interrupt but she won't have it.

'No. Listen to me now. Walter's dead! There's nothing
left to do, don't you see? You too could have done more,
but you didn't. And Walter didn't, and Jenö didn't, and I

didn't. There comes a time when all this fury is useless against it all.' There's a voice in the background; maybe it's her husband, Teddy. 'Please,' Irmi says. 'Come for me, at least. For us. For old times' sake; for what we had! I want to see you.'

'I can't. I'm sorry.'

'Go on,' she says, her voice gentle again. 'I'm broke. You still owe me for that ticket to Amsterdam. How much is a hundred marks after inflation?'

This is how much she lent me to get me out of Germany. 'I'll wire it to you.'

'Forget it,' she says, her tone hardening. 'I don't care. I don't want it unless you're here.'

Because I don't know what else to say, I hang up and listen to the telephone's song, watching the beach huts below as people take dips in the sea in the last of the day's warmth.

It won't make a difference whether I am in Berlin or not. Walter König can be buried without me.

# 9

## Weimar

We were a week into the fast when I saw something that made me think my eyes were playing tricks on me.

It was after one of my shifts at Mr Steiner's studio. We had been working on a commission of Christ ascending, all halo and fat cherubs. It was for a Jewish bank in Hamburg, Steiner said, laughing: something to make their customers feel at ease. It was a straight-forward commission because the light was so refulgent and frankly ridiculous, and Ernst said I could go a little earlier than usual. Thank goodness he did.

Once I hit town I went directly to the station bakery. It wasn't as good as the one nearest my lodgings, but by the time I cycled there, inflation meant I'd only be able to buy half a loaf. Like the others I wheeled my bicycle inside to offload Steiner's marks, and I heard the shop-keeper make his regular joke about preferring the basket to the cash.

The baker poured me a coffee – made from turnip, or chicory, it was only about a quarter coffee, anyway – then sliced the black bread that would be my breakfast and dinner. He knew to keep all the painters sweet – we were his first customers of the day, and besides I think he liked our company so early in the morning.

It was as I was finishing my coffee that I saw Jenö walking past the bakery window. It was not yet four thirty and still dark, but the light of the baker's captured his expression perfectly: he looked worried and full of remorse. Instinctively I wanted to ask him if he was all right, since I couldn't work out what on earth he was doing at this hour, and on the wrong side of the railway tracks to boot, but his manner made me hesitate. He had such an air of melancholy that perhaps a conversation would be useless, and instead I watched as he walked away, around the corner, and into the city. He had been so lost in thought that he hadn't seen me, on the other side of the glass, only a few feet away.

I went to bed thinking little more about Jenö's appearance at the baker's. It was so early, and I'd been so hungry, that I assumed I'd dreamt him up, a ghost in the fasted streets.

What with the late night, I spent most of Saturday asleep. Bed was also the easiest place not to think of food, so that's where I stayed. Every time I woke I was surprised that Charlotte wasn't standing above me, asking me whether I thought it a good idea that Steiner's studio had made me miss a whole day of my life. We usually spent the weekends together, preparing work for school, or cycling the woods, or strolling the Ilm. I gave her hanging lantern a tap, hoping it might invoke her presence here.

All afternoon I spent sketching, something I hadn't done in a while. My boarding house was on a hairpin turn, where the town's prostitutes often solicited business. Opposite was where the Communists met on a Thursday, and a bigger band of the NSDAP met on a Tuesday, although that wasn't hard, given the Kozis in Weimar might be counted on two hands. Below my rooms was the city's cemetery packed with famous dead men, and the striped Russian church, and the statue of a helmeted warrior with his sword up, whose name I never knew. I always liked him, perhaps because I fancied I saw myself in him: here was a man ready for action.

All afternoon I sketched the women below. Though it denied me a muse, I was always pleased when one of them found a customer. I imagined the meal she'd be able to eat afterward, and I wondered whether, with each man, she thought 'there's breakfast' and, with another, 'there's schnitzel'.

Later, when I heard a voice travelling the staircase, shouting my name, I assumed it was Charlotte, coming to explain her delay. But when I opened the door it was Irmi, standing on Mrs Kramer's WELCOME mat, her eyes scooting my room. 'Paul,' she said, her voice breathless. 'Where have you been?'

'Here,' I said. 'I've been here.'

I invited her in but she didn't sit down. 'All day?'

'Yes,' I said. 'Why?'

'Something's happened. With Jenö and Walter,' Irmi said, coming down heavily on the *r*. 'They're in trouble. Maybe we all are.' Irmi looked at my scalp. 'I don't know why you all had to shave your heads. It's only going to make things worse. Get your shoes and coat. We have to go.'

We took the staircase, but we hadn't escaped before my landlady shouted at me from her open window. 'No more noise, Mr Beckermann! I can't stand all this hollering.'

'Yes, Mrs Kramer!'

I wondered if Jenö's melancholic appearance outside the baker's was linked to whatever trouble he now found himself in. 'Where are we going?' I said as I caught up with Irmi.

'To the Bauhaus, of course.'

In the dark the cafeteria was as lit as a proscenium. Bald Walter and Jenö were hunched over the same table where I had first talked to Charlotte many moons ago. Charlotte and Kaspar were there too: bussing plates of food from the serving station. It wasn't yet dinner time, and no one else was in there. I felt left out, and wondered what they had all been up to without me, but I told myself not to be silly and put this feeling away. 'What's happening? Is the fast done?'

'I don't know,' said Irmi. She wasn't the one usually dispatched to run errands, and I wondered why she had let herself be. 'They just told me to fetch you.'

'We've only just begun,' I said, thinking about the high

by the river, and that I didn't really want to stop whatever that feeling had promised.

Inside, the cafeteria lamps lit Jenö's face more clearly. There were bruises along his jaw and another on his cheek. I couldn't remember seeing any bruises at the bakery, but then perhaps they hadn't come up yet. His big hands were on the table and they looked scuffed and sore. Maybe he'd been in a brawl. Maybe someone had picked on him at the Swan. Maybe it was one of Steiner's men. Walter didn't have a mark on him.

'Jenö, what happened?'

Charlotte placed a bowl in front of herself. Pulling herself erect, she began to eat.

'Charlotte, what's going on? What about the fast?'

She began to eat the stew slowly, and we all watched. 'Director's orders.' She chewed at her food. 'We all have to eat.'

'The Director cancelled the fast?'

'The Director doesn't want us doing this *funny business* any more. The fast is done.'

'But I was only just getting somewhere.'

Charlotte looked at Walter. 'You explain.'

Walter shifted in his seat and it was then that I noticed he looked different. Usually he went around with a high toss of his head as if he owned a good deal of the land you walked on, but now there was diffidence there. 'Something happened at the Bath-house.' He straightened his knife and fork as he geared up to his story. 'Forgive me for repeating myself. Everyone's heard this already.'

'Why didn't you fetch me earlier?'

'Too busy recounting the story,' he said. 'Well; I'll be brief. Jenö fainted in the sauna. It was very hot; naturally. And we were hungry from the fast.'

'You fainted?'

Jenö made a noise. I'd never thought of Jenö as a fainter. I could pass out easily with only a sighting of blood. But I'd never known Jenö – brickhouse that he was – to faint.

'I couldn't move him,' Walter continued. 'I called for help. A man came in; he worked for the Baths. He was slapping Jenö, trying to wake him. And when Jenö came to, well, he must have thought he was starting a fight. There were blows on either side.'

'What does the other man look like?'

'Worse,' Jenö said. Maybe it was the pain in Jenö's jaw that made Walter the storyteller. 'Much worse.'

'When was this?'

'Last night,' said Jenö.

'What time?'

'Late.'

'But what time?'

'Why does it matter?' said Kaspar, who was heartily eating his meal, finally out in the open.

'About midnight,' said Walter. 'The man's name is Sommer. He lives above Reinhardt's cobbler's.'

Jenö's hands tapped the table. 'He might press charges.'

'But he was the only one to witness it,' said Charlotte.

'Who will a judge believe? A citizen or a student? Besides, it's hardly honourable to argue my way out of what I did. I caused him harm. It's my responsibility.'

'The Director's talking to Mr Sommer,' Walter said confidingly. 'To persuade him not to press charges.'

'I'm so sorry,' Jenö burst out, penitent: 'I lost control of my temper!'

Walter moved his hand to cover Jenö's; it was the first time I had ever seen the two men touch like this. 'It was because of the faint,' Walter said. 'Obviously you didn't *intend* to hurt him.'

Jenö looked at him, searchingly. 'Still.' He touched his lips. 'Not much of an excuse.'

'You got off rather lightly,' I said to Walter, who, as I said, didn't have a scratch or a bruise on him.

'Not much I could do.' He looked at his hands. 'I'm hardly built for brawling.'

'What do we do now?' asked Irmi.

'No ostentatious behaviour,' Charlotte said. 'No more fasts. At the Bauhaus, and in town, we're as good as gold.'

Walter coughed. 'There is one more thing.'

'What now?' said Irmi, who seemed just about as irked as I was, and I saw Charlotte shoot her a look.

'We're under curfew.'

'What?' said Kaspar. '*All* of us?'

Walter nodded. 'The Director said "you six". "Master Itten's folk," he called us. "The acolytes. The bald ones." We're to stick to the Bauhaus and our rooms. And, once it's dark, nowhere else. We're under curfew until this whole thing blows over.'

Kaspar threw his cutlery down. 'Brilliant.'

Walter lowered his voice. 'The Director thinks there's a threat of retaliation. And the school's relationship with the city is fragile. I think he's scared we might get beaten up.'

'Right,' I said, but not knowing really what to say.

'I'm sorry,' Jenö said again. 'I got us all in this mess.'

Charlotte put her hands on the table. Her bowl was empty. She regarded Jenö's bruises. 'If I hadn't started the fast, this wouldn't have happened. We were foolish to have done it.'

I saw Walter try to arrange his thoughts; Charlotte's contrition was obviously unexpected. 'You can't blame yourself.'

'You said it was the fast that made Jenö faint.'

Walter made a kissing noise. 'The fast; the heat; it was a number of things.'

'It's my fault. I want to help.'

'Thank you, but there's little that can be done.'

'If the police press charges,' I asked, wanting to distract Charlotte from her guilt, 'what then?'

'Then it's curtains for the both of us.'

'Surely not?' said Kaspar, suddenly bereft.

'We can't go around beating up the citizens of *Weimar*, Kas. It won't do. The Director won't have it.'

I stood. The disordering of our six made me want to quit this place. Also: I had no desire to eat, and I wasn't going to squander my hard-won labours so far. It was no one else's business what I did or didn't do with my time.

'Where are you going?'

'Home. We're under curfew, remember?'

I expected Charlotte to come with me, but she stayed, and I left her to it.

I caught them one last time before I turned the corner for home. They looked a lonely group: rather exposed, and just ever so slightly stupid, as if I were viewing them with the eyes of the Director, or the baited citizens of Weimar, who had us now in their sights. The scene had an elegiac feel; no one looking at anyone else. Not long ago we'd been horsing about in the woods. Now we were menaced: because of stupid Jenö, and his stupid temper.

I watched them for longer than I meant to, until Walter caught my eye. And then I saw something I hadn't seen during the conversation: a look of pleasure drifting across his gaze, like happiness itself. It was then that I realised why Walter looked so different: he was without his spectacles.

# 10

## Weimar

The story was all quite strange. I had never known Jenö to faint, and though he could be mute when the situation warranted it, the fact that he hadn't offered a defence struck me as odd. All he'd done was apologise for his temper. Still, I chalked it up to misadventure: the police were never going to prosecute a couple of budding art students for a minor brawl, and so I spent Sunday preparing for Itten's class.

The next day we were to explore the properties of newspaper, identify where it was strongest and would bear the most weight, and how this might be applied to a three-dimensional structure. I spent the morning trying to make preparatory forms, working out how I could roll it, cut it, and bend it at different angles. But my mind couldn't keep itself on the task. Instead I kept on thinking about Walter's story. The incident had happened at midnight, and I'd seen Jenö at the bakery at four thirty. What had they done in between? And how had Walter been able to see what had happened in so much detail at the Bath-house, without his spectacles?

Later, in the afternoon, I went to find my friends, but they weren't in the Bauhaus, nor were they at the Ilm, and I didn't think that on a day such as today, when we were all meant to be doing our best impressions of altar boys, they'd be up at the woods cavorting. (What had I dreamt of in the woodland? Bacchanalian rites and witchcraft?) Besides, if they were, they would have invited me.

I called round to Walter's, and then Charlotte's, but neither was there. Kaspar was at Irmi's. She said she hadn't seen them all day; she'd been to church that morning 'on a whim', and Kaspar said he would leave shortly before our curfew began. I looked at Charlotte's rooms, but the windows were shuttered.

I went home, wondering why I had been the last to know the story last night. What had Walter said? *Forgive me for repeating myself?* Maybe it was just bad luck that I was the last to be fetched. After all, somebody had to be the last.

Inevitably, the whores came to the hairpin turn – no Sunday Sabbath off for them – and I heard Mrs Kramer's music, a Viennese waltz, sounding like it belonged to a different century, which put me in a melancholy mood. Things felt out of joint.

Without anything else to do I was a little lonely. I longed to eat but reminded myself of the promise of new vision: a state of fluorescence. I thought it'd be a struggle to get myself to sleep, but perhaps I was still tired from Friday night's shift at the studio, because after a shot of hot lemon water, I drifted off to sleep with surprising ease.

The next morning I felt clearer and brighter than I had done in a while. I ate some bread and drank some of Mrs Kramer's sticky morning coffee. I knew the Bauhaus would be rife with gossip from the Bath-house, and I didn't much want to get involved. That morning, I left it as late as I could.

When I arrived at school almost everyone from the first year was already in the atelier. What was odd was the way our group had split. There was Jenö, Walter and Charlotte on one side, with Kaspar and Irmi on the other. I don't know why I didn't go over to speak to Charlotte, but I wanted to ask Irmi about her trip to church, whether she'd been moved to religious feeling by the fast. Perhaps she'd felt the same thing as I had done by the river: that curious sense of omniscience and power. But Irmi was deep in conversation with Kaspar. 'Bloody Jenö,' Irmi was saying as I sat with them. 'Turns out Sommer is a friend of a local judge. They're goners.'

Kaspar, who was in all black as usual, nursed a coffee. 'Surely not for a few thrown punches.'

'Apparently Mr Sommer is black and blue.'

'According to who?'

'He came in this morning for a talk with the Director. Max saw him.'

'Jenö's dad,' said Kaspar, 'will have him working on his farm in no time. I'd rather be dead than go back to my old life.' This struck me as odd, because Kaspar, a Berliner, sounded like he'd had quite an exciting life before the

Bauhaus. It wouldn't be like me going back to tea and butter balls in Dresden; or Walter to some province of Westphalia.

'Will Sommer go to the police?' I asked. I knew I sounded naive, but I really hadn't thought it would escalate that far.

'Irmi has a theory,' said Kaspar.

Irmi looked at Kaspar.

'Go on,' I said. 'What is it?'

'Nothing.' She seemed peeved with Kaspar. 'Don't tell me you believe their story?'

'Why not?'

'I've never seen Jenö faint. You, yes' – she jabbed a finger in my ribs – 'but not Jenö.'

'Oh, Irmi,' Kaspar said, putting his hand on hers, 'do stop with the theories.'

She took his hand away. 'Paul doesn't think it's true either.'

'Don't you, Pauli?'

'I have no idea,' I said, with absolute certainty, since I didn't.

'Has Walter mentioned anything else?'

'No. I mean, I haven't seen anyone all weekend.'

'Jenö fainting. It's all hokum, I reckon.' She sawed the blunt part of a carving knife into her palm and the sound made me feel a bit sick. 'I think Walter did all the fighting himself and Jenö's covering for him.' And then she let out a throaty laugh and dropped the knife.

'Walter's a weed,' Kaspar said drily. 'He wouldn't hurt a fly.'

For a while I watched the others before Master Itten joined us. Walter was being particularly attentive to Jenö, but Jenö looked like he was keeping to himself. His bruises were yellower. Charlotte kept her head down, scrawling on a piece of paper.

Master Itten ignored our groupings when he walked in later. He asked us to close our eyes, and we began our meditation as usual. I expected someone to join me in my ritual espionage, but no one did; not even Kaspar. He probably didn't want to get caught; not right now.

Time passed slowly. I watched the room but everyone stayed still. I had the odd feeling that we were made from very fine powder, and with only a breeze we might be blown apart. If the police were to come for Jenö, then they would come for Walter too. How easy it would be to take us from our specialness here: some thrown punches and Jenö would be back to farm work. How quickly all this beauty could come unstrung!

Just before the Master's bell I closed my eyes so that people might think I'd been deep elsewhere. I came to in a faked dreaminess, but Itten was not watching me; he was looking at Jenö. 'Did you fall over, Mr Fiedler?'

This was for show: surely Itten had heard about the Bath-house. I'd be surprised if the Director himself hadn't cautioned Itten with what he was allowed to do with the students now. No more private conferences; no more fasts.

'Yes,' Jenö said.

Over the class I kept on trying to catch Charlotte's eye,

but she was deep in the exercise. We had an hour to make a new form from several sheets of newspaper. After yesterday's preparations I had decided on a boat: it was a shape that best exploited the material's properties. Everyone worked noiselessly. Even Elena, Hannah and Eve – whom we called the Three Graces – were quieter than usual, fashioning, in turn, an African-style hat, a blazer, and a big chunky necklace.

The Master roamed the classroom, commenting on the newspaper's materiality and its uncommon strength. 'Fold it six times and it's impossible to rip. Roll it up and bend it in two' – he flashed a look at Jenö – 'and it could kill a man.'

Afterward, he dismissed all of our creations – boats, hats, and aeroplanes – in favour of Gerhard's simple construction: he'd simply stood the paper on its edges. 'There it is!' Itten shouted in delight, which made the whole class simultaneously stop and also give up. 'Look! A material stiff and yet pliable enough it can stand where it's narrowest. The rest of it' – his look took in our vehicles and jewels – 'is just junk.'

My boat belonged in the bin.

'Better luck next time,' Irmi said. 'Mine's useless too.'

I felt a pang for whatever compliment Ernst might throw me for an oiled moon.

'Attention please,' Itten was saying. 'For next week's figuration class, I want everyone to have drawn someone else, full length. The body does not stop at the torso, oh no, and you may paint them in as many – or as few! – clothes as you choose, in any medium you choose. We'll be looking at the human form. The Bauhaus is not always about the will to abstraction. We must also give in to the caprices of the organic.'

There were smiles all round. This would be something at which I could excel. Steiner's studio had proved this, and in turn I could prove to Charlotte that the two disciplines might yet be complementary. 'Disassemble, please.'

There was never any wastage at the Bauhaus; everyone unfolded their newspapers and packed the sheets away. I smiled as Elena hid her necklace in her bag. Sometimes, there were little rebellions like this; sometimes, we did not do as we were told.

As I filed the newspapers in the storeroom I overheard Kaspar talking to Irmi. 'Jenö was caught doing this before, you know. In Munich. It's why his parents pay for his art school. To keep him out of trouble.'

I took a few steps back into the workshop so that I could hear them better. Irmi's expression was hard to work out, but then expressive people are often hard to read. 'Charlotte gave him quite a lecture in the cafeteria after Paul went. All about temperament and self-possession. Sometimes I think Charlotte has so much self-possession she might be dead.'

I'd always thought the two women were good friends; but maybe there was some cruelty in Irmi of which I wasn't aware. Both she and Kaspar were watching Charlotte now, who was looking at the beech forest framed in the window. When Jenö joined her they quickly became deep in conversation.

'I wish I could be like that.' Irmi wore a strange

expression; not envy, not quite, but as if she, too, yearned to have some of Charlotte's coolness. 'Yesterday I saw her sneaking off in the middle of the night.'

'She broke the curfew?'

'She didn't head to the Bauhaus, either.'

'Peeping at her from behind the Fürstenplatz, Spy Irmi Schüpfer?'

'I happened to be at the window, that's all. She had a big bag with her and a hat with a brim,' Irmi said. 'Now where was she going?'

'You and Paul! Why can't you just accept what Walter told us?'

'You, my dear,' she chucked him on the cheek, 'need to be less of an ingénue and more interested in the truth.'

'*Truths are illusions which we have forgotten are illusions.*'

'Oh, go back to bed, Mr Nietzsche.' Irmi gave Kaspar an elbow in the ribs but also a kiss. How easily I could watch them from my hidey-hole; how real and lovely was their affection for each other!

Walter walked into the storeroom just then. 'Stupid Walter,' he said. 'Not listening.'

Strips of paper hung from his forearm: he'd been reprimanded by Itten, since changing the material had not been part of the brief. 'Don't believe what they're saying about Jenö. He didn't mean to beat Sommer. It was a mistake.'

'They said he was arrested for something similar at home.'

'Even if that's true, he was defending me this time.'

'Against who?'

'Why, whoever he dreamed up in the faint.'

We went back into the workshop; Master Itten had already gone.

'Do you think Sommer will press charges?'

'Oh,' said Walter. 'I wouldn't be able to bear it if he did.'

I knew how he felt. If it had been Charlotte I would have been beside myself.

'Say they won't, Pauli.'

'They won't. Not for a skirmish in the Bath-house.'

When I turned back to the window, Charlotte had gone. And when I looked to the classroom – damn fool spy that I was – I saw that Jenö, too, had followed her out. I wanted to ask Walter – unbruised, unseeing Walter – to have a coffee with me, so that I could mine him for what had really happened at the Baths – but by the time I'd packed my things, he too had disappeared.

# 11

## Weimar

Those first nights spent under curfew were dull; life can be when you're not eating, and not allowed to go out. Rumours were circulating that city thugs were looking to avenge Mr Sommer's beating, and so, every evening, we all dutifully sloped to our lodgings alone. None of us wanted to get ourselves, or Master Itten for that matter, in any more trouble. Jenö especially was keen to observe the curfew, and often left before the last class had finished.

It felt strange to be alone, given that in our time here we had never been out of each other's pockets. Not knowing what else to do, I did my breathing exercises, put a few acupuncture needles in my legs (to draw out the poisons; this is what the Master had advised), and I imagined Charlotte doing the same in her candle-lit bedroom alone.

Hunger was everywhere. Though my appetite split my sides, I was surprised that my abstinence didn't so much exhaust as energise me. In many moments I teetered on a prolific transparency: the city felt mine for the taking.

I was sure, too, that soon my fasted vision would let me see through Walter's story. Like Irmi, I didn't believe all this hokum about Jenö fainting in the Baths. I wondered what it was that didn't add up. There were the unmentioned, and absent, spectacles. There was the lapse between the midnight fight and Jenö's appearance at the bakery. Then there was Charlotte's odd sortie on Sunday night, with her big bag and a hat, like a caricature of a grave-robber. I suppose she had a capacity for guilt that I didn't, and the fast had been no one's idea but her own. And what had she said to me? That she was a zealot; an obsessive – hadn't she compared herself with Margaret of Cortona, who was herself a penitent? I'd leave her to it. When she was on some private mission it was best not to distract her. This was, for her, just another form of escalation.

On Wednesday I heard the happy news that Sommer would not press charges. Walter and Jenö had been summoned to the Director's office that morning and told to expect instead a school tribunal. Everyone would be heard: Mr Sommer, Mr König, Mr Fiedler. And the Director would chair the meeting: no town representative or magistrate.

No one could believe the threat of police action had been removed so quickly. It was a triumph. All around the room the message travelled quickly: Jenö and Walter would avoid jail! Merely questioned by the Director, and didn't the Director think Jenö, especially, a fine and fee-paying student, who ought to stay? There was general consensus in the ateliers, in the Craft Building and the Prellerhaus, that Walter and Jenö would be all right, and that the Bauhaus in general would emerge unscathed.

They were not yet scot-free, but to see Walter's face over breakfast that morning, well, it was as if the future had been wiped clean. In fact, he seemed more positive and less melancholic than he'd been all week. 'It's all working out!' he said.

Over breakfast, which I ignored, we discussed Jenö and Walter's approach to the tribunal. There was the question of whether to mention that Master Itten had initiated the fast, and therefore whether it had been 'sponsored' by the faculty; whether Jenö should deny the previous brawls in Munich, should the Director have got wind of them; how Mr Sommer should be treated with the utmost courtesy and even deference – and that the fullest apology should be made within the Director's earshot: Jenö ultimately would own all responsibility for the brawl. Then it would come down to what was out of our control: the Director's mercy. Jenö was a good student, but he was also one of Itten's acolytes, and there was an awareness that perhaps the Director might take the opportunity to purge the school of its more eccentric, or at least expressionistic, elements.

Charlotte asked me if I wasn't thrilled. Of course I was: I said they'd sail through the tribunal, since that's what I'd overheard Hannah saying to Eve. I couldn't admit to her that the prospect of losing Jenö had looked increasingly attractive, that in the past week I had wondered whether it might not be a good thing if he were on his way. If he had done this before, might not he do this again? And if it were done again, wouldn't it plunge our group into even more serious peril? But these were impermissible feelings, and impermissible questions, and I pushed them away. Jenö was my friend. I should do right by him. Charlotte gave me a watchful look, then left to go to class.

'Not hungry?' asked Irmi, when the conversation between the others was tailing off.

'Lost my appetite.'

'You should eat. It'll keep your energy up.'

'What are you doing with your curfew?'

'Me? I'm cross-stitching chapels.' This was a joke. Irmi's work at the loom was modern and geometric. Her woven work was as fabulous as skyscrapers. 'Women's work. Nothing ever came of stitches in fabric.' Irmi raised her brows. 'What about you?'

'Oh, nothing much. Sketching lots.'

'And you're not fasting?'

'I'm on three square meals a day.'

'And I'm embroidering chapels.'

'Exactly.'

Irmi looked about to say something: but then decided not to.

'Irmi?'

'I shouldn't,' she said, biting her lip, watching Charlotte disappear into the Prellerhaus. 'I feel like I'm reporting on her. You know I can see her rooms from mine?'

'Yes?'

'She's been breaking the curfew. Heading off some-where: wearing a hat, holding a bag. Where's she going?'

'No idea. You think it's the same place she went on Sunday night too?'

'Did you see her as well?' Irmi asked.

'I overheard you telling Kaspar. Didn't you follow her?' I had meant it to sound off-hand, but the words came out seriously.

'I'm not spying on her, Paul.'

'I didn't say you were.'

Jenö and Kaspar left for the Prellerhaus, and Walter finished the last of his porridge.

Irmi lowered her voice: 'I didn't want to break the curfew. She might break her neck, but I'm not going out for the sake of Jenö Fiedler and Walter König. Will you ask her?'

'What?'

'Where she's going. But make it look as if it wasn't me who told you, will you?'

'How should I do that?'

'I don't know,' she said, 'I'm sure you'll think of some-thing.'

'Paul,' said Walter, interrupting us, his eyes shifting from me to Irmi. 'Any chance I might do a shift at the studio soon?'

'Is everything okay?'

Irmi was packing her things, readying to go.

His voice was all breeze: 'Just a few extra expenses. Because of the Sommer affair.'

'You won't be able to paint without your glasses, will you?'

Walter looked caught out. Irmi, too, paused. I'd been storing this gem since the weekend.

'It's only distance I can't see. I'll be fine.'

I told him to meet me outside the statue of the soldier at eleven thirty tomorrow night.

'What about the curfew?' asked Irmi.

'No one will catch us at that time.'

'Be careful,' she said. 'Won't you? We don't want more trouble.'

Walter got to the cafeteria door when he turned back. 'Aren't you coming?'

'No,' I said, 'I have a little job to do, first.'

He shrugged, and both Irmi and Walter left me to it. The fast had indeed delivered: I'd woken this morning with a plan. I don't know whether it was the patchy sleep or the hunger, but as I had gazed up at Charlotte's paper lantern swaying idly above me, its chambered rooms visible, I knew what it was I should do. If Walter hadn't recovered his spectacles, that meant they might still be in the Bathhouse, and that he was probably too afraid to retrieve them for himself. If he came to do a shift in the studio tomorrow night – well, so much the better. In the woods, I'd give him back his glasses in exchange for the truth. And then I'd be able to get the story down to zero.

During the fast my sense of smell had heightened. In my rooms the scent of mouse was stronger; the cafeteria I found by turns revolting and exquisite; the pigments in Kandinsky's class smelled of the reeded lake where my family holidayed in Moritzburg; and now, inside the Bath-house, the chemicals in the building's pipes were an unpleasant odour. All this time I had been banking on clearer sight, not a more accurate nose.

I was wary. This was the scene of the crime, and I knew if I should be caught in the Bath-house I'd be in trouble. Maybe I'd be found by Mr Sommer himself, who wouldn't mind throwing a few punches at a man much slighter than Jenö Fiedler.

In the locker room I put on a cap to disguise my bald head, and changed into my swimming costume. Some men gave me suspicious looks but didn't say anything, and I made my way to the poolside. The day's light hit the water hard, and it made me think of that rip of sunshine against the River Ilm that had moved Charlotte's hand to mine, and which had opened a boulevard in my heart. I had missed her these past few days. I'd call for her later: see if she wanted to start on the Master's figurative portrait together.

I went down some grubby backstairs, my footsteps alone on the staircase. I hoped it would bring me out directly to the sauna; I was relieved when it did, and I had not been followed.

The sauna door was fitted with glass, and for a moment I stood outside, imagining I was Mr Sommer looking in at the two men in the room. Jenö would have been unconscious on the floor; Walter, who wasn't always helpful in an emergency, would've been flapping around his friend. Sommer would then open the door to help Jenö, only to be knocked around as soon as the man came to, and

Walter would have been screaming at Jenö to stop. In fact, maybe Walter had been on the bench, keeping away from their fists, since he had emerged without a scratch. But if he hadn't been caught in the fight – as the question came to me I simultaneously cheered myself for the genius of having come here – how had he lost his spectacles?

The door gave with a shove. I sat down in case someone should find me here doing nothing, and pulled off my cap. I wondered how vulnerable I was. If someone was to come in here, would they hesitate in teaching me a lesson? It was quiet; only the benches creaked, and the air was dry and clear. It must have been a real scrap in a room this hot. On the floor there was a halo of ash or charcoal; perhaps still left over from Jenö.

How large his body would have been in this space; how much Walter would have loved to stake his claim. Surely it had been a tease for Jenö to come here with Walter alone. Walter couldn't swim, so the sauna must have been their only destination. Jenö knew they'd be naked, and light-headed, and hungry. Four hours later he'd be ghosting outside the baker's: a man half mad with hunger – or something else.

The door swung open; a man – not one of those from the changing rooms – waddled in and sat down. He looked at my shaved head but gave me a nod, and the swinging door flashed light under the other bench. I smiled, and though he didn't return the gesture, he also didn't appear too aggressive, and I thought I could just about get away with it.

I already knew what was under the bench. The fast had

given me this vision, and it had been correct. Crossing the room, I bent over to collect what I knew was there: the flashing object was Walter's tortoise-shell glasses, cracked on one lens. The man stared at me, obviously wondering what I was up to. And without really knowing what I was doing, I put on Walter's glasses, as if they were my own.

# 12

## Weimar

Before the war, my family holidayed in Obersee. Every summer we trained down from Dresden, stopping at Nuremberg, then Munich, then taking the tourist train out to the lake: my father fussing about whether we would make our onward connection; my mother, who could be an absent woman, vaguely enduring my devotion – I wanted to sit nowhere except for her lap, and stroke her hair, and lay my cheek against hers. Something about my mother has always made me sentimental, and to commune with her for endless hours was usually enough to keep me occupied; this, Peter found revolting. The day after our arrival (we weren't allowed down to the lake immediately, for a specific reason never explained to either me or my brother) we went out in the boat my father had chartered.

The lake at Obersee has an unsettling effect. The chemistry of the water traps the world's image in uncanny perfection: the mountains duplicate, the houses flipped, and the horizon such a thin seam as to be almost imperceptible. This liquefaction of the world induced in me a kind of vertigo: horizons and skylines wobbled perilously. It was why, I was sure, my mother wouldn't come on the boat. She said it turned her head: the glass lake, the ghost reflection, the beauty's queasy perfection.

Obersee's literal beauty is rather kitsch: its strident colours would appeal to a man like Ernst Steiner. It's a sentimental place, too, since when my brother went to the Front, my family stopped going, and it always now makes me think of a place that is innocent, and unwounded, and untouched by tragedy.

As I cycled from the Bath-house, Weimar metamorphosed into another kind of Obersee. The buildings receded; rocked; and the eagles and cherubs unpeeled from the brickwork. I could still with some acuteness smell the Baths, as if the city too were chlorinated and drenched. I could no longer be sure – it was the same feeling that I had on the boat in Obersee – that if I put my foot down it would hit hard ground.

In the market the reddening apples flared.

Worrying I was about to fall off my bike, I dismounted at the Frauenplan. My vision began to prick and dot. Maybe this was what had happened to Jenö. An energetic cycle, the heat of the sauna, the forfeiture of the fast: it was enough, yes, to make a man faint. I put my hand to my pocket; Walter's spectacles were still there. I held on to them. Soon, I would find their bigger meaning.

I heard my name called; I turned, there was my friend,

Kaspar Lemke, wheeling his bicycle over. I tried to steady my vision on him. Closer to, I saw he had a coil of rope, and he was without a jacket, oblivious to the cold. 'Are you all right?' he said. 'You're white as a sheet.'

'I might have overdone it at the pool.'

'Not breaking the Director's orders, are you?'

'I lost my breath, that's all.' Indeed, I already felt better, just for talking to someone else.

Kaspar's gaze wasn't without tenderness, but it wasn't without its sense of challenge, too. There were sweeps of masonry dust on his suit. I envied him his hair, its luxury. 'I don't think it would be a good idea to carry on with the fast. After all this stuff with Jenö. We don't need more trouble. Can't have *you* fainting as well.'

'I told you, I'm fine.'

He evidently didn't believe me, but decided to drop it. 'Did you skip class this afternoon?'

'I had to run an errand. Who told you that Jenö had been done for brawling in Munich?'

'Elena or Eve or Hannah. Can't remember which. One of the troika. What were you doing at the Baths?'

'I wanted to see where it happened.' I wondered whether I should mention Walter's spectacles: ask Kaspar how Walter had been able to narrate the story so well without being able to see clearly, but I remembered his admonishments on Monday.

'What's there to check on?'

'Walter's story just felt off. Didn't you think so?'

'No,' he said, but then Kaspar hadn't seen Jenö outside the bakery. 'You and Irmi might do better supporting them this Saturday rather than doing your own little investigations.'

'Of course,' I said, blushing, because he doubted my alliances. 'What's on Saturday?'

'The tribunal, of course.'

'Right.' And then I added, too heavily, 'It's brilliant the police aren't going to pursue this.'

He looked as if he didn't believe me, but then our attention moved to a shutter which banged in the old Goethe house. The house was so big there must have been twenty or so windows across its front. I remembered what Walter had said about Charlotte von Stein, roaming the woods, moaning Goethe's name. Such a big grand house had surely been his wife's house, not his mistress's.

Another student showed up, but Kaspar didn't introduce me. Instead he said he was going to the dump. 'Where are you off to?' he asked.

'Charlotte's.'

'Oh. I think she's back at school,' Kaspar said, swinging a leg over his bike. 'Masterminding their defence. Everyone's ecstatic they're not going to prison. But it's rather worth remembering,' he said, in a solemn tone, 'that they're not out of the woods yet.' Then he said goodbye in Italian, as if we were in Rome.

Our conversation had settled the world; the city was flat and unperturbed once more. Outside the Fürstenplatz there was a union leader preaching, and other men warming their hands at a burning can. Charlotte's rooms were in the damson-pink house in one corner of the square. At the doorway I looked to see if Irmi was at her window, watching me as she had watched Charlotte, but it was the middle of the day, and there was no one there.

The landlady shrugged when I asked if Charlotte was in, which I took as a good sign that she might be by now. There wasn't a response, however, to my knocking. I put my ear to the door but there was no sound aside from a faint percussive noise. Charlotte and I went freely into each other's rooms, but walking in alone always felt a touch transgressive.

The room had an unvisited feel. The tables were stacked with cloths and paints. Everything was piled on Biedermeier furniture. An easel was set up and an uphol-stered chair was positioned in front of it. All around there were touching examples of her failed weaves. Even three or four were enough to surprise me; I thought she had quitted the loom altogether. I found a tobacco tin of acu-puncture needles, and candles, and I wondered if she, like me, were continuing to fast. I imagined her putting the needles in her skin. The room would be warm and the light tinselled from so many candles burning down to nearly nothing.

It was the shutter that was bumping against the frame: that had been the noise I'd heard. Funny that I'd seen the same image at Goethe's house. I fastened it and sat facing the easel in the high-winged chair. I turned over Walter's horn-rim spectacles, tempted to pull one of the arms straight. My prints were on the other lens. I wondered what I should say when I presented them to him. I wondered whether they would be a gift, or a sting.

After a while I found some paper to leave a note. Charlotte's haphazard writing was on the back: a scrawl of sums: big numbers, into the hundreds of thousands. Master Itten had once teased her about her handwriting, asking how students were taught to write in Prague. You would never guess it was her, from her writing; or at least her loose style suggested a person she wasn't. I wrote her a quick message, asking if she'd like to get Itten's portrait done soon, then left it on the mat.

But just as I was about to go I heard footsteps ascending, and didn't have time to snatch it before Charlotte walked in. She was startled. Her cheeks crept with crimson. 'Oh, Paul!' she said, and she held her throat.

Jenö followed. 'Hullo,' he said. He had walked in whistling, as if a packet of good news had fallen on his lap. I suppose it had; the police weren't going to arrest him: that was reason enough to make a man whistle. There was a certain wizardry in Charlotte's eyes too: perhaps she was still fasting.

'We've been at school—'

'Masterminding a defence,' I said.

'Yes.' She looked at me oddly. 'Exactly.'

I wanted to know what was going on, but I also didn't want to have to ask. Her heeled boot was on my note. Jenö went to the fire, which was dead, and fanned the coals. A flame began to flare. The magic touch.

'How do you feel about the tribunal?' I asked him.

It was almost comic, how grave both of them became.

'Jenö feels really bad about it,' she said (as if Jenö were unable to ever speak of the matter directly). There was that stitch in her forehead again. 'He lost all sense of himself. You must know that feeling. After a faint.'

'Sure,' I said, though I didn't. After a faint, I hardly had enough energy to stand, never mind box someone's lights out.

'Do you think you could lend something for Walter to wear? He can't afford a new suit. And you're the same size.'

'All right.'

Jenö sat bonelessly on the chair. He didn't look like he felt bad at all; instead, he looked dreamily to the parkland's river and sheep. Charlotte went to the easel and flipped a few sheets over, rubbing out some green chalked marks, which came off on her hand. Then she scrunched the paper into a ball. Jenö frowned.

I held Walter's spectacles in my pocket: feeling their sleek curves. 'I was at the baker's on Saturday morning, Jenö. The one near the station.'

I watched in her expression how she suppressed her interest.

'You came past. I'd just finished at the studio.'

'I couldn't sleep,' Jenö said at last. 'Too keyed up.'

'It's near Reinhardt's cobbler's.'

'Yes. I went to talk to Sommer.'

'Did you?' Charlotte said. 'You didn't tell me that.'

'At four in the morning?'

I wanted to coax from him all the words he was stopping

himself from saying but I didn't know how. When they had come in both of them had seemed almost high; now Jenö was alert and quick-witted. I noticed his throat work. 'I went to apologise.'

'You have to tell me these things,' she said. 'There can't be any secrets.'

'And what did Sommer say?'

'Obviously he didn't want to talk to me for long. I just told him how sorry I was.' He offered up his hands, a *mea culpa*. 'I admitted it was my fault. That the faint had made me confused. That I'd lost my wits.'

'Good, that's good,' said Charlotte. 'It was a bad idea: the fast, and all that. Master Itten's in trouble now too. The Director wants things to be straightforward. He can't stand a scandal.'

She disappeared into the kitchen, and Jenö and I didn't really look at each other, and we certainly didn't talk to each other. In fact, he closed his eyes, and I was left standing at the door, doing nothing. When Charlotte came back her skin looked rinsed and her eyes more fierce. She massaged her scalp; I could see the skin move under the stubble. 'Your job at the studio. Do they need help?'

'I don't think Mr Steiner accepts women.'

'Not for me. For Walter. He's going to need the money.'

'Oh, he already asked me. We're going tomorrow night.'

'Oh, good,' she said.

'What happened to your objections?'

'Needs must,' she said, smiling.

I looked at Jenö, who still had his eyes closed. I realised then he'd dropped off to sleep.

Charlotte laughed. 'Have you ever seen anything so ridiculous?'

Wake him up? Tow him out? I couldn't think what else to do; I would have to leave him here. 'I miss you,' I ventured. 'I haven't seen you all week. It's not your fault Jenö lost his temper.'

'I just don't want either of them to go. And I feel responsible. If I hadn't suggested the fast—'

'He wouldn't have fainted. I know. You're not still fasting, are you? With all this going on,' I said, thinking if I used Kaspar's words she might believe me, 'it might not be a good idea.'

'Oh no. I ate the most enormous sandwich for lunch.' She gave a cheery laugh, which convinced me she was being sincere.

'You're thinking Sommer might want compensation? That's why Walter needs a shift at the studio?'

'That's the best-case scenario.'

'The other?'

'That they might go, Paul. It's serious,' she said, her tone changing again. She looked at sleeping Jenö. 'Don't you see? All week it's as if you haven't really cared.'

'I do, Charlotte, how can you say that? I'm taking Walter to the studio tomorrow. I'll lend him a suit. I'll help how I can.'

'That's not it. You've been disengaged.'

I wanted to say to her: I'm not disengaged, I'm wary; that everything felt embroidered; that everything felt like a fiction. And I suppose I too had my part to play. 'The last thing in the world I want is for Jenö to go.'

'Well, act like it, then. Pretend you care.'

'You've hardly been around to know I do care.'

'I'm sorry,' she said, puffing her cheeks. 'I just want it over.'

'The curfew's lonely.'

'Oh, Paul, it's only been a few nights.'

I held her hand. 'What am I meant to do on my own?'

'Oh, I'm sure you can keep yourself occupied.'

'Where do you go? In the curfew? With your bag and hat?'

'Are you spying on me? That must mean you've broken the curfew too.'

I shrugged. 'I got bored,' I said, hoping the lie would cover Irmi's tracks.

'Nowhere. I haven't been going anywhere. Tell Irmi to mind her own business.'

Evidently not. 'Can you come around tonight? Keep me company?'

At which point Jenö let out a deep, rumbling snore.

She laughed. 'I will if I can wake him up. If not, tomorrow.'

'Tomorrow I'm at Steiner's.' I added: 'With Walter.'

'Well. We'll work something out.'

I kissed her goodbye, and it was then that I could smell the bar-room off her. And I was so busy in my realisation that the chemical smell wasn't the chlorine from the Baths, but alcohol, that I forgot to pick up my note. As I walked down the spiral staircase, my mind was alive with this new knowledge: they weren't fasting: they were, in fact, both drunk.

I don't know which one nettled me more that evening as I spent another night alone: that my message would expose me even more as completely uncaring of Jenö's situation, or that I had left him alone, and sleeping, in her rooms.

As if in confirmation of my feelings, overnight the fast's expansiveness disappeared. I slept badly. I kept on obsessing about the note and how much I wished I hadn't written it. If there was one thing she believed in – in this she was so like Kaspar, always wanting us to stick together – it was our sacred six. We should not be put asunder. She would not want dissent. The note exposed that I didn't care.

Her lantern swayed above the bed. I don't know why it bothered me, but it was keeping me awake. Unwiring it made it collapse: all the rooms folded in. I laid it on my desk.

It was very cold when I opened the window. Even with the first brushstrokes of light there was a guilty air to the streets: there might be thugs lurking, or a band of Kozis looking for a fight. Maybe I'd see Charlotte, with her bag or cap, or see Jenö skulking as I had done outside the baker's. But no one was around. Even the whores had gone to bed.

Just then I had the rushing sensation that things were happening over which I had no control. One can speak of disquiet, but what does it mean? A feeling in the bones; in your eyes; the pit of your stomach. I didn't know its source. Things did not feel right, but I didn't know where this feeling came from – or whether it was simply the paranoiac vapours of the fast. In the mirror my gaze reminded me of a painting of a turbaned Coleridge stumbling from an opium den into the outside light. I put Walter's spectacles on the sill. They were the answer, I thought. They would reveal the truth.

Thankfully, by the morning, my unease had lifted. The nightmarish thoughts were gone. There was a vibration in my left eye but I put this down to the fact that over the past few days I'd eaten nearly nothing and had very little sleep. Perception, now, if it came at all, would come *in extremis*.

# 13

## Weimar

Though Paul Klee painted *Bird Garden* a year after everything that happened at the Bath-house, I find that painting strangely congruent with how I view those weeks which disarranged us for the next decade, so that, even in Berlin, we were forever changed by those events. Because it was during this week that Walter learnt to hate; and perhaps all that hate began when lies were told, and secrets kept, and allegiances slipped.

Klee's *Bird Garden* is a procession of waterfowl. The paint is applied so thinly that the leaves and even the newspaper it's painted on – Klee was no richer than the rest of us – are visible behind the negligible birds. We don't realise at first how flyaway, how transparent, is each form. There's a delicacy to the birds' footing, and the sense that with only a breath each shape would roll away as easily as cigarette paper. Whenever I look at this painting, there seems more depth than there really is: we are not looking into a garden but a pool – and yet, peer closer, and that depth is an illusion. There's really nothing there.

I still believe that my version of that week could be blown away as easily as those birds; that my story is simply a layer upon someone else's, and that theirs is a layer on mine. Even now Irmi could tell me that my understanding of what happened in Weimar is false; the pool is depthless, the stories were real.

Klee of course wouldn't have known what happened at the Bath-house, and neither would the Director, nor Master Itten, who was let go, anyway, months after the incident. It wouldn't have really mattered to the staff; these details. To them, two fasting men went to the Bath-house. A student fainted. A townsperson tried to revive him. The student was confused and threw some punches. And then, much later, the Bauhaus closed.

This is my whole story perhaps. Recollection scratched against recollection.

The next day we had tours of the ateliers (Metal, Stone, Weaving, Wall-painting) that we would choose for our second-year specialism. No one else had opted for Wall-painting, despite the fact Master Kandinsky would teach it; more fool them, I thought. Like Jenö, Charlotte had chosen Metal, though she must have known the Director would never admit a woman into that workshop.

That afternoon Master Kandinsky gave the Wall-painters a long speech. He was a tall man who gesticulated wildly with his Russian-inflected German. He talked for a long time about the aesthetics of colour and their natural forms, about metamorphosis, and seeing and not seeing, but it must have been impenetrable (his teaching often was), because I can hardly remember a sentence of what he said.

Walter and I kept our curfew separately that evening. I had figured the worst time to break the curfew would be in the evening, but no one would be spoiling for a fight as late as midnight. And so, perhaps because of Master Kandinsky's class, when we cycled to the woods together that night I imagined myself like Kandinsky's magnificent *Blue Rider* on his horse, going at such a gallop as to render the autumn in which he rides nothing but speeding trees.

In the studio, Walter was timid at first. Like me, he wore a cloth cap to disguise his baldness, and he kept to the corner of the room until I beckoned him over to the pearly skin of an already ravished Leda. Her retinue were still only outlines, and the courier was coming tomorrow. It boded well for Walter's chances.

When he saw the painting, Walter's expression changed completely. 'Why don't we make things like this at the Bauhaus?'

'Because it's useless?'

'But still,' he said, 'magnificent.'

I took him to Mr Steiner's office and Walter took off his cap. I shut the office door so that the other men couldn't see his bald head.

'Yes?' Steiner said, his face still buried in the ledger. I saw the anchor tattoo on his neck. The thing about Mr Steiner was that despite his ability to work the market, or put the money in the right dealer or politician's hand, he still had quite poor taste.

'My friend needs some work, Mr Steiner. You said you needed all hands on deck. For Leda and the Swan?'

He hadn't quite said this, and he knew it. As he looked Walter over I wondered if this was a good idea or insanity. If the other workers found out that Walter was part of the Bath-house brawl, would he be beaten up? And what would I do? See blood and faint? There was something else to Mr Steiner's gaze. Maybe he recognised Walter from the Swan. 'He's a painter?'

'Yes.'

'At the Bauhaus too?'

'That's right.'

'It's a bit early to be introducing apprentices, isn't it, Mr Beckermann? He might do you out of a job.'

I shrugged: I had no answer for this.

'Half pay. If everyone else rates him, he can stay.' He looked at Walter. 'When you paint the women, think of your sister.'

'I don't have a sister.'

'Your mum then. Don't mess them up.'

'Thank you, Mr Steiner,' said Walter.

'Call me Ernst.' This was odd. He had never given me such permission. 'Aren't you meant to be under curfew?' he asked, as Walter returned to the canvas.

'Yes. But I need the money. You know how it is. Spend a hundred, lose a thousand.'

This softened him, and he let me go.

I painted the big sky for a few hours while Walter worked on Leda's crowd. He worked close to the canvas, to make up for his lack of spectacles. Other men on other canvases worked elsewhere. Leo the courier came to take a commission even while the paint was still wet. All the padlocks took the same combination: 1919 – the year Ernst had founded the studio; the year, too, of the founding of the Bauhaus.

'Are you all right, Pauli?' asked Walter.

'Fine,' I said, giving Walter a thin smile, and gesturing at the skittering clouds. 'Just working out the direction of the wind.'

'Does Mr Steiner make lots of money from this?'

'Tons,' I said. 'But we'll see only a fraction.'

'Who does he sell to?'

'Foreigners. Anyone with *valuta*.'

A few steps back I saw that the sky's light was too approximate: Ernst liked it literal and disambiguated. I'd have to go over it.

'Do you ever think about why you paint?'

'I don't know,' I said, taken off guard. 'I guess it's always been a way to make sense of things.'

Walter nodded, brush held aloft. Without his glasses he stood close to the canvas. 'It's a form of truth-telling?'

'Not exactly' – though it had started out as that – 'more a way of understanding what's already there.'

'Does this picture hold any truth to you?'

'This?' I analysed the commission. The women were not so different from Kirchner's *Bathers at Moritzburg*. 'I don't know.'

'It's my father's taste, but I can see why someone might like it,' said Walter. 'There's beauty in it. Do you see beauty in it?'

'Isn't it a little deceptive? Look at the way the brush-work disappears; it's all surface.'

Ernst told us to get back to work. Were we a couple of old wives, come for a chat? Walter stared at him for longer than I did, but then returned to Leda's army, staying with the nymphs all night. His brushwork was lovely: his paint dazzled their hair.

During the shift break we went outside. I loved the woods like this. The air in the forest was so cold and the trees creaked in the dark. Ernst passed around beers and someone else shared a flask of coffee. My one meal of the day – black bread and butter – tasted deliciously of turpentine and paint.

'Have you ever brought Charlotte here?'

'To the studio? I don't think she'd be allowed.'

He looked at my mouth and my eyes. 'Ah,' he said, 'but I think she'd like it.' There was something about Walter tonight: he had swung into happiness again. Really all week he had been either marching to the gallows or walking down the aisle. I beckoned him over to where we couldn't be heard or seen. To let him continue with his nose a quarter of an inch from the canvas would be embarrassing. I brought out his spectacles from my overalls.

'You never found them! Where were they?'

'In the sauna. At the Bath-house. They were on the floor. Why didn't you get them yourself?'

'No chance I was going back there. Thank you.'

'What happened?'

'I told you. They were knocked off. During the fight.'

'But that doesn't make sense. You said you weren't hit.'

The trees squeaked in the wind. 'And you didn't have a mark on you.'

'It was just my glasses that went for a sail, then.'

'Of their own volition?'

Then the smile, full, unbridled; and a display of his palms.

'Come on,' I said. 'Why didn't Jenö tell his side of the story?'

'I think his jaw hurt.'

'And Charlotte keeps on breaking the curfew with big bags. What's going on?'

'Did Irmi see that? Yes. She sees things, doesn't she?'

'No one believes the story you've told.'

'Don't they? I thought Kaspar had bought it. All that Nietzsche and yet he'll swallow any story.'

The bell was rung for time, and the painters began to head into the studio. 'Look, I'll tell you everything after the shift.'

'What if we're seen? It's still the curfew, and people might be around.'

'In the cemetery, then. No one will be there at five in the morning. Oh, Paul, I don't think I've ever felt so happy!' He put his glasses on. The wonky spectacles made him look rather mad. 'Lucky my left eye is the stronger one.' He winked either eye, trying to find his sight, then finished his beer in one. He strolled into the studio like a man who couldn't throw his happiness off him. 'Lucky, lucky!' he shouted.

Walter König, half blind, unrequited, accused of attacking a citizen he had not laid a hand on, on the brink of expulsion from the school he loved: as he disappeared into the studio, it struck me that he wasn't a lucky man in the slightest.

A while into my brother's military training, we started going on holiday to the Moritzburg Lakes. Without Peter, my father said the trip to Obersee wasn't really worth it, and Moritzburg was closer to home. But Moritzburg was no mirror lake. The reeds were thick and the water silted. The woodland around it was dark even at midday, and there were several places I was not allowed to go. I missed my brother terribly.

In lighter moods I heard my mother laughing to my father, asking if they shouldn't take a trip on the lake and leave me behind. Behind? And be left with whom? The nanny had gone on her own holiday and there was no Peter to keep an eye out against these secluded groves; these needs for privacy. Travelling at speed in my father's motorcar I'd often spot a rushing between the branches: bird-flight, probably, and then my mother would make some incongruous comment about the weather, though I kept on questioning what was between the flickering elms.

Seeing Kirchner's *Bathers at Moritzburg* – a group of naked swimmers kissing and carousing by the water – convinced me that I wanted to be an artist. I was sixteen when I saw the painting. Not only did the veil drop from my eyes, as if Kirchner himself had parted the trees and revealed the naked bodies to the young boy's stare, but it was the painting itself which seemed to awaken me from all stupor – the primitive forms, the block colours, the thickness of the impasto: all this had combined into an astonishing seduction of my gaze.

From that moment on, I wanted to make work like that. After seeing the Kirchner painting I would forever see art (and it was an unfashionable notion, even then) as a means to the truth. The painting had lanced the woodland and revealed the truth. Though Obersee might astonish, it was the silted Dresden lakes that really changed how I viewed the world.

And the Bauhaus was the culmination of all this. I had heard of the new art school as soon as it had opened. I had read its manifesto, its ideas of putting men and women, and the arts and crafts, on equal footing. Utopia in Weimar: which it was, at least for a little while.

Besides, it was the only place a modern artist would dream of studying. Despite all of my father's reservations (he wanted me to attend Dresden Art Academy), I persuaded him to pay my fees: I appealed to his nature that genuinely believed, as I did, that there was a truth in beauty that could be captured by the brush on the page.

When Walter asked me whether the Steiner painting told a truth, I had lied, to seem worldly and impervious to what I knew were old-fashioned values. Of course, truth meant something to me, even in the butchered form we gave it in the Steiner Studio. After all, that had been the whole point of the fast: that with enough work, the world's transparency would eventually reveal itself.

# 14
## Weimar

In the cool of the morning Walter and I walked the cemetery path in silence, our bikes held by their necks. We weren't meant to go in there after sunset, and the dark as well as the curfew intensified our sense of trespass. Under the trees were bright mushrooms and spring flowers. Everywhere there were dead Walters on the gravestones: Walter Schwarz, Walter Richter, Walter Beck. I only hoped Walter König didn't notice them as well.

We stopped by a ruin, moss creeping its walls. Walter ditched his bike outside, Steiner's cash still inside the basket. It was lighter inside, as if the stone threw off the dark. He leant against the wall; and I saw that smile again, like a man three leagues in love. 'Thanks for sharing your work with me,' he said. 'I know there's not much around.'

'It's nothing. Mr Steiner liked you.'

'You can tell that already?'

'I'm sure you'll be invited back. If that's what you want.'

'I think it would take care of expenses, yes.' He slid down the wall. 'You know I'm in love with Jenö?'

'Yes.'

'Oh, but Paul! Something *magical* has happened!'

'What's that?'

'I think he's falling in love with me too.'

'Really?' I thought of seeing Jenö in Charlotte's room, with that dreamy gaze as he looked at the parkland. Yes, it clicked into place: I'd been looking at a man in love. 'Jenö didn't faint, did he?'

Walter shook his head. 'He told me not to tell anyone. He told me that I must keep absolutely quiet.' He waited for something inside him to give him a cue, then he said, 'Mr Sommer walked in on us. Kissing.'

'Ah. I see. No faint?'

'No: no faint.'

That's why his specs were off: he had taken them off to kiss Jenö. They hadn't been swatted away during a fight.

'Do you think this is it? Do you think he has feelings for me?'

'I don't know. Have you asked him?'

'I can't,' he said, choked. 'I can't.'

'Why didn't you tell me the truth?'

'Jenö made me promise. Oh God, you won't tell him, will you? It would ruin everything.'

'I won't. Don't worry. I promise.'

Walter's laughter was a little bark. 'All this time I haven't known what to do with myself. I swing from hysteria to misery within an hour. It's all I've ever wanted. I'm on the edge of getting it, and the uncertainty is killing me.'

'What has Jenö said?'

'Not much. I think he's trying to work out what it all means.'

He stood. We reclaimed our bikes and wheeled them through the cemetery's paths: passing grave after grave – even Goethe's crypt, which Walter nodded at respectfully – until we neared the Russian Church. The building was striped in ochre and gold, its domes teal. 'Shall we go in?' Walter asked, his voice a dare, his shoulder already pushing the heavy door.

Inside, the church was smaller than it looked from the outside. There was a portrait of the Virgin and the baby against the altar. The emptiness of her gaze reminded me of Charlotte's neon stare.

'Oh, Paul. It's all so much!'

'But Walter,' I said, unable to resist smiling, 'isn't this what you've been hoping for? Why are you sad?'

'Somehow,' his voice gave a squeak, 'it was – it is! But I've no idea if there's a future in it.'

'Give it time. Jenö doesn't know if he has a future at the Bauhaus. Let alone with you. He's still got Saturday's tribunal. If the Director decides he's not fit to study—'

Something passed over his expression, as if there were reserves of information I still didn't know. 'The trial's a dud. Sommer's been paid off.'

I thought about Charlotte breaking the curfew; how Irmi had seen her leave at night with a sack. It must have been filled with cash. I wondered how much the bribe was. Thousands? Or hundreds of thousands? 'Did Charlotte do that?'

He nodded. 'She feels ever so guilty about the faint.'

'But there was no faint! That's not fair, Walter. Is it her money?'

'I'm paying her back, don't worry. A few shifts at the studio and I should see the deal right.'

'What's everyone worrying about then?' I thought about Kaspar's words at the square, that she had been 'masterminding their defence'. 'If the trial's a dud?'

'A whole lot of nothings. Do you think Jenö might feel something for me?'

'Well, did he stop you, when you kissed him?'

'Pauli, no, you don't understand,' he said, searching my face, looking for how to say this: 'He kissed me,' he said, 'he kissed *me*.'

And, just as I had thought that perhaps, for Walter, this was the great pinnacle of his time here, the ghost of Jenö walked past the glass front of the baker's, and I saw again his expression of profound regret; his visible pain.

My heart sank. I don't know why I needed to lie to my friend just then: why I couldn't simply accommodate his worry rather than give him false hope. 'Well, there you are,' I said, feeling Walter's body relax against the church bench: 'Take heart. He made the first move. Now you just have to wait.'

# 15

## Weimar

We worked quietly the day before the trial. Our class was in Kandinsky's atelier with its view of the city's buildings, and the sea of trees over at the beech forest. Master Itten was talking to the Director in his workshop; we'd been left without a teacher, and given junk from the scrapheap to demonstrate varying textures. It was a task designed to keep us occupied.

All day people gathered around Walter and Jenö. I guess everybody had their cautious words of counsel: what to do in the tribunal, and what should be said to the Director. Charlotte acted as a gatekeeper: letting in certain people; rebuffing others. A rumour was going around that as well as Jenö and Walter, Master Itten too might be expelled. Itten, however, had no one to pay off. He had avoided us all week since news of the fight had broken. Understandable: he had no wish to jeopardise his job. Walter, unsurprisingly, looked completely relaxed. The trial was a dud; that's what he'd said just hours ago.

I felt curiously deflated. I tried to read Jenö's behaviour, to see in him the habit of returned love that Walter had hoped for. Jenö looked dazed, but that could be down to anything; the trial tomorrow, as well as all of this unwanted attention.

Though I kept on looking over at him – imagining their kiss in the sauna, the press of their bodies in the heat, an image so visceral it stirred in me a desire to be the third in that closed chamber – Jenö avoided returning my gaze. Maybe he *was* in love with Walter, and when I'd seen him outside the bakery his regret had been for the violence he'd inflicted on Mr Sommer, and not for the kiss.

Indeed, as Walter talked to his well-wishers, Jenö was looking at him with frank astonishment, and, yes, almost love. At one point, Walter clocked me watching, and he nodded, as if to say: here we are; this is what I told you; here's all the evidence in droves.

It wasn't melancholy in the room that day: more like quiet solidarity, and I felt bad for not going over to them, to give a specious word or two for a junk trial. Charlotte kept on looking at me: probably wondering when I would talk to them. But in my head there was a high sort of pressure. When I'd woken this morning, with only a few hours of sleep after the trip to the cemetery, my peripheral vision had all but gone. In the past this had been a warning of a headache, or, even worse, a migraine. But I thought perhaps it was the last augury of the fast: that I was on the verge of seeing anew.

At one point I caught Charlotte with her hand outstretched. Jenö said something, she shook her head, and from her fist out sprang a tiny man made from newspaper. He laughed.

The fast made me wobble the grommets and hairpins I was forcing into a sculpture, but I couldn't hold everything as I wanted to. Over a meagre breakfast – I had dreamed, after the graveyard, of buttered toast and croissants big as hammers – I had wondered if everything Walter had told me was, at worst, a lie; or, at best, a complete invention: not only that they'd kissed, but that Jenö had kissed *him*. Neither had he left me with anyone to corroborate the story. Only we three knew. And I had promised not to breathe a word of it.

Irmi came in later; I wondered where she had been; she wasn't one for skipping class. She looked at Charlotte rather mutinously. She set up next to me, unloading what she'd found at the dump; metal washers and bicycle handlebars.

I wanted to tell her what I knew, but I could not imperil the secret; not when everything was so finely balanced.

'I saw Mr Sommer leave the Director's office,' she said immediately after sitting down.

'How'd you know it was him?'

'The bruises gave him away.'

'And?'

'He's *ancient*, Paul, he's ancient. Why would Jenö ever believe a man that old would be a threat?'

Walter hadn't mentioned Mr Sommer's age: not in the cafeteria, not in the cemetery. But then why would he have? This new fact cast Jenö in a terrible light.

Most of the student body came to the Swan on Saturday when word got out that neither Walter nor Jenö would be expelled. The school tribunal had – unsurprisingly, at least for the four of us – been a brilliant success. In the pub Walter regaled us with his version of the trial (doing the voices of both Sommer and the Director and even an exaggerated form of Jenö's Bavarian twang) while we waited for Charlotte and also Jenö, who had been detained the longest, and who was the star of this show.

'A hundred thousand marks a week, every week for eight weeks,' Walter said, holding court at the bar – although Mr Sommer, too poor or too stupid, had not demanded the payments go up with inflation. 'In a month or so,' Walter said, 'he'll be wishing he'd asked for a bag of marbles instead.'

Everyone laughed, and I looked at Irmi. She was inspecting the shabby carpet. I knew we were both thinking of Mr Sommer's age. He's *ancient*, Paul, *ancient*. I don't know why Walter had to crow so cruelly, especially given they'd won.

'It's Germany's new Bath-house Plan!' he announced, and he said it in English as if he were David Lloyd George himself.

Even in Jenö's rolling walk you could tell the manner of his mood. 'Everything's fine!' he announced as he came into the Swan and Irmi let out a noise which was like a celebration. Jenö shook our hands, Walter's and mine, and then took Charlotte into his arms and I heard him whisper, 'Thank you,' in her ear.

I was pleased that Walter and even Jenö could stay, but it was in Charlotte that the happiness was truly expansive. 'Isn't it a relief! It's such good news! Jenö can stay!'

'You never needed to feel so bad about the fast,' I said. 'It wasn't your fault.'

Jenö's features were animated. 'Like that,' he made a big gesture: 'swept under the rug.'

We clinked our glasses, and I watched Walter finish his drink as if he hadn't had three beers earlier.

'Everything's back to how it's always been,' Jenö said, and his expression, I thought, was the opposite to what I'd seen at the baker's last weekend: today he was a soul sprung free.

The six of us stood awkwardly. We hadn't been together since the cafeteria. I felt quite gone, drinking as I had been on an empty stomach, and had to remind myself to keep step with their cheer, but the headache was massing, and I longed for home. Anyway, Charlotte's manner told me I couldn't leave. Not yet. I had to be here.

'No more punch-ups,' said Kaspar.

Jenö did a little jab: a one-two, then he dusted off his knuckles and put them away. 'I shall be as good as gold for the rest of my artistic career.'

'I wouldn't bet on it,' said Irmi.

'Is the curfew over?' said Kaspar.

'Yes,' said Walter, 'we're free to roam. Just be careful of the Bath-house. I think there's still a price on our heads there.'

Sunlight flooded into the room. I'm sure it made everyone feel doubly drunk because we were carrying on as if it were three in the morning rather than the afternoon. Jenö stood on a table and shook at a stuck window. 'Fuck, it's hot in here,' he said, pulling at his shirt.

One of the locals told him to get down.

But then a cloud moved over the sun and the room's temperature dropped. Jenö's face turned exuberant. 'Ha ha!' he shouted, then beat his chest. 'I am Jenö! The all-powerful!'

Everyone laughed. Irmi tried to pull him down by a trouser leg, but Jenö (he must have been very drunk, this was so unlike him) swung her up to dance. There wasn't much space on the table-top, and he took up the bulk of it.

'All right, Jenö, enough!' Irmi said. 'We're going to fall!'

'Come down!' shouted Charlotte, but she was laughing too. 'No more *funny business*!'

Jenö ambled down but Irmi was still there, looking like a figurine on top of a cake. Irmi looked ready to make an announcement. I hoped she wouldn't. Even if the student body knew Mr Sommer's age, I doubted she'd have the room's support. Everyone was in the mood to celebrate; this had been a victory. 'Won't you come down?' I asked.

'Am I the only one who doesn't think this is right?' she said, jumping to the floor. 'It's all just disgusting. He's old enough to be your grandfather.'

For the next hour Jenö burped between his retelling of the Director's homilies and drinking beer like it was water. That afternoon he behaved so strangely that even Walter kept him at bay. My head hurt, but it still felt too early to leave.

At the bar I bought my last drink, and it was here I found Ernst Steiner. I had assumed that he slept between shifts. But perhaps he came to the Swan, to sink a beer with old friends; perhaps that's what he had been doing when he'd picked me up the first time. 'Mr Steiner,' I said. My headache also waved a greeting. It was becoming painful to talk.

'What's everyone celebrating?'

Before I had a chance to make something up, he said, 'Was Walter in trouble?'

'A small scrape with the law.'

'Didn't have anything to do with the Bath-house, did he?' Mr Steiner kept his voice low enough that no one overheard him.

I didn't know what to say, and I certainly didn't want to jeopardise Walter's work. Inflation or no inflation, he still had to find the money for Sommer's payments. 'No, that wasn't them.'

'Your school hasn't treated him well.'

'What do you mean?'

'Chicken feed. That's what they've thrown at him. And Sommer's too dim to have demanded more. It's not a good day. Not a good day at all for the Bauhaus.'

My friends would have all begged to differ.

'But your lot are celebrating. So I suppose I should be congratulating you.' He pushed two glasses together and held them in his fists. 'There's Walter,' he said. 'He did a good job with Leda. I'll go say hello.'

When he went over to Walter I wondered if he would fire him. But Walter merely adjusted his taped-up spectacles and laughed with whatever Ernst was saying. I caught Charlotte talking to Kaspar, explaining who Steiner was. The last image I had was of Jenö and an attractive woman conferring closely in a dark corner, and Charlotte and Walter arguing about something they both knew little about. Kaspar had disappeared a long time before, probably to see some girl somewhere, and at some point, with my poor head roaring, I decided to call it a night.

# 16

## Weimar

In the middle of the night I woke to a sensation of sawing from my left ear to my eye. I drank a glass of water, threw it up, then tried to stay as still as possible on the bed. By morning I was pinned to the bed. Even the smallest of movements made the headache worse, and it was all I could do to lie very still under the blankets, waiting for time to pass. So much for transparencies and new Jerusalems. After weeks of fasting, this was my deliverance: a migraine had come.

Vaguely the church bell scraped its hours, and I knew the weekend was disappearing, and I wanted desperately to be elsewhere. I heard the wind scratch the trees. Remembered lights flashed in my vision: the retinal cafeteria, the Virgin's glare, the forest's strobing trees, flickering fast. The air in my bedroom had the chlorinated stink of the Baths.

All weekend, my friends visited. Sometimes they were ghostly; at other times it was only their voices I heard. There was old Mr Sommer, creaking about the bedroom;

Irmi alone on the pub table, not wanting to take my hand. Jenö, too, ghosting past the baker's window, then summiting the table, declaring, 'Everything's forgotten!' (Poor Walter: *Do you think this is it? Do you think he has feelings for me?'* and my phoney reply: *'You'll just have to wait.'*) Charlotte pressed her cool hands to my face, and combed my hair; then she too turned to shimmer and I was once again alone. In a moment of clear thinking I wondered why no one had checked on me. It was the weekend, wasn't it? Surely Charlotte would come soon. Surely Irmi. But then the waking dreams of the migraine would push on me once more, and I was lost, like this, for days.

Joan Miró painted *The Birth of the World* while he too was hallucinatory with hunger. The canvas is unevenly primed: the colours saturate some parts and fall away at others. The dark painting is all storm. When I look at *The Birth of the World* I see a visual reminder of the migraine after my inconclusive fast. The promised vision – that I would clasp an as yet uncomprehended truth – was gone. The fast had got me nowhere. Instead, this is what I had won from my fortnight's labours: hallucinated friends; polluted smells, flashing lights. I was much too gone for thought. I was too gone for anything aside from the sickness which came at me in waves. All weekend I spent in bed.

All pain must end, and eventually the migraine lifted. No more flashes in my vision, and each limb again was free. I was surprisingly euphoric; I hadn't died.

By the time I arrived at the cafeteria (it was somehow Monday) I'd put together a theory about my friends' absences: they'd been working at the studio all weekend to pay for Jenö and Walter's fines. Even Irmi and Kaspar would have been there, joshing with Ernst Steiner and painting in the nymphs' breasts. Love would set them hard to work. The question would not be: *why did no one visit me?* But: *Paul, where have you been!*

That morning I feasted on a delicious breakfast of porridge and coffee. My heart was gladdened to be here, waiting for the friends I loved. And then I saw her! Tricked from the air, Charlotte in trousers and blouse, walking over. She looked so carefree and happy. There was a black case swinging from her hand and I remembered: today we were to present our life drawings. I hadn't done mine, but Itten would forgive me: the Master was good; the world beneficent; Jenö and Walter were free from trouble, and they'd make a happy couple.

And after this week, Charlotte could come back to me.

She waved as she picked up her breakfast, and Jenö came in minutes later, and Irmi and Kaspar too. Everyone was in high spirits as food was fetched and coffee poured. Charlotte told me about the celebrations on Saturday – after the Swan they'd ended up at Kaspar's girlfriend's (I didn't even know he had a girlfriend) until she'd chucked them out the following morning. Then they'd spent the whole day mopping the school floors (the Director's punishment) but they'd shared a bottle of schnapps and it hadn't been – all agreed – too bad.

Charlotte's laughter, naked and rich, was lovely to hear. I savoured what would be. Spring was here; summer soon. We would celebrate the new warmth at the Ilm, and up in the woods, and we'd forget all about the fasted havoc of these weeks.

But breakfast too soon was finished and I saw that Charlotte and Jenö were getting ready for class. I wanted to say – *hold on! Wait!* All morning I'd been thinking of the best phrases to describe the sensations of the migraine – the ghosts of them in my bedroom, the blooming visions and odd smells – but now I felt like Irmi, standing on the table in the Swan, not knowing how to stop people; not knowing what it was I should say.

Instead I watched them from a distance as they made their way from the cafeteria, as if the distance between us was yards, a road, a city: Jenö and Charlotte, two golden creatures edged in April light. And then I saw it. (So this was my vision at last; the fast's broken epiphany.) My goodness. It felt as if my heart was breaking. All weekend, she hadn't even noticed I'd been gone.

# 17
## England

An old feeling this afternoon: that if I don't work, I'll only brood. There's a feeling I should do something with my hands but I don't know what. My seaside wanderings do nothing to keep my mind from things. Since Walter died I can't think of anything but the Bauhaus. I have had a life elsewhere – other friendships, other love affairs, several decades in my adopted country – and yet after the news of his stroke I can't think of anything but what happened to us.

Work is the antidote; it always has been. But I also know I can't make any more of what Irmi calls my 'breezeblock abstractions', and so I have decided on a self-portrait. I've never done one before. It will be my confession in paint: I will show myself how I really am.

For a while all I do is look in the mirror. Master Itten would be proud of me: how long I delay marking the page. Instead I use my fingers to learn the form of my face: the unshaven cheeks, the sunken eyes, the proud nose. My neck is soft, an old man's, and I'm as bald as I ever was in

Weimar. I spend a long time like this, trying to find what Master Itten called the *instress*; my singularity.

It is an age since I've worked figuratively, and it's not unwelcome. Usually, my paintings are blocks of colours, bright as ice creams. Usually, I play with the colours' saturations, which give, like Klee's *Bird Garden*, a sense of moving transparencies. I can't remember when my work showed this orientation toward flatness; it was after the war, in any case. (Worringer would explain my urge to abstraction as 'an immense spiritual dread of space', which doesn't sound entirely wrong.) I'd even paint with a spatula. I got bored of objects and representations; even fairly unguessable ones. I guess I had finally outgrown my imitative impulse.

Over the decades, critics have noted the heat of the paintings' colours; but to me it is the unprimed corridors that are of interest: unlit and chilly, no bleed between. They're meant as edges you could drop off. These paintings reference Charlotte's woven black squares, with their lightning strikes of panic, but no one knows who she is, and so they can't read into the painting how much her absence and her influence has been left.

Sometimes these zips – I'm borrowing Barnett Newman's phrase – are at the perimeter, at other times the white caption goes right through the mass, dry as a gone riverbed. Whatever these late works are, their spaces are all Charlotte. Beware the oncoming colour, they say; watch out where it isn't happening.

# 18

## Weimar

Looking back, I still fail to see when it was that Charlotte and Jenö came together during my hapless fast. Was it when I had left him in her rooms, drunk and sound asleep? Maybe he had spent the night there, and they had ended up in bed together. Was it as she chalked his green portrait, and he had reached out a hand to hers behind the canvas, and I'd caught them later, him looking dreamily to the parkland? Or maybe it had been when I'd been staring out from the luckless window at five in the morning, and I'd had that prophetic rush that things were ending; the lantern collapsed; that something odd stirred abroad; that our group, as we knew it, was over. At that point I had pushed the feeling aside, but maybe some part of me knew.

But all this is conjecture. Really, it could have been any curfewed night I'd spent alone; it could have been the weekend of the migraine. I will not know. I won't ever know.

I had thought the fast would give me clearer sight: instead I'd only been getting blinder. Hour by hour, day by day, I failed to see what was in front of me. Charlotte and Jenö, two perfect creatures. Of course. Why wouldn't they be together? They made sense; they made sense.

Jenö's dalliance with Walter in the Bath-house had been nothing. In the church at dawn I had given Walter a future with Jenö that had seemed viable. And over the week, as I'd been snooping around, fancying myself a hungry detective, I had been watching Walter, when really I should have been watching them.

Walter too must have gone over these weeks, trying to work out when they had come together; or the moment, more precisely, when we had failed. We knew we had. As soon as we saw her take Jenö's portrait from the port-folio case in Master Itten's class that Monday morning, we both knew. Here was a man beloved.

The worst thing was that now both the future was dead and the past had to be reassessed. What promises had she given me all year? None! What love tokens? A few doodled messages, some scrawled portraits, a hand held on the banks of the Ilm. I hadn't been kissed in the Bath-house. I didn't even have that to resent. I didn't even know whether I had the right to be angry. Heartbreak. *Herzschmerz*. What a common wretched thing it is. Most of April I spent bewildered.

Pain gathers. It hardens.

We were witness to their growing closeness in the classroom and in the cafeteria; their in-jokes and soft smiles; their conversations in the windowed light; their collaborations on new projects; their picnics in the woods. It's not hard to see a relationship forming: their new love came off them in beams.

If I had felt left out of the secret weeks ago, it was nothing compared to this. I had a mania to find them out: I wanted to know what they were doing. I wanted to know where they were doing it. More than ever before, I wanted to be around her.

Charlotte came to see me often enough but the visits were empty; as if she had discussed with Jenö that I should be let down gradually. In any case my behaviour clipped her visits short. I hated her going but I hated her company more. My meanness that April shocked my September self, who had fallen in love with this golden girl and thought she could inspire me only to good. Charlotte tried desperately for normality, but it was a dream of how we were, and it made things worse. I could tell she checked her mood when her happiness unsettled me.

When I had arrived at the Bauhaus last September I had fashioned a future life – narrow-minded magistrate that I was – of my little Dresden wedding to my little Dresden wife. By May it all looked impossible; laughable; silly. I waited for her to say something, but she didn't, and I said nothing to her.

I had thought the future unshakeable; I was wrong.

Weimar soon lost its memory of winter. Blossom was rich in the air or else browning in the streets. In the cemetery, full of dead Walters, the tulips opened; hydrangea offered their heads. It was very dry that spring, almost no rain, and the bees in the air were fat as beans, and the birds unendingly cheerful.

Walter and I spent most of May at the studio: him, working out Sommer's reparations; me, keeping away from the Bauhaus. As we painted nymphs at the reeds, or Alpine mountains, Walter's pain so mirrored my own that coming to the woods after a long day at the Bauhaus was hardly the distraction I longed for. Still, sorrow made committed painters of us both.

Every morning, after our shifts, we'd go to the baker's to exchange our gargantuan salaries for bread. We'd wait for the bakery to open (the ghost of Jenö's regret materialising in the gas lamp) and buy a black loaf. And then, with the remoteness that was now part of Walter's heartache, he said he'd see me later, and I wondered what he did with his mornings, when it was early and the moon was still in the sky. After a shift we used to go for a walk in the cemetery, or go for a cycle around town, but now he went off by himself. And I wondered whether he'd return to the Bathhouse, to think of the promise of Jenö's body, or whether he'd go to Charlotte's, to see of them what he might.

That May, money turned; it ripened. It was in the butcher's and the baker's and the beer-hall. Money was under beds, in bicycle baskets, in wheelbarrows, in pockets, stuffed into pillowcases. It was on the roads, in cars, in fires; it made wallpaper, wrapping paper; the homeless lined their jackets with it when the nights for a time were cooler than usual. To push a limb into a day's wages would see an arm or leg gone. Useless, it gathered in the gutter, in bins, in the sewers, off the river. At school we used it as material for papier-mâché towers. Soup kitchens appeared, women volunteers ladling out food to kids; men hung around the Frauenplan, waiting for something to happen outside Schiller's house, Goethe's house, Liszt's house, Cranach's house; famous men who could do nothing for them. Soon our lives were measured in the billions. That spring, Charlotte and Jenö too felt like a soaring kind of money – they could not stop their ascension even if they wanted to; even if they had tried.

# 19

## Weimar

I found out what Walter was up to on the night we finished Mr Steiner's last Hamburg commission. How he had been spending his melancholic mornings had been bothering me all month: I had become intensely wary of people keeping secrets.

Mr Steiner's painting was smaller than usual and we finished it quickly: bowers and light and some comic ducks. At the end of the shift, Ernst gave Walter a funny look and told us Daniel would finish it off. They had a few private words, and I waited for Walter outside.

We cycled down from the studio as usual, stopping off at the baker's. I expected Walter to go off, as was his normal fashion, but this morning he invited me up to his rooms for coffee.

There was a fusty smell as soon as the door was opened, and the light was dim. It was the opening of the curtains that exposed the secret of what Walter had been up to. There were bags of salt, broken chairs, vegetables and meat; a salami, even a phonograph. Here was his heartbreak, his *Herzschmerz*: Walter had been stockpiling.

He grinned. 'My empire!'

'What is all of this?'

'I have turned into a merchant.'

My gaze went immediately to the pencil drawings propped on one shelf: both recognizable as Kandinsky's. There were a couple of others too: boggy abstractions, which I didn't much like. I picked up the smaller of the Kandinskys. 'How did you get this?'

Every morning, Walter explained, after a shift at Mr Steiner's, he'd go straight to the baker's. From there, he'd trade the loaf for a book of matches, matches for carrots, carrots for pencils, pencils for a tin of luncheon meat, and finally he'd find one of the Masters' wives and trade in the tin for a sketch. 'My uncle,' he said, 'the art dealer in London. He's going to get me *valuta* for one of these! British sterling. Can you imagine! Corned beef into a Kandinsky, then maybe into a house!'

'You'll never give them away,' I said, my eye following the loveliness of Kandinsky's line. 'You'd rather die.'

'Last week I read about a man in Berlin. He withdrew all his life savings – a hundred thousand marks – to buy a subway ticket. He saw the sights, went to the zoo, the palace, the Tiergarten, then locked himself in his rooms and starved himself to death. It's a dangerous time to be alive.'

'Not if you're Walter König.'

On the side table there was a photograph of Walter with his mother and father, looking how he had when he'd arrived in September: bony and aristocratic. It made me realise how plump he'd grown. Maybe he was eating the stock as he went. Walter hardly ever talked about his parents, but then maybe none of us did. They were the ones we were running from.

He brought out some coffee. He'd changed out of his painter's smock into a collarless shirt. I saw how he carried this new weight awkwardly; he still moved like a thinner man. Seated on the sofa he was framed by tins and cured meats.

'Won't it go off?'

'Even rotting food is better than money.'

'When did you do all this?'

'The past month. I had to keep my mind on something else.'

There it was, the tacit mention of the happy couple. I let it go, not knowing what to do with it. We hadn't yet talked about them. 'You've paid off Mr Sommer then?'

'Oh. Ernst's money took care of that in two shifts. I owe Ernst a great deal.' He made a dismissive gesture, and it sent irritation down me. What had happened to Sommer was grubby, and it had split the group. Irmi had distanced herself from us, preferring the company of the Three Graces, and Kaspar more and more took himself home on the weekends.

Walter waved a nearly empty bottle of vodka. Before I could answer he topped up the coffee with what was left. Unsleeping Walter, trading all day, painting all night, when did he rest? I had cycled past his curtained rooms many times, and had always assumed he'd been asleep. I had retreated into myself, while Walter had become a tsar of all things.

'Chin, chin,' he said, our cups clinking together.

The coffee and booze warmed me up. I looked again at the marshy paintings. 'Whose are those?'

'They're Charlotte's.'

'Oh. Really?' I felt bad that I didn't like them. I stood to get a closer look: the brushwork on both was thick, as if she'd used a palette knife. Walter would have chosen this specifically, since everything, now, was measured in how *much* of the thing it was. I looked for her initials but couldn't find them.

'What did you trade them for?'

'A bag of salt.'

'You could have just given it to her.'

'Do you think she deserves that? After what she did to us?'

'Well,' I said, 'whatever she did to us, Jenö did too.'

'She worked on him. Between the Bath-house and the tribunal, she *worked* on him.'

'Rubbish. If there's anyone you should be angry at, it's Jenö. He went with you, and then with her, of his own free will.'

'No. She lured him away. Persuading him he wasn't in love with me. Making him believe he was in love with her. It's a treachery.'

'No, Walter, it's a disaster. That's what makes it sad.'

Walter dusted the divan cushions. 'I must have put him off quite violently.'

'That's not what I'm saying. I'm saying that it's not just

her to blame. Jenö acted badly. He shouldn't have kissed you—'

'Kissed me! He didn't just kiss me, Paul, we went home together.'

'What?'

'When you saw Jenö outside the baker's, he was walking home from my rooms.'

I thought back to what Jenö had said in Charlotte's room. 'I thought he was apologising to Sommer?'

'Old Sommer didn't get an *apology*. He got money, not an apology.'

'Fine. You slept together. You didn't get engaged.'

'He made me a promise! With his body.'

I didn't know whether I believed what I had said. Charlotte had never made any such promise. We hadn't even ever talked about our relationship, and yet still I was full of indignation.

Walter opened the window and leant out. There was a florist on the ground floor of his building, and the new air brought in a smell of lilies. When he turned his face was twisted. 'Oh, Paul! My heart is breaking.'

'Well,' I said, shocked that I was being so cold, but I didn't know why it was Walter who got to feel everything, 'that's the one thing you shouldn't be surprised about.'

My tone led him back to anger. 'Has she even apologised? For leading you one way and offering nothing the next?'

'She didn't lead me one way: I did it all on my own.'

'Come on! Decency might permit her an apology. She took what she wanted without regard for anyone else. People have been hurt.'

'Look, I don't know what happened. They've fallen in love, and that may have been a mistake. I don't think it's as simple as just blaming Charlotte.'

'She worked on him!'

'Nonsense. She was helping.'

'*Think*, Paul. It was her idea to pay Sommer off. There was nothing to *help* with; the trial was sorted from the Sunday when she first gave Sommer the money. It was just an opportunity to spend all that time with Jenö.'

'Look, I don't know about all this.'

'You do! I'm *telling* you. Ask Irmi. She feels very bad for you. And she knows Charlotte hasn't treated you right either. Ernst says the same thing.'

'You told Ernst about all of this?'

'Ernst knows a thing or two about heartbreak. Let me tell you that.'

'Walter, don't listen to Ernst.'

'Why shouldn't I? *He* has experience. *He* has lived.'

'Ernst is not to be trusted. He hates the Bauhaus. Always has.'

'Jenö's a child,' he said, and I wondered if these were Ernst's words. 'His attitudes haven't quite left the nursery.'

Tears threatened. Poor Walter; an emperor of all things and nothing. Jenö had no need for him; Jenö was done. I remembered, then, Jenö's expression as he had stepped over the threshold of the Swan: when he had looked to all the world like a free man with no past.

'I can get anything; *anything*. But I can't get what I want.' Walter wiped a tear away but another came just as quickly.

'There's nothing we can do.'

'Don't you get bored,' he spat, 'with your own inertia?'

It was too late to get into all of this and so I said nothing.

'Sometimes you're so passive I think you might just implode.'

I stood and Walter leapt up too and held me by the shoulders. 'How can you go around as if nothing has happened?'

'What is it?' I asked. 'What would you have me do?'

'Fight for something!'

'There's nothing left! We're done. They have fallen in love!'

He let go of me. 'I cannot accept things with your God-awful equanimity.'

'It's not equanimity, Walter, it's forbearance!'

He looked at me, down to my lips. For a moment I thought he might kiss me too. 'I would rather be me than you, Paul Beckermann, a hundred times over.'

'What is that meant to mean?'

'Nothing. That's your favourite word, isn't it?' He fanned out his hands as if he were playing cards. '*Nothing, nothing, nothing.*'

# 20
## Weimar

Of course, there were times when nothing much happened. If my memory serves me well, I can't enrich the next few weeks with much of relevance. I put in my choice for next year's specialism, and went less and less to the studio. My argument with Walter and his cosiness with Ernst Steiner made me not want to go any more, and I left my skies to someone else.

I saw Ernst occasionally in the Swan, but he didn't talk to me, and I was glad we didn't have to make conversation. The end of the school year came into view. Some would stay for the Summer Exhibition; others would go. I had decided to head back to Dresden for the holidays; I couldn't be around Charlotte and Jenö any more. I didn't want to put on my public face every time I caught Irmi watching me, watching them, with something like – it was – pity.

Waiting for term to end, I roamed the warm city. Weimar was maddening in its prettiness: the palace, the castle, and the statues of its philosophers. But in the

Bauhaus, with its aprons of cut glass, I couldn't get any rest either.

Walter, too, became a ghost that May. Oh, one could find him easily enough: everyone in the Bauhaus knew that he was the man who could get you what you needed now that money meant nothing. But he sat elsewhere with a different crowd at the cafeteria and in class; Elena especially became his new friend. He gave her cigarettes, asking for nothing in return. I wondered if he hoped Charlotte would hear of his largesse.

At the cafeteria I would catch him looking at us. Charlotte, too, would watch him in return. She probably knew nothing of his claim to Jenö; I was sure Jenö hadn't told her the truth. A man fainted. A man was beaten. This was still the Bath-house story.

Before term finished our choices for next year's ateliers were pinned up at the school office. This was clever: many of the staff had already left on holiday, so there was nobody to complain to, aside from an administrator who wielded no power. Minus Walter, we all went to the Craft Building and climbed the staircase. Painted on the walls was Oskar Schlemmer's mural of red, yellow, and blue dancing figures, making me think of a happier time when we too had been braced in all that freedom.

There were already foundation students there, running their fingers down the board to find their names under the workshops – Metal, Carpentry, Wall-painting, Weaving, Stone. It felt the same as when they had put up posters of our grades at school, and it seemed curiously retrogressive for the Bauhaus to operate like this. We looked around the boards, ducking under other people to find our names. Irmi had been admitted into her first choice of Weaving, Jenö into Metal, Kaspar into Stone, and I found *Beckermann, Paul*, under Wall-painting, just as I had chosen. My atelier was, unfortunately, entirely male.

Charlotte hung back. Above her a gridded window threw its shadow on the wall like a gate. I tried to find her name. She hadn't told me her specialism, but I couldn't find *Feldekova* among the German surnames. But then Irmi pointed to Charlotte's name in the Weaving list. And when Jenö saw it, he too blanched. In the corner of my eye I saw him comfort her. Then, for the first time, I saw him kiss her. It stung, and I turned away.

'Perhaps it's a mistake?' Irmi asked me, very quietly, to draw my attention from them. But it wasn't a mistake. I knew that. What the Director was saying was clear: this was where the female students belonged.

I looked for *König*. Walter was in Metal: very close, of course, to Jenö Fiedler.

'You know,' said Irmi, as we went down the central staircase, leaving the lovers to it, 'Walter's staying here all summer?'

'With them?' Charlotte and Jenö were showing their work at the Summer Exhibition.

'I think it is a bad idea. Don't you? Very bad indeed. What will you do?'

'I'm going to my parents'.'

'You shouldn't do that. You should come to Berlin with me and Kaspar.'

'I've got a job in Dresden.'

'I'll find you one in Berlin.'

But I said I needed the money, and Irmi let it go.

That night Charlotte and Jenö came to my room, two pale saints knocking gravely at my door. I lied about having been asleep and poured them big drinks. I felt blurry but also generous. It was as if we were having a party, though I knew they'd come to apologise. The alcohol from the schnapps made me sit there dumbly. My suitcase was packed for Dresden: all summer I was destined for my father's shoe factory. Better than being here – with them, in Weimar; or with Walter, at the studio.

I smiled as Charlotte explained how it had all happened out of nowhere, that this business of falling in love hadn't been done in the week of the Bath-house, but some time after. They had come . . . Here, she stumbled. What had she come to do? I'd never admitted my love to her – it was another secret in our web – so she could not walk in here and presume I needed an apology.

Jenö took up her case: they wanted to make sure I was all right with everything that was happening, he said.

Flushed with alcohol, I put on a fine performance: smoothing away their worries with murmuring rebuttals – *no, no, no, it's fine, I am happy* – kissing her cheek, shaking the square of his hand, pouring more schnapps, and there we all were: the party had begun, their love affair anointed. I heard Walter's words – *Fight for something!* – even as I sat there, beneficent as a priest, with Jenö's head nodding along to the rhythm of mine. I detested more and more his honeyed features and blond-tipped lashes; in the summer he was a creature dipped in gold. But I smiled, I drank, I watched their pretty heads. All the while I thought – *go, you must go, you must leave, I cannot bear this*. What if I vomit? Or take a knife to Jenö's throat? Or what if I simply blurt out the secret of what Jenö had done to Walter? Inside I felt propelled toward a violence I'd never enact but which possessed me anyway: I wanted the cage of him to shake.

# 21

In the decade after the Berlin Wall went up, I received the handful of Walter's letters which I still have to this day. They reveal very few personal details. He taught art to school kids, which had been a challenge to secure, given Charlotte had got him expelled in Dessau, and the expulsion had left him without a diploma.

He didn't mention what had happened to Ernst Steiner; whether he still lived with him, or if he was dead, or exiled. He talked instead of his life in the East and some memories of the Bauhaus that I couldn't recall. Then the final plea: for a 'cultural invitation' to England.

These letters were phrased in a stiff register that worked hard at concealing our mutual embarrassment. Apart from a drunken letter about Franz, where I could hear his old lively voice, not once did he mention what had happened to Charlotte in the camp.

I heard that the people of Weimar were marched five miles north when Buchenwald was liberated. It took days for the residents, dressed in their Sunday best, to file through the camp. It must have been the barmaid from the Swan, the attendants from the Bath-house, the guides from Goethe's house, the new teachers at the art school with Schlemmer's painted-over murals, traipsing along the rail track to see what had happened in Goethe's golden forest. 'We didn't know,' they said, which must have been true and also not true, in the way that horror can be acknowledged but also ignored. (Disavowal; *Verleugnung*.) Then there is the fact that even what is known we do not admit; that in our minds we disperse the unthinkable. It is possible to know of horror vaguely.

But Irmi's right: I cannot judge. I was in England from 1934, and later I'd also be ignoring Walter's letters, because I too didn't know what to do, and ignoring him was the easiest option. Though I knew he must be suffering, that East Berlin was a prison, I simply didn't reply.

I too looked away. It was easy.

## Weimar

In tone the letters I received from Walter that summer of 1923 were the same as those he sent me after the war: polite, and very formal. I had expected Walter's normal spleen – Charlotte was a whore, a tease, a seductress – but instead these summer letters were all restraint. He wrote that he'd been seeing lots of them, and having an excellent time; that all three picnicked together in the woods; that a pool had formed in one of the clearings near Goethe's Oak, where they could take dips to keep themselves cool.

But a liar can sniff out another liar, and my performance of goodwill toward them was mostly a sham. I wondered what was really going on: whether I'd return from Dresden to Jenö and Charlotte bludgeoned in bed (a tabloid picture of *Lustmord*) or whether (and perhaps it was not unthinkable for a utopia like the Bauhaus) all three of them might have simply hopped into bed together.

When I returned to Weimar in September it took me a while to track Walter down. I couldn't find him in his rooms. He wasn't at the second-year registration, nor was he at the party for the Bauhaus babies (the civilians of Weimar looking gravely on) and neither Irmi nor Kaspar had seen him since they had (joyously, triumphantly) returned from Berlin. Though I didn't want to go there, I decided Walter must be hiding at the studio. It seemed like a test; that he would know the last place I'd want to look, and the first place he'd hide out, would be the woods.

I headed to the forest. The woods were so still they could have been a photograph were it not for the beating of birds' wings as I cycled past. All that could be heard was my wheels on the forest floor, and my own thin whistle I'd nervously begun. I don't know why but I felt panicked on going back to the studio. I thought about Walter mooning about as Charlotte von Stein (back in that magicked spring when all six of us had been together, unexploded) – but I hadn't been there in months, and I had a feeling that Mr Steiner was angry with me for leaving without telling him why.

At the top of the hill I rested, and looked down at the

city. I had forgotten the new term would start with a lantern festival to welcome the new students. The city roads were rivers of light.

When I reached the studio the door was locked. Even when there was no one there the big door normally slid open without a key; no one, after all, was going to steal a six-by-four painting of Persephone in the underworld. I still had the key and I unlocked the door. There were voices on the upper level, though I couldn't hear Walter's. Bizarrely a picture flashed in my mind of Walter modelling naked for the painters before him.

It was this image I had to clear as Ernst greeted me on the studio floor. 'Pauli!' he said, his mouth big, his small teeth numerous.

'Hello, Mr Steiner.'

There were some men gathered around a canvas. On its reverse there'd be, I knew, patrols of doves and women. Walter wasn't amongst the workers. If he wasn't here, then I had run out of options, and it struck me for the first time that he might have left the Bauhaus altogether.

'Where've you been hiding?' said Mr Steiner.

'Dresden. I went home for the summer.'

'What's Dresden got that Weimar hasn't?'

'Nothing.'

'You missed the Great Exhibition.'

'I know.'

'Albert Einstein came. And Shostakovich.'

'I heard.'

'It was fun. Though of course it persuaded nobody that the school's fit for purpose.'

I followed Ernst into his office. On the desk there were commissions, ledgers and newspapers, and on the walls a few paintings of an Expressionist tilt. There was also a new painting hanging above his desk: a yellow triangle, a red square, a blue circle – just like the one Kandinsky used in his seminars. 'Didn't know you were a fan.'

'I bought it at the exhibition.'

'It's a Kandinsky?'

He nodded. 'Collectors have rotten taste.'

'Was it expensive?'

He tapped his nose. Though it was cool in the studio I noticed he was sweaty. I was about to ask him about Walter, but Ernst brought him up instead: 'He's so funny, your friend,' he said, snapping the ledger shut.

I waited for him to elaborate but he didn't. 'How do you mean?'

'He's quite an emotional person, isn't he?'

'Yes. I suppose so.'

'This Jenö fellow's a waste of time. Still, he insists on seeing him, and that awful woman Charlotte. The Czechoslovak.'

'He saw them a lot?' I doubted Walter's version of the summer, but there was no reason for Ernst to lie.

'Oh, he was never out of their pockets! I did try to tell him it wasn't any good.' He snapped his jaws. 'That's why I swapped his shifts. I thought it would be advantageous, to keep him busy during the day. You know, not to have to see them all the time.'

'Thanks,' I said, alarm growing in me. 'I mean, for looking out for him. Is he here?'

'He's really such a terrific painter, Pauli, you should see him go. He has this . . . this thing he does with light. He's a genius. I owe you for bringing him to us.'

Walter appeared just then, visible through the office glass, rubbing his hands on a rag and sporting a beard.

'And, ho! Here he is!' Ernst shouted, walking over to him. 'Our very own Caspar Friedrich David. What have you been doing out there? Disposing of bodies?'

Walter hadn't seen me yet. Instead I could see he was watching whether his handsome features were having their effect on Mr Steiner. But when he clocked me his expression froze and his eyes darted over Ernst's desk.

Mr Steiner picked up the Christmas scene which was evidently the new commission: baby Jesus sweetly sleeping, and Mary and Joseph kneeling by the crib. 'It's for a bank in New York.' Names were written inside the outlines: Daniel in the faces, Hans for the fabrics, and Walter's name, written across the sky, in the hay-bales of light. 'Do you want me to add you, Pauli?' He gestured to the straw manger. 'Maybe this?'

'No,' I said, surprising myself.

'No?'

He gave me some moments to reconsider.

'I'm fine for money,' I said, though it was untrue: the trillions I'd made in August had lost all value, and soon I'd have to beg my father for the fees again. 'I'm concentrating on my studies.'

'Suit yourself,' Ernst said, and something like relief passed over Walter's expression.

'How long's your shift?' I said to him.

'Still got a few more hours.'

'Everything all right?'

'Fine. Good.'

'Do you want me to wait for you?' I asked.

'No, no. You go on. It's the lantern festival.'

'I'll see you tomorrow at school, then?'

Walter nodded. It was unlike him to be so taciturn.

'All right. See you later.'

On my way out I went over to the painting, knowing I would find Walter's paintwork on my skies. I don't know why I felt upset: I knew someone would have to do my job if I didn't show up, but I also didn't really want it to be him.

There was, however, an altogether different surprise. The commission was a strange painting, quite beautiful. It was a field scene with a couple of heavy horses in the background. In the foreground there was a farmhouse and a trio of girls, all blazing petticoats and rosebud lips, playing with chickens. The birds' wings were open in alarm. The field was nearly all ploughed, ready for the drop of seeds. The clouds were tissuey, and well done.

I scanned the painting, trying to find the trick of it: in the seeds thrown, the terror of the flightless birds, the horse's moronic tread. I couldn't work out why the painting was so unsettling. Walter had done something funny with the light. I couldn't name its technique; couldn't work out the painting's code.

When I looked over Walter was still in the office. Ernst

was talking to him, gesturing at the sky and the holy figures supplicant, waiting for the gift of kings. But Walter
kept his eyes on me, as if he were willing me not to see
what, this summer, he had buried inside the painting.

# 22
## Weimar

The festival torches were stacked in the school foyer the following morning. There was something of the gang to them, their blackened heads waiting for the firing squad. Several of the lanterns had been discarded overnight: a ship, a tree, an aeroplane, a car, a lipstick. In patches the lanterns had been burned brown or the heat had opened holes in the paper. I wondered which one was Charlotte's, which Jenö's, whether Irmi and Kaspar had been there too, while I was puzzling over that painting and the strangely anaesthetised Walter.

I breakfasted with Irmi in the cafeteria. No longer was she the bony girl last seen in Weimar. She had filled out, and had new freckles on her nose, and a bob cut at her jaw. 'Kaspar,' she said, 'has led me astray. You should see him! He's as dark as a gypsy.'

'Did you have fun?'

'In Berlin? It was wild. And Dresden?'

'Not so wild.' I laughed. 'But it was fine. I'm now a dab hand at gluing plimsolls.'

Irmi said she'd found a summer job waiting tables at a ritzy hotel called the Kaiserhof, which served famous singers and writers and actors. Though I knew she didn't want to talk about it, I also couldn't resist asking her opinion. 'I saw Walter last night at the studio. You know they spent the summer here? Together? All three of them?'

'I heard.'

I couldn't help myself. 'And?'

'And what?'

'What do you think of that?'

She let out the air from her cheeks. 'Well. He spent all summer with one person he hates, and one person he loves and can't have, and pretends to be best friends with them both. It's bizarre, but for someone like Walter, it also makes sense.'

'Do you know what really happened at the Baths?'

'Walter wrote to me. It was a bit of a shock, reading the details over my lunch break.'

'Does Kaspar know?'

'I assume so. We haven't discussed it.'

'Everyone knows,' I said. 'Even Mr Steiner. Is it not wrong to keep Charlotte in the dark?'

'She's happy, Paul,' Irmi said quietly, 'I know that's hard for you. But I'd leave her alone. It would only make things difficult.'

I let this one go. 'I just don't see why Walter didn't go somewhere. He would have had a remarkable time in Berlin.'

Irmi smiled mournfully and finished her breakfast. 'Well, yes. People are strange.'

I wondered why Irmi was frustrated with me. I didn't dare mention Walter's painting, since I thought this might actually end her patience altogether. I was starting to think there might be an alternative drawing under its surface. Fresco painters had often made sketches of cherubs and saints on the *intonaco*. Maybe there was a ghosted image underneath: a naked Jenö; a grotesque Charlotte; some clue as to what might have happened while they were all playing nice in the woods. Perhaps, as Irmi would have me believe, the performance of goodwill was real, and Walter had been trying to make amends. But I didn't believe it. Walter was too much in love with Jenö for a hot summer to have baked that dry.

At our second-year introduction meeting I shook hands with Jenö, and gave Charlotte a kiss. Kaspar squeezed me into a cuddle. Irmi was right: his tan had depth.

Walter offered me a thin smile. 'Sorry again, Paul. About doing your skies. It doesn't feel very sporting. After all you did for—'

'Doesn't matter,' I said, and I was being honest; it wasn't that that was bothering me. 'Really.'

'You're sure?'

'Don't think about it.'

Masters Kandinsky and Klee began by explaining how we would take our elective options and how we'd be working toward our diploma in a few years' time. While Klee was speaking I noticed Charlotte had a black mark where she had held her torch last night.

The school secretary came in some way through, asking for Stefan: the Director wanted to see him. Kandinsky and Klee continued. Then she came back, asking for Masha. I heard Charlotte asking Jenö what was going on but couldn't catch his reply. Neither Stefan nor Masha had yet returned when the secretary came back for the third time. Before she could speak Master Klee told her to take everyone she needed at once.

The secretary was dressed like one of the war widows in the square. Her mouth tightened.

'Well?' said Klee.

She looked around the room: the whole of the second year was squeezed in there. 'I am to take all foreign nationals. And,' she paused here, perhaps from discomfort, 'people of Jewish descent or Communist membership.'

The students rose when she read out their names. I saw in the secretary's face some pleasure as Charlotte stood; she would be glad to have netted one of Itten's followers.

'And us too?' said Master Kandinsky very quietly. 'Madam, you are looking at a Russian and a Swiss.'

'No,' said the secretary. 'The Director did not say anything about staff.'

During the First World War the German military had conducted a count of the Jews in the army: it was called the *Judenzählung*. Now we had our own census; a *Bauhauszählung*. After the Director's meetings with Stefan, and Masha, and Charlotte, it filtered down to the rest of us that the *Republik*, a right-wing newspaper none of us read, was threatening the school with the publication of a report: a Citizens' Survey. It would detail the names and numbers of the school's foreigners, Jews and Communists.

The Director had got wind of the article early. It was an awful way to start the academic year, and there was a mood of siege in the school once more. It had been silly to assume the city had forgotten the incident at the Baths, just because time had passed, Mr Sommer had gone off meekly, and all the trifling payments had been made. Last night the students had advanced with their rocking lanterns burning; once again, we were now in retreat.

Charlotte said the Director didn't know whether he could retain the same number of foreign students. The report might force him to revoke foreigners' places, because it was German money funding places for French, Russian, American, and indeed Czechoslovak students at the Bauhaus. 'I might be told to go,' she said. 'If they take away my place, I'll have no papers.'

I couldn't imagine the Bauhaus without Charlotte. Jenö, yes; even Walter I was prepared to see go last April. But Charlotte, in Prague? And us, continuing here, as if nothing had changed?

'German money?' said Kaspar. 'There's no such thing as German money. Who cares what it funds? It can't fund a thing.'

'The point is the principle, I guess.'

'The point is,' said Masha, 'they don't want to subsidise anyone who is not their own.'

'They're going to get rid of me,' Charlotte said, in her rooms later, 'they're going to kick me out. I'm not only a foreigner, I'm linked to the Sommer case. I could be sacrificed to save the school. I don't know what to do. I can't live in Prague, Paul: what would I do in Prague?'

'That won't happen.'

She picked up a weave, the yarn falling from the warp. 'Why would they keep me on?'

'You have as much right to be here as anyone else.'

'I'm not sure that's true.'

On one wall was the green chalked portrait of Jenö, his feet prominent, his torso foreshortened. Master Itten had praised it for its mastery of perspective: Jenö sleeping, the vanishing point receding beyond the plane; as if a dove might hover there.

Now Charlotte fell onto the bed. 'I'm a woman. A foreigner. And a weaver, of whom there are already too many, and I'm probably the worst in my class. I wouldn't be missed.'

I remembered the false confidence I had given to Walter in the Orthodox Church, and I said nothing.

'It's hopeless,' she said, and I saw the tears in her eyes leak, and neither of us said anything for a good long while. Then she sat bolt upright, and offered me her fist outstretched.

'Close your eyes,' she said. 'And count.'

I remembered the hiding game, how we had played it at the river, when the world was all mine. How much I had shrunk in the months since then! I counted, and opened my eyes.

'Sheep,' she said. 'Braided. Future.'

'A weave?'

'Smaller than that.' Charlotte opened her hand: inside her fist was a yellow thread. 'Yarn. If they let me stay, I'm going to have to get better at this.'

That week we kept our heads down. Walter was mostly up at the studio while the rest of us attended school meetings. There was talk that the Director was not doing enough: there were fears he would pogrom his own students; get rid of the alien within. It was no secret that he neither wanted too many women nor too many Jews, and that this might be an opportune moment to recast the school. There were petitions and letter-writing campaigns.

I spent my time making murals for the fundraising nights. We were experimenting with different shapes and colours in tension, so that they appeared like a child's mobile gathering upon a flat plane. We painted in the hall, since none of the ateliers were big enough. Though the Director said the Survey didn't apply to staff, I knew Kandinsky was worried he was about to be exiled to St Petersburg. Before he'd arrived at the Bauhaus I'd heard he'd not bought a new pair of shoes in eight years. Indeed, I knew Walter could still entice Mrs Kandinsky into a sale of a sketch with merely a tin of corned beef.

'Why's Walter not here?' Kaspar asked, over lunch.

I wanted to tell him about the strange painting, but I didn't know how to explain my apprehension about a horse, some chickens and a trio of girls. I wondered anyway whether Kaspar hadn't had enough of my suspicions.

Since the Bath-house he too had been distant with me, although that might have been because he had a new girl on the go. 'There's a commission at the studio,' I said. 'He's busy with that.'

'He's not in trouble? With the Survey? I heard the Director wanted to speak to him.'

'I think he's just preoccupied with other things.'

Kaspar frowned. 'I really don't know what's more important than this. Is something funny going on? I haven't seen him for weeks. He's not a Communist. His family go back centuries in Detmold. What's he got to worry about?'

'I don't know,' I said, being honest. 'I really don't.'

'Well, if you see him around, tell him we miss him, won't you?'

'I will,' I said, but I doubted I would see him anywhere but the studio, and I had so firmly cut my ties with Mr Steiner that it was unlikely I was going to bump into him any time soon.

# 23

## Weimar

None of us, the Director included, thought the Citizens' Survey would bring us down altogether. Looking back, I might even be tempted to say the Survey was a brilliant move, because in the end, Weimar didn't serve just the foreigners with their exit papers, but all of us. Though the Director had persuaded them not to print the names of the Jews and the French and the Americans and the Czechoslovaks, the numbers had been printed – and the numbers had done enough.

Shortly after the article, and in a stroke of good luck for the city, the new mark was brought in, and the *Republik* revised how much money – in suddenly sober terms – these Jews, foreigners and Communists were costing the country. There had been a wildness to the inflation that had let the Bauhaus flourish: if nothing had value then anything was possible. But when the new money came in, Reichswehr officers raided the school, looking, ostensibly, for Communist activity. When they didn't find any Communists, well: the school was shut down anyway.

The day after they cancelled the old money there were people everywhere wheeling their rubbish to the dump. Up at Walter's apartment there were trillion-mark notes snowing onto the pavement below, and Walter himself was seated on his lodging's window as on a horse: a leg over the sill and another in the apartment, as he watched the wind carry off the cash. His silk gown revealed his stomach and the bulge of his genitals against the sill. There was a foul heaviness in the air from the florist, and the day was cool and muggy. I was surprised I'd found him. As Kaspar had said, he'd been something of a ghost since the semester began.

'Walter! What are you doing? Stop!'

The light hitting his taped-up spectacles meant I couldn't quite see his eyes. 'Why?'

'At least keep it for kindling.'

'Ah, Pauli, ever the pragmatist.'

His landlady let me in, and the doorway to his flat was open when I'd made it up the stairs. Inside, there was mess everywhere. 'It's all garbage,' he said, looking around the room. Overnight, he'd become a pauper. In his gown he looked like a figure from the *Hochadel*: an aristocrat's ruination to him. 'I can at least make you a coffee. I have,' he said, 'tons of the stuff.' He came in with two small cups. 'No milk. Sorry.'

We hadn't really spoken since I'd seen him in the woods. I'd finished my coffee by the time I could think of something to say. 'I haven't seen you for a while.'

'I've been busy,' he said, packing up the stuff. 'Baby Jesus. The Magi, et cetera.'

'Walter,' I said, 'I hope you don't mind me asking. I mean, us not seeing you all this time, since the Survey . . .' I was messing this up, because I didn't really know how it was I should say it. 'I know that article came as a surprise.'

He tensed. I knew I was on to something, then. He stopped packing, waiting to hear what I had to say. I thought of the painting in the woods: the thrown light, the disquiet, its curious mood of intimacy and confession. I kept my focus on anything but him in the room. 'It's all right,' I said. 'If you're Jewish. We won't let anything happen to you. Or Charlotte.'

He laughed, then. 'Why would you think I'm Jewish?'

'I thought maybe you were keeping a low profile . . . On account of being Jewish.'

'No,' he said, almost sadly, as if he wished he were. 'I'm not.'

'Kaspar said you'd been avoiding the Director—'

'It's nothing,' he said. 'I'm not Jewish. You don't need to worry.' He took the cups to the kitchen.

Poor, inscrutable friend. It had been in this room that we'd argued, and from here that he'd written those lonely letters. *We picnic in the park. The light is lovely against the lake. When will you be home? Ernst is asking if he might tempt you back.* I resolved not to let things ever get so bad again. We were friends, good friends, and, most importantly, we were torch-bearers together.

When Walter returned he seemed more energised. He pulled a hand through his hair. 'Can you spare an hour? There's so much stuff to get through.'

We packed the junk into three big suitcases and cleared most of it quickly. Just before we were about to tow it to the dump, I noticed the absent sketches. 'Where are the Kandinskys?'

A look of guilt swept his features. 'I traded them in.'

All the air went from me. 'No! Walter! For what?'

'Trillions. I couldn't say no.'

'What's a trillion worth? I thought you were waiting for *valuta*.'

'Uncle König didn't come through.'

'Who did?'

He shrugged, but I knew it had to have been Ernst Steiner. Walter would never have made this error of judgement if he'd been in his right mind. No way would he ever have sold one of those paintings for anything less than they were worth.

We walked from Walter's apartment to the dump, and there was something funereal about our slow procession. In the city, money once again meant something, and the grey light hardened around the buildings, and the Reichswehr officers, unbeknownst to us, were readying to raid the Bauhaus a few hundred yards away. New money changed hands in the shops. Whatever we had kept in abeyance – responsibility, perhaps – was hard on our heels as we transported Walter's scrap toward the accountable future.

Everyone else was doing the same. How smelly it all was: what people had once cherished, and would have fought over, for the chance of an egg. Walter had not, I noticed, brought Charlotte's boggy paintings.

At the dump he rid himself of everything that had made him rich. It was then that I noticed the whistling sound as he bent to his work. I tried to work out what it was, then I realised he was sobbing. He howled, as if some lesson had pierced him, or the whole dead summer had finally broken him. I didn't know what to do, and so I stood by, letting him weep, in the fields and fields of Weimar's old junk.

# DESSAU, 1929

# 24
## Dessau

A hundred miles north of Weimar, our new school in Dessau was an enclosure of wall and glass. Glacial in winter's dark fields, everything about the building was essential: white walls, windows gridded in iron; no timber to speak of. It threw off light in great profusion; to stand beside it even on a summer's day could take tones from your skin. The building aroused in us our devotion; to enter into it was to ascend skywards: it was held only skimmingly to the world. From the outside you could see many floors at the same time, and the way people disappeared and then materialised made them appear like actors in a jump cut. Outsized on the black plains, the building was a spaceship. Within a day of its finishing it was hailed as the Director's finest monument.

I like to think the Director had imagined his building not when he had seen the plot in Dessau, not when he had designed it at his studio desk, but when those Reichswehr officers had turned up at the school, and he had thought:

*enough*. If the Bauhaus were to survive, it would have to get out of Weimar.

When the Director opened the school to us in 1926 – his students, his Journeymen, his Masters, and a thousand others come to celebrate – he kissed his wife's hand so that people would not see his tears. He had not lost a single person: not Stefan, not Masha, not Charlotte; not Paul Klee nor Wassily Kandinsky. And walking into its cool laboratories of art and design, the building did seem to exempt us from all the hardness of this world.

It was before the first snow that winter that I caught Walter heading to the Georgium Park. I watched him from my balcony, wondering if I should follow. The looseness of his stride gave him a sorrowful air. Our improbable twinness made me sensitive to his moods: Walter, after his weekend trips to Weimar to work for Ernst Steiner, could be tender and snappish, and I often questioned whether I wanted to be dragged into the remembrance of what we had lost. Weimar was a long time ago, and I had worked hard to forget it. Below the balconies his thick chestnut hair was blown about by the wind. After a while I put out my cigarette and went after him; I knew he wouldn't begrudge the company, even if he did protest.

The Georgium Park, just next to the Bauhaus, was full of neo-classical follies, dreamt up by whoever had committed the park so irreversibly to the nineteenth century. There was a garden house that went unused, and a ducal summerhouse, flanked by two mossy maids. Presumably the statuary was to give the park an air of wealth; instead it amplified its menace. Blank-eyed sphinxes guarded the mausoleum; a one-armed goddess stared forlorn from her plinth. As you walked through the whips tangled with snowberry, these open-mouthed statues sprang from nowhere. Empty nests darkened the light-fall to the path. The snow always took longer to melt here, and when it did the River Elbe turned rich and smoky and dark. The Georgium was not at all like the Ilm.

An inlet of reeds and grasses was where the river had broken its banks, and this was where I found Walter: his shoulders slack, his mouth a line, his eyes on the water, reading into its surface some manner of trouble. Maybe he would wade into the river with rocks in his pockets and put a stop to things. Over the years he had once or twice mentioned suicide. But really I knew Walter's life-force to be resilient: it was just sometimes he got caught in these big nets of mood and found it difficult to go on. Whereas my love for Charlotte had become an acceptable fact of everyday life, as natural but as ignorable as breathing, one felt there hadn't been much in the way of love's diminishment – not for Walter.

'Oh, Paul,' he said, looking up at me, startled.

'Aren't your shoes getting soggy?'

'They're all right.' He gave me a tense grin, a flash of teeth. He was quite a bit rounder these days: his flesh was graspable; a hand could paddle into it. He didn't look like he was carrying more fat so much as more water. His skin was stretched like the top of a pie, and it made you want to press a thumb in to see how far it would go. The darkness under his eyes was the result, I imagined, of last night spent in the woods with a bottle of vodka and the ear of any painter he'd persuaded to stay up late. I wondered if the forest had had its first snow; the beech trees blacker, the branches ravishing. 'How was Weimar?'

'Same old thing.' I watched his eyes skate the water. 'Pretty girls; chickens.'

'And Ernst?'

'Ernst, well; Ernst is still very fat.'

Walter's own extra weight made his mouth a heaviness; his forehead was higher as he had lost some hair. There was always a soreness in my heart to see him aged and bigger. I followed his line of sight to the school.

'Do you ever feel like it's going to eat you alive?' he said. 'Sometimes I think I might die if I stay any longer.'

His words made me imagine him as Ophelia, floating down the river, his loafers engorged. 'Every time you go to Weimar you say things like this.'

'Do I? I'm sorry; I must be very dull.'

'Walter, come on: that's not what I meant. Surely you've saved enough for years' worth of school fees. I don't understand why you go back.'

'Ernst kissed me. Behind the studio.'

'Oh.' I couldn't remember whether this had been expected. 'That's nice. Isn't it?'

'I suppose so. He asked if I was still in love with that man from the Bauhaus. Jenö.'

'What did you say?'

'Yes,' he said, without pausing. 'As soon as I said it, I felt like a fool. To be in love with the same man for six years!

How can I be so stupid?' He looked dumbfounded at the water. 'What a waste of time, and effort.'

We never really talked this frankly; we usually skirted the issue. This had become the easier way of doing things. 'It's not stupid,' I said. 'To be in love with someone.'

'It's beginning to feel that way.'

'You haven't exactly had a choice.'

'But how long can I carry this torch!' Pain made his voice rich. He took off his glasses and his eyes were smaller without the lenses. 'Jenö once said to me I had too many feelings. It was early on, in the autumn when we'd all just met. I had no idea what he meant. I didn't know what it was like not to feel things like I did – to be a man who felt things come and go, as if it were a case of watching the clouds go by; *skitter, skitter*. I wanted to say: do you not *feel* things? How is it that out of everyone I'm the only one to ever *feel* anything? But now I've learnt: best to pretend everything is fine. Whatever you do, don't say what's on your mind. That's what will save you. Say nothing. Do nothing.' He looked at me bitterly, and I knew what he was going to say before he said it, and I knew already that I would lie. 'Do you still have feelings for Charlotte?'

'No,' I said, and I felt relief in my heart for the deceit.

'You always were so much more sensible. I envy you that. You knew how to keep your cool.'

A flock of birds set off from the trees, spooked by something.

'Do you want to see him again? Ernst? Like that, I mean?'

'I'd like to be with someone, yes,' he said, by way of an

answer. I thought about Ernst and Walter together, two bodies pressed between the trees.

'Well, why not have a little fun then? You deserve it.'

His hand slipped to his pocket again. I wondered what was in there. Rocks to drown himself with? Or his wages from the studio? 'Shall we head back?'

Walter went, scowling. It was cold and the trees were noisy with wind. Things were in disarray: the sunshine so quickly changing into wet squalls and thunderstorms, and then days of this: nothing but cloud. Even today the iced school shone. The bottom of the building was painted grey, which gave the illusion that the school was hovering. I often found it a confusing place to find my way around; each leg of the building drawing you away from its centre like a switchblade.

We walked toward the big letters spelled in metal and shadow: BAUHAUS. The word ran vertically. As we reached the doors – painted in red, the only real colour at the school – there was a knocking above us: it was Jenö and Charlotte, grinning down at us from the Metal Workshop.

I felt a lurch of feeling, seeing them there, then I put it away. It might even have been rage: in the time that I had buried my feelings the entrance to the honest state of things was now slender as a keyhole. It made me smile that I had once been obsessed with truth and transparency; now I had a synthetic life with no great passions; and it wasn't all that bad. I knew I was a little dead. But in a funny way it was the only means I had to stay alive.

We waved up at them. We were both well practised in pretending that we were fine, though Walter occasionally let slip a lash of his tongue, a droplet of poison. Charlotte made a moony face, then turned away, the yellow silk of her hair following. Walter mimicked her expression. Jenö didn't look like he knew what to do, and so he followed Charlotte back into the workshop. 'They're idiots,' Walter said, 'but we're fools. What should I do? Tell me, won't you, what should I do now?'

He didn't understand that nothing could be done. We lived in the same stack of bedrooms and balconies: should I crane my neck from my balcony to Charlotte's room, I could see right inside it. Walter lived on top of me, and he could see my room from his own. In fact, we could all see each other all of the time. There was no escape.

# 25

## Dessau

Given my inauspicious beginnings at the Bauhaus, it was surprising I had become a fixture at the school. I had only really landed my role as a Journeyman due to luck: an apprentice had left when I'd graduated in 1926, and I stepped into the position as Josef Albers' assistant. Because I knew how it felt to be bottom of the class, I considered myself a good teacher: even to those who showed minimal promise.

It was a week or so after seeing Walter at the watery reeds that I was teaching the foundation year *Vorkurs*. My class was a good bunch of students, and they reminded me a little of ourselves as first-years: they were that curious mix of optimism as well as fatalism that Germany had been forever ruined by their parents. There was, I suppose, no other way to be; this attitude was the right one.

Josef Albers – Master Itten's replacement – had taken them for the morning session, and this meant they would work hard for me in the afternoon. Josef could be severe, even with the Bauhaus babies. He was a good-looking

man: his hair dense and grey-blond; his sharp nose dom-
inant. Like Walter he was a Westphalian, and always wore
a suit.

Josef had spent a large part of the first semester stripping
the students back: he called it their year of 'forgetting'. He
began his first workshop with a box of drinking straws:
'Take what you need,' he would say. 'Make something
that could only be made of drinking straws: not knitting
needles, wire, or spaghetti.' And, after the students' ini-
tial confusion – lessons from the lemon continued – they
would start to make things: straws were split, flattened,
glued, even used as spatulas and paintbrushes.

Most of them came around to it. Some dragged their
heels, wondering, I think, what it was they had come to
the Bauhaus to do. It all looked too much like child's play,
and not enough like fine art. I always had my eye on the
man or woman who was most resistant; someone like me
who clung to the imitative impulse. I tried my hardest
with them.

Today I would continue Josef's themes of spatial cre-
ation. The babies gathered at their work tables. Most of
them looked like they could do with a good meal, and I
wondered that they didn't stock up at the cafeteria, as we
Journeymen did. Most of the students were blond, but
there was also Michiko, a student visiting from Japan, and
a tall dark man: Howard, an American. Before I began I
felt self-possessed and powerful; how good it felt, to be
their teacher; to have the students in my hands.

Beside me were stacks of colourless cardboard. 'I want
you to find new ways of dividing and joining the cardboard.

Obviously, cutting and gluing are uninteresting. Can we make this cardboard do something it has never done before? Something it is particularly suited for?'

It was always best to leave them unobserved, because even the suggestion of authority could impede their experimentation. And so I left them to get on with the task, and in my room I worked on a painting that was turning out better than expected: a simple grid of berry-bright colour. Now I was living, as well as teaching, Master Itten's methodology, which was not to care too much about what was produced.

When I returned to the classroom an hour later the results were ingenious. One of the students had wetted the cardboard into spirals which retained their shapes when dried. Another – this was Michiko, who was particularly talented – had made a design on the board by stippling its layers of laminated fibre. No other material would have achieved such textural difference; she had discovered its unique properties. 'Was it accidental?' I asked her. 'This discovery?'

She nodded.

'What knife did you use?'

'No knife.' Michiko brought out something from her handbag. 'My eyebrow tweezers.'

We surveyed the offerings. Some students had scored and folded, so that the sculptures formed buildings and bridges; others had found ways of curving the board into wheels, stars, bowls. We assembled everything at the front. 'We need to pay attention to create things *material-gerecht*,' I said. 'The Wilhelmian Age delighted in making things that appeared what they were not. How could iron sprout acanthus leaves and blossom? Why would tin ever look like wood?' (Whenever I gave this speech I always thought of my mother's fruit bowl, shaped, unthinkably, like a swan. It had caused a big argument between me and my father about truth in art, and he'd called me humourless, which was probably accurate; it wasn't long after I'd lost Charlotte.) 'A station shouldn't pretend to be a Scottish castle! A hotel shouldn't be the Alhambra! Truth to materials – in their technical treatment, and truth to purpose in form – should be the target of all our efforts. What we do in here is not art,' I said, 'but experiment. Beautiful design may come from it. But that's a way off until we understand the material's innate properties, and how we can exploit them for our function.'

After that I gave them a shoebox of gramophone needles to share amongst themselves. Several students ran their hands through the cool needles. This would be a tricky task for them, since they probably wouldn't be able to build or construct with them. 'Have a good think about them,' I said, realising I was hungry, and therefore warming to my words as hunger could make me do. 'How do they feel? What are their properties? How does light interact with them? I don't care about the *painterliness* of what you do. I care about *invention*. Classical ideas of form and symmetry may still be in your system. Eradicate them! Forget them! Is not the balance of unequals more exciting than symmetry? After the war, what is order? Form? Perfection? It is not a thing; it is not in this world. Tension is everything. Avoid hammers and nails and glue and tape and thread, but concentrate on what the needle itself can do. What would it do standing upright, cast in light, spilled across different textures: velvet, hair, grass? And what would the needle do,' I said, getting edgy, 'in skin?'

I could just as well hit my hand on the table and shout, '*Licenza! Licenza! Licenza!*'

They looked up from their notebooks. I knew this was the moment when they wondered if I would let them keep their work. I was more indulgent than Josef, and didn't make them destroy what I had just asked them to create. 'You can keep your things,' I said, 'but don't sentimentalise them. We'll do the gramophone work in a couple of weeks. You'll notice I've given you double the time as usual. That's on purpose. Only in boredom will you understand. Boredom is very helpful to the artist. And come down to the cafeteria, won't you? You all need feeding up.'

Day to day, the Bauhaus operated just as it had done in Weimar. Breakfast, lunch and dinner were eaten in the cool expansiveness of the school's modernist cafeteria (Marcel Breuer's chairs; Marianne Brandt's lighting). It was Charlotte and Jenö who could be found there most mealtimes, sitting away from the other Journeymen and students. Though Charlotte had never ceased to be the centre of our quartet (Irmi and Kaspar had gone to Berlin after graduating) I think the rest of the school found her standoffish. As Journeymen we were permitted to sit with the Masters, but when we did it only promoted the idea that our gang, by proxy, was a little aloof.

While Jenö and Charlotte were creatures of habit, Walter was ambulatory and carousing: king of the jailhouse; pals with everyone. Really he could have sat at any table and any students or Journeymen would have made space for him. He was even friendly with Marianne Brandt, the one female Journeyman in the Metal Workshop, who had a famous *froideur* with almost everyone.

'What was today?' asked Charlotte as we settled down with potatoes and sausages.

'Twisty bits of cardboard.'

'Ah; that one. Josef doesn't like to change things too much, does he? Did you do the "eradicate" speech? About the war?'

'Yes,' I said, laughing. We had all heard this speech in one of his lectures.

'I do that one too,' said Jenö. 'Did they understand?'

'They looked bamboozled. I was rather hungry. I went on too long. But in a funny way they remind me of us.'

They both nodded. How alike they were. Being around them was like being with a brother and sister. Or twins, perhaps.

'There's a woman in my class,' Charlotte said, 'she's just like me. She's determined to fight it: the work, the loom, the wool. Everything she makes is rough and coarse. I haven't worked out what to do with her: I want her to fight, but I also want her to survive. I think I should probably give her the order to surrender.'

'Probably,' said Jenö, putting a hand on hers. 'Look at you, and Otti and Anni; none of you were naturals; at least, not to begin with.'

She tucked her ash-blonde bob behind her ears and frowned. 'I do wonder about the cost, though. Both of you got your first choice. It's not exactly fair.'

'I know, I know,' Jenö said, putting an arm around her, and placing his forehead against hers.

If I were any other man I'd have been able to simply observe Jenö's tenderness, but it was in these moments that my ancient feelings flared. 'Where's Walter?'

'With Franz,' said Jenö, 'I think.'

'Is he in one of his Weimar moods?' she asked. 'I haven't seen him since Sunday.'

'Yes,' I said. 'A big one.'

'I don't know why he continues there,' said Jenö. 'It plunges him into a depression every time.'

'Someone has to pay his school fees. Why not Mr Steiner?'

'His school fees! He should just take whatever diploma he can get.' Charlotte's mouth turned flat. 'What do you make of him?'

'Ernst Steiner?'

'Franz Ehrlich.'

'Oh; I don't know. Walter seems very attached to him all of a sudden. Apparently he's an excellent Print student.'

We'd first met Franz when he'd been a Bauhaus baby. He had so enjoyed being baptised in the city fountain that, drunk, he'd gone for a swim in its shallow waters. He had that kind of reputation. Instead of taking the staircase, for example, he'd slide down the bannister with his legs in a V. His intelligent eyes were always on the move, trying to find what fun could be had in the most ordinary of situations. I knew that Walter had had his eye on him all autumn: here was someone who might provide diversion. And, after the moody conversation at the river, Franz and Walter were suddenly best friends. I didn't begrudge him it. Walter had had a tougher time than most.

'Did you know Kaspar and Franz know each other?' said Charlotte, who was a regular letter-writer to Kaspar. 'Something to do with Berlin. Kaspar says they didn't get on, as kids.'

'Franz gives me the creeps,' said Jenö.

'You're just jealous,' said Charlotte, giving up on her food. 'You're used to being Walter's star. You don't know what it's like to be in the shade.'

# 26

## Dessau

Dessau was a small town, and well kept for working people. It had none of Weimar's classical beauty, but it was a little more honest, and this drew me in. It had a church, a square, a shopping arcade, and a cinema of silent movies, where the workers from the Junkers factory spent their money; as well as the Lamb, where I liked to drink, sometimes with Walter, sometimes with Walter and Jenö, on the fine boulevard of Cavalierstrasse.

As well as the Brownshirts on the streets that winter, there were also Communists and Anarchists, and every other idiot that could dress in a uniform who had idle time after shifts at the sugar factory. Most of the Junkers men, who were better paid than the rest, dismissed them as kids. The Brownshirts drank in the beer-halls and sometimes the Metropol, but they were usually shooed away, since they were known as trouble-makers.

After dinner with Jenö and Charlotte that evening I had a few drinks in the Lamb. I often came to the city on my own. I liked getting away: the school, with its multiple balconies, could be a grid of surveillance. There were a few Brownshirts in the Lamb: younger than me, and good-looking. One, with green eyes and an aquiline nose, kept on looking over, knowing that I was a Bauhäusler. I didn't like his scrutiny, and finishing my drink, I soon left.

As I headed to school the traffic was coming from the factory, and the cars had the sleek edges of the aeroplanes manufactured there; cruising, remote. I walked past the Metropol, the air inside blue with smoke, and the noise of people having a good time. A woman stumbled onto the pavement; she gave me a hobnailed smile. A man ran his hands down her sacklike dress. They kissed as if I weren't even there.

I felt myself observed as I too did my watching, and a man dematerialised in the dark then formed again in the gas lamp's reach. I thought it might be the green-eyed Nazi; I don't know why. It was just the way he had looked at me with intent, though it hadn't been all menace, either. He turned into the Metropol, and I walked on, somehow a little disappointed that he had not talked to me, or even approached me.

Beyond the rail tracks the Bauhaus was luminous. Outside its walls the world was in rapture. I could hear the noise from the other side of the building: the students and Journeymen would be out on their balconies until the small hours.

My bedroom was simple. A Brandt lamp lit the room, and one of Charlotte's weaves hung above the bed. Long gone were her knotted plots of displeasure. Instead, her most recent work had a hovering beauty. Now that she had mastered the loom she was intent on extracting from it increasingly granular levels of blackness. They were very dark, her weaves, so dark that one had to search hard for bolts of lighter aluminium or graded cellophane. She called them 'Beinahe Nichts' – Almost Nothings. When you looked inside them it was like falling down a hole.

I began one of Itten's breathing exercises. I still did this every so often. I thought of the couple outside the Metropol. I moved away the image of the green-eyed Nazi looking at me, but it kept on returning unbidden.

Later I changed into my pyjamas and went out on the balcony. The tip of the cigarette was the only point of colour in the wintry grounds, and though all around me was greys and whites, my brain felt newly filamented with an electricity I had assumed was all but dead. Something about the Metropol couple, or maybe even the Nazi in his uniform, had awakened in me a desire for another human being. I thought of how Jenö, very gently, had placed his brow against Charlotte's at dinner. Such a simple thing to do. Such a small gesture of love.

I hadn't felt desire for a long time. Over the years I had gone through nearly every woman in the Weaving Work-shop: Grete; Trudi; Margaret, the American. There had been something promising with Magdalena – even talk of an engagement – but she'd said I was too distractible. In any case she broke things off when I didn't take the next step. She had probably been right.

A voice shouted my name from a balcony above mine. 'Paul!'

When I twisted my neck to see who it was I was

surprised to find that the movement unloosed tears from my eyes.

'Come up!' It was Franz, waving from Walter's balcony. He threw down a knotted sheet, as if I were a prince about to climb Rapunzel's hair. There was more schoolboy giggling. 'Climb up! Climb up!' I thought about it: taking the sheet, leaping off the balcony, quitting this Arcadia altogether, but laughed instead, and told him I would take the stairs.

When the door to Walter's room opened, it was Franz who greeted me. He had black hair, a soft jawline and a stomach at full sail. He raked the hair from his eyes. 'Pyjamas!' he said. 'Wonderful!'

'I was going to bed.'

'Come in! Come in!'

Walter was smoking on the balcony. He tapped the ash over the railing. 'Paul,' he said, 'hallo. You didn't fancy our other method of transport?'

The knotted bed sheet still hung from the railings. I heard raised voices from the direction of Charlotte's room. 'What's going on?'

'Oh, they get like this occasionally. Ever since Rügen.'

'Really?'

He dropped the cigarette off the balcony. 'Did you hear the noises earlier?'

'What noises?'

'The wolves of Anhalt county!' said Franz, ambling outside, his cocktail spilling. I wondered how drunk they were.

'There aren't any wolves in Germany. Never mind Anhalt. Are there?' I said, suddenly doubting myself.

Franz gave a howl to the half moon. Walter laughed, then someone else on another balcony joined in, as another howl began, and another.

'Lunacy,' I said.

And Walter gnashed his teeth. 'You're not wrong.'

We went inside. There was a ruler and a compass resting on Walter's desk; beside it, paper, ink, a fountain pen. 'Look at this,' said Franz, assessing the drawing. 'All this Expressionist shit.'

Walter frowned. 'Please, I have to hand that in tomorrow. Franz is the only person who you can rely on for a good time and yet when it comes to work he's a beast. A wolf.'

Franz picked up Walter's work. 'Everything's in disorder. The letters hook into one another. The bowls are too big, the tails have too much flourish. Where's the baseline, Walter?'

'I think it's lovely,' I said. 'It's more a picture than a word.'

'It's not even finished,' Walter defended himself. 'It's not so much a type as—'

'It's capricious. The stress is variable. It creates confusion.' Franz took three paces away from me. 'Look, it's not even legible. It's worse than any of that old Blackletter stuff . . .'

'What's Blackletter?' I asked, feeling lost.

'A Gothic type,' Walter said.

Franz seemed harder and more talkative than normal, but I put this down to his dismissal of Walter's lawless homework. 'At least Fraktur doesn't have this terrible whiff of modernity.'

Walter addressed me. 'Franz wants everything straight and clean. As if the type had to burn through something. Not everything needs to have such a will to purity, Mr Erlich.'

But Franz wasn't really listening. 'It's not even legible. What does it even say?'

But this, Walter chose to ignore. I tried to stop the letters swimming, but couldn't work them out. I felt like they would have meaning if only I could decipher them. Franz was fairly obsessive about work, and he wouldn't let anyone denigrate his much beloved Print Workshop.

'Where've you been all night?' asked Walter.

'The Lamb.'

'On your own? The Lamb customers scare me.'

I thought about the young man in uniform and the intensity of his stare. 'They're not so bad. You know, if you're discreet.'

'I've never not been discreet in my life.'

'Oh, sure.'

'Were you going to bed so early?'

Behind him I saw Franz drop the paper.

I shrugged. 'It's nearly midnight.'

'Oh,' he flashed a look at Franz, 'we must have lost track of time.'

'Too busy having fun,' said Franz, and they both burst out laughing.

I stayed for a while longer but these two, when they got going, could be their own private universe, and I lost track of what they were talking about – types, Frakturs, Blackletters – as I fell in and out of sleep on Walter's bed, listening to the sounds of the school's consolatory plumbing, which had the deep resonance of Dresden's cathedral bells.

●

At the time, Franz didn't seem a bad guy; just young. His place in history of course is much more ambiguous. Personally, I have never known what to make of him, nor how we should judge him. Blameless, I suppose. And yet; and yet. Had he not found himself in the same camp as Charlotte, I believe I would have forgotten him entirely, or at least remembered him only from photos, since his significance only comes after the fact: he was freed from Buchenwald, and Charlotte wasn't.

I was surprised when Walter wrote to me, boasting he had sprung Franz from the camp and into a desk job as one of the camp's architects. The looseness of the handwriting suggested Walter was drunk; the warmer tone, too. He had addressed the letter to *Pauli*, just as he used to call me. As I've said, the rest of his letters were stiff and circumspect.

After Walter had worked his magic, Franz designed the type for the Buchenwald gate: JEDEM DAS SEINE – to each what they are due. Three words thieved from a Bach cantata. Carmine on zinc, and to be read from the inside looking out. After that, I suppose Franz gave them what they wanted: new bunkers, new dorms. I don't judge him on any of these counts. As Irmi reminds me: I wasn't there. I wasn't tested. Or at least my test was never quite so public; my own failings (and they are numerous) are not in the historic record, not like Franz's thirteen letters.

I often wonder whether Charlotte noticed Franz's alphabet as she walked under its signage in 1944. The type's Bauhaus character would have been abundantly clear. I wonder, too, if she would net the six of us in her memory and traverse those woods with us at liberty. That forest; it could give such days – skies of fluffed clouds; days dipped in gold. How we would fly on our bicycles, chasing each other down to Weimar, a city infinite in its prettiness and voluptuous in its charms, dreaming of violence elsewhere.

Now the camp is rubble, and the pain is in its stone. Goethe's Oak is burnt; a stump. The wind whistles through Franz's lettering on the gate.

And the trees; they stand witness.

# 27

## Dessau

Snow came. The whole building soon turned freezing, its high ceilings doing nothing to warm us. Klee, Kandinsky and the Director all had their necks scarved and their hands gloved, even while teaching. I sat out on my balcony smoking in the mornings as long as I could take the temperature, and looking across to the other balconies, inevitably finding someone to talk to, most often Anni Albers or Otti Berger, from the Weaving Workshop. Otti was a Yugoslav weaver with soulful eyes and a crowded mouth, who was able to trick from the loom rainbows of colour. She spoke German with an accent that reminded me of Charlotte's eastern inflections. Anni, Josef's wife, was also a weaver. When my brother had come here he had got on very well with her, but then everybody did get on marvellously with Anni. 'He's such a gentle soul,' she had said, when Peter had gone inside for a lie down. She had noticed his tremors. 'What happened to him?'

'Shell shock.'

'How does he show it?' she asked. 'What are the signs?'

'He's sensitive to noise. Panics easily. He gets head-aches for days, and awful nightmares. Long depressions, too.'

'Your parents must be distraught.'

'My parents don't know what to do. My mother thinks it's all her fault. My father on the other hand blames every-one he can: the Bolsheviks, the Jews, the artists; God and Bismarck too if they were contenders. The worst thing is they drive Peter crazy, but he can't keep a job, so he's stuck with only my mother for company.'

'What about friends?'

'His friends are dead. Or they're worse than him.'

That week Anni made a beautiful weave, textures of sand and pebble, and sent it to Peter as a gift. She hung it on a branch she'd found at the Georgium: it looked as if it had been washed up from the sea. I thought of my brother often and it grieved me to see his wretchedness. I wished I could do something to help, but every time he came to the Bauhaus I saw his deep sensitivity to its loveliness, which only made him worse. Better to live with the idea that life was no good than see your fellow man find in it so many pleasures. What we could talk about were only distant memories; what he could not talk of was his life as a med-ical student, how he had passed the *Physicum* exam with top marks, his meticulously imagined Berlin doctor's clinic. That life was gone. And the truth was, very little remained.

There were terrible storms that week and our balconies were the best places to watch the strange weather in Anhalt. The lightning strikes were prolific, and lit the snowflakes blue, and the wind so fierce that the snow appeared like tiny birds thrown this way and that. It was a wonder not much settled, but in the mornings the snow wasn't much more than sugar, and it was gone by noon, and the day could be placid, even bright, until the weather changed again and the sky resembled a nineteenth-century painting of ships lost to the boiling sea.

I was on my balcony with my coffee and cigarette watching one of these electrical shows when there was a knocking I didn't recognise. My first thought was that it would be Franz – he'd taken an interest in me since our night in Walter's room and I suppose his attentions were quite flattering. But when I opened the door I saw instead a courier in uniform, and the embroidered logo on his overalls stirred my memory. There were wet patches on his shoulders where the snow had melted. His face was smooth. Without meeting my eye he said he had a delivery for Mr König.

'His room's upstairs.'

'He's not in. No one's in. Can't you take it?'

'What is it?'

He gestured at the box, about a yard by a yard, and I realised the logo was from the same courier company Ernst had used. 'All right. Leave it here.'

He asked for a signature, which for some reason I was reluctant to give. I would have preferred it if Mr Steiner had forgotten me completely, and I put down a scrawl.

The courier scowled, looked at my nameplate, and printed BECKERMANN and my Christian name too, so all of my efforts anyway were for nothing.

'Leo?' I said, suddenly remembering.

'No,' he said, scowling. 'That's not me.' Without a further word he pushed the box into my room and left.

Before Walter's package was even in the room I knew I wouldn't be able to resist peeking inside. I slipped the padlock to '1919' – thinking that Mr Steiner would surely have changed the code by now – but it worked first time.

There was a burst of excitement: what could be inside? At the top was one of Charlotte's bog paintings that neither Walter nor I had liked. I wondered why he had kept it, and why Mr Steiner had sent it. Underneath were navy ledgers, the kind that had been everywhere around the studio. Inside them were compositions, measurements and portraits of some of the painters, a few of whom I recognised.

As I went through the ledgers I began to understand how involved Walter had become in the planning of Steiner's commissions. He'd obviously become more important than just a hired hand. No wonder the job kept on pulling him back. I hoped Ernst was paying him properly – but then Walter was one of the few Bauhaus students who was never out of pocket.

At the bottom of the box was a painting wrapped in paper and string. I undid the bows, wondering what bucolic landscape it would reveal, but what I hadn't expected was this painting in particular. I propped it against the wardrobe to take a better look at the September image which had stayed with me so vividly over the years: perhaps because of the image, perhaps because of the shiftiness that Walter had exhibited around it. It was from the week that Walter had disappeared.

And now here it was in all its glory, lit even better by the flashes of winter storm: the gabled cottage; the blur of orange chickens; the draught horse; and the three girls playing, looking apprehensively sideways.

The years gone had given me fresh eyes and it took me only a moment now to see its trick. There's a painting by an old Dutch master – a big Netherlandish landscape, which looks on first viewing like a normal scene of canals, narrow boats, Dutch houses, until you realise the light is pouring in from two directions. Everything is light; nothing is unlit, and it's not the high midday sun either, but a blast from east and west. It's an impossibility, and somehow Walter had managed to achieve this same doubleness.

It was a lovely piece. It didn't make sense that Ernst hadn't sold it. The paintings that didn't sell he simply used for firewood. Maybe Walter had convinced him of its sentimental value, but I couldn't see why: it was only the technique that made it special, not its subject, and Ernst was only ever interested in subject.

'What's this?'

I hadn't noticed Charlotte in the doorway. 'A delivery for Walter,' I said.

'What is it all?'

I looked at the notebooks and old paintings on my bedspread. 'Don't know,' I said. The dust made me want to sneeze. We hadn't ordinarily been allowed to leave our things at the studio. But Walter, as he was proving, had always been a different case to the rest of us. 'Remember this?' I said, pulling out the bog painting she'd sold for salt.

'Oh, God!' she said, but she was laughing. 'Don't remind me! It's awful! What's it doing here?'

'I've always thought it's more interesting than you ever gave it credit for.'

'For a frog, maybe. Is there another one? Didn't I sell him two?'

'Maybe Walter sold it.' I looked into the box. 'Its twin is gone.'

Charlotte studied the marshy brushstrokes. 'Maybe it was used as firewood. Probably the best use for it, at the time.' There was another lightning flash that blued the room. 'It's odd, this weather, isn't it?' she said, putting down the frame.

We both wandered over to the glass, from where we had an uninterrupted view of the sky. 'Otti said it's something to do with weather fronts and jet streams. Warm air and cold air. She actually said the words *extratropical instability*.'

'That,' I said, 'is not a surprise.'

The thing about Otti was that despite her charm she also liked to fake her expertise on matters of which she had no idea. And, because she was a little hard of hearing, I think people were ready to listen to her for longer. I'd heard her talk at length about the Republic's constitution, about reform in Bavaria, and wine production in Zmajevac – once, on a winter's night, how to slaughter a pig. I asked her if she really knew how to do that, and she said, 'We're Jews. Of course not.' (I wondered why I adored the sight of her crooked teeth, looking so infantile and sweet; why her smile, almost always extended a quarter-inch with a rolled-up cigarette, provoked my own.) 'I suppose Otti knows what she's talking about.'

'Otti knows what she's talking about thirty per cent of the time.'

'As low as that!'

'I'll give her forty, but that's generous.' Another leap of lightning. 'All the snow will be gone by tomorrow,' she said. 'I wish it would settle so we could do something with it.'

Behind us the bedspread was hardly visible what with all of Walter's things. 'Here, help me get everything into the box,' I said. 'I don't want Walter to know we've been through it.'

'Naughty Paul,' she said. 'How'd you get in?'

'I remembered the combination. All this time and Ernst hasn't thought to change it.'

While I piled the notebooks into the box, Charlotte rewrapped the large painting: she frowned, summarising it as *awful*. The light was all wrong, she said, but then, of course, she wasn't able to see its doubleness; its lit deception. Now, I saw, this was not so much the painting's technical fault as it was the animating reason why the landscape – with its throwaway tropes and images – was so haunting.

'Is there something going on between Walter and his boss?' she asked, retying the string around the painting.

'He's always liked Walter.'

She frowned. 'I thought you didn't like him very much.'

'Ernst Steiner? I don't. But if Walter's happy . . .'

'I thought something was going on between him and Franz.'

'Oh, I don't know. It changes every week.'

Charlotte watched with interest as I fastened the buckles and slipped the numbers on the padlock. 'Nineteen-sixteen?'

'Nineteen. The year Mr Steiner went into business.'

'And the Bauhaus.'

'That's right. Though I don't think Ernst Steiner cares a fig for the Bauhaus. Don't tell Walter we've been in here, will you? He doesn't like people interfering with his stuff.'

'I won't.' Together we pulled the box from the bed, and I checked it over, to see whether there were any tell-tale signs of our meddling; there weren't. We looked at each other and smiled.

# 28

## Dessau

Like Dresden, Dessau was built on floodplains. There were years in high summer when you couldn't see the street-car lines, when there were sandbags lining the shops, and people used makeshift boats to row down the central street. The Mulde could climb twenty feet, the Elbe several more, but it had always been an opportunity for carnival, with the factories in danger of flooding, and everyone taking it as a moment to slack off.

The Elbe today was full of moving shadows though the day was bright on the leftover snow. At the river's banks the water was starting to ice. Walter and I were on the iron bridge, in our heavy coats and scarves. 'Dare me to jump?' Walter said, his eyes shining.

'You'll smash your ankles,' I said. 'Besides, you can't swim.'

He leant on the rail. Wrinkles fanned his eyes as he looked into the sun. For some reason I fancied putting my nose into his scarf to see what he might smell like. It struck me as strange that I didn't know this about my friend; what odour he went around with, day to day.

From the bridge we watched Charlotte and Jenö walk hand in hand towards the mausoleum, which towered over the Georgium pond. This was where men and women spent their leisured hours in the spring and summer, and where the willows trailed their branches on the water's top. Behind them were the Masters' houses: white cuboid structures built by the Director for his staff. I had always wondered what it might be like to be inside them: whether it might be cosy, or stark, and whether, for a joke, they might have pastoral scenes on their walls like the ones Walter would touch up tonight in Weimar.

'You've lost some weight,' I said. Maybe Franz had put him on a diet, although I couldn't imagine fattish Franz would ever exert limits on Walter.

'How can you tell under all these clothes?'

'I can see your cheekbones again.'

He smiled. 'I've found something in the pharmacy which suppresses my appetite.' He bagged out the sides of his coat. 'I don't actually like being this heavy.'

'What is it? A magic pill?'

'Just a little thing Ernst picks up for me.'

'You'll have to tell Franz. He carries a little extra, doesn't he?'

'I think he always has.'

'He seems a serious man.'

'He's a buffoon really. He has the most enormous appetite.'

'That will explain it then,' I said.

'What?'

'The extra weight.'

'Hmmm. Why do you think he's so serious?'

'I suppose I mean about work,' I said. 'That whole lecture about type and the will to purity. Is he always like that?'

'The thing about Franz is that he's an obsessive, and if you're not, you're a dilettante. He's a purist. He thinks Otti's a fake for using too much chenille. If you're a weaver, use wool. If you're a sculptor, use stone. If you're a typographer, then for God's sake make it legible.'

'I'd like to see Otti and Franz in an argument.'

Walter rolled his eyes. 'It would never end.' We watched what the river's current could drag with it. 'I think Otti likes you.'

'Otti Berger? Why?'

'Because she goes into hyperinflation when she's around you. All her facts and figures. You make her nervous.'

This was a nice thing to hear, though I wasn't sure I believed him. Otti was the same with everyone: there was no difference between her behaviour to me or Charlotte or Anni. 'Are you excited about seeing Ernst tonight?'

'Yes,' he said, his smile warm and real. 'I think I am.'

'That's good,' I said. 'It's your turn. For a little sweetness.'

'Do you think that?'

I hesitated. I was wary that I had perhaps over-promised him things in the past. 'I want you to be happy, that's all.'

'Well, that means you deserve something too. I was sad nothing happened with Magdalena.'

'What was in that box he sent you?'

'Oh, stuff from the studio. It was too heavy for the train.'

'What'll you do tonight?'

I don't think I've ever seen Walter blush as scarlet as he did on the snowy bridge.

'I meant in your painting!'

'Oh,' he said, laughing. 'Glades and girls. The usual. Come on, let's catch them up.'

In the puddles the ice broke under our boots. We walked toward a trapped bar of light and reached the mausoleum: Christ in the stucco, stone bears below. We heard their footsteps first, then Charlotte and Jenö emerged around the corner.

'I've never been in,' said Charlotte, looking up at its dome.

I'd been inside in summer, and it had felt wintry even in the height of the hot weather. It would be an icebox in February.

'Who's in there?'

'Goethe once came here with Charlotte von Stein,' said Walter, who said it seriously but laughed straight afterward.

'You and your Goethe!'

'It was built *years* after he died,' Jenö said. 'Look.' He found the Roman numerals. 'Eighteen hundred—'

'And eighty-eight,' said Walter.

'Ninety-eight,' Charlotte said. 'Mad to think the Director built the Bauhaus thirty or so years after this monstrosity.'

Jenö grinned. He warmed his hands with his breath.

Putting the weight on one foot, he ran and then scaled the gate to the top. You could see in his speed how strong he was.

'Bravo!' Walter called. 'But what will you do now?'

The chained door yielded a gap that was small but not impossible. Jenö put his shoulder into it and, inch by inch, he flattened himself inside. 'Who's going to join me?' he said, inside.

We told our students to avoid these kinds of hi-jinks: this was exactly the kind of thing that would trick any conservative into thinking us Bauhäuslers were grave-robbing Bolsheviks. Still. I didn't want to be the last one to volunteer, so I followed Jenö's lead. But I was halfway in when, with some dismay, I saw that neither Charlotte nor Walter was following. 'Aren't you coming?'

They looked at each other. Perhaps they were both wondering what the best of the two bad options was: spend some time together or trespass into the dark. 'You go ahead,' said Walter, 'I'll keep Charlotte company.'

'Suit yourselves.'

Inside, the mausoleum was freezing. There was a golden mosaic high above us in the cupola which gave the only light. 'Echo,' Jenö said, into the atrium, to hear his voice thrown back to him. I marvelled again that Charlotte had opted for him; this boy-child.

'Jenö?'

There were sounds of things falling. 'Looks like this is where the Prince keeps his garden furniture.'

I found him rifling through trowels and rakes. The smell of cut grass came off the box. I felt a strike of irrational terror: that Jenö might take one of these rakes and swing it to my skull. 'Don't,' I said. 'It's not ours.'

In the gloom I saw him looking for the next thing to do. 'Down here,' he said.

We took the steps to the crypt. I followed the brightness of his hair. In the wet basement there were several tombs. In the dark I touched their lettering, trying to make out the names of those who had died, but the type was too decayed to work out who the dead had been. As I did this I realised it was the first time I'd been alone with Jenö in years. I had him, in the darkness, all to myself. I wondered what Walter would be talking about with Charlotte outside. I remembered what he had said down at the reeds – *Am I the only one who has ever felt anything?* And I wondered what it would be like – how it might feel – to be honest. I hadn't been honest, not with anyone, let alone myself, for so long. 'It's not been easy, these past few years,' I said. 'With Charlotte and you and me.'

After some time, Jenö spoke, and I was surprised his voice was a little scalding. 'It's not always easy on the other side either.' I hadn't thought about this. I hadn't thought that what they had given us, as well as what we had given them, had been a performance.

'I know about you and Walter at the Bath-house.'

I heard his tongue on his lips. 'It was a mistake. I still feel terrible about that night.'

'Does Charlotte know?'

'I told her in Rügen.'

'Ah, I see.' Walter had said their arguments were more frequent after our holiday there.

Jenö struck a match and the flame guttered in the wet air. He stood holding it until he couldn't any more. 'I saw the spa in Binz, and then felt like the time to confess. Now I think I shouldn't have. It's caused problems, naturally. About what she did and didn't know. About what's happened as a result.'

The match went out and I didn't get to see his expression. I lit another, but by then he'd already started speaking. 'I should have been more careful. Foolish; to have treated Walter's feelings with so little care. I simply wanted to see what it was like. To be with another man like that – well, it was nothing more than curiosity. I apologised, but he didn't really hear it. And by the summer it had blown over. He'd forgiven us.'

I thought of the strange September oil painting and wondered if that were true. 'Walter said you'd told him you loved him. The autumn before. When we'd all just started.'

'That's not true. I never said that. I promised him nothing.'

I wondered why I would so quickly believe Jenö over my friend. 'There's enough promise in a body.'

'I agree. But people make mistakes. People make mistakes with their bodies too. I have apologised, over and over. There was nothing else for me to say. Nothing else for me to do.'

The dark was so black it amplified all sound in here. I heard him lick his lips again, I heard the shifting of his body. I vaguely wondered if he might kiss me too, down here in the dark, where no one could see us, and no one would know.

'And then Charlotte came along.'

'Yes. And then Charlotte came along.'

Suddenly I felt revolted: that I had thought Jenö would kiss me with those lips that had kissed Walter and Charlotte; that we were such a foul merry-go-round of desires and bodies. I wondered whether Walter and Charlotte would be enjoying the same kind of heart-to-heart. Outside, the world would be rolling: the unknown trees soughing; the placid swans; perfect roads of smashed-up stones; the city waiting for its summer floods in the wind-blasted plains, Brownshirts crawling the city like lice; and Walter and Charlotte looking at the sky, his hatred of her like an arrow prone; not far away, the Bauhaus signifying something of worship to all of us and yet sometimes not so much a school as a cage wherein our madnesses multiplied. To think that a friend might take a club and wing it to my head! Being pent up like this: no wonder we thought such fevered things.

Irmi was right – as always. I should get out of here.

There was a crashing sound in the atrium. 'Time to go?'

Upstairs Jenö gestured for me to go ahead of him through the narrow gap. But before I did he evidently changed his mind, and, without warning, embraced me where I stood. The moment's intimacy – inexplicable – flushed my heart; then, just as soon, it left.

Outside, the world was bright, and Jenö and I both stood blinking off the darkness, waiting for Walter and Charlotte to materialise, but they did not. They had left without saying goodbye.

# 29

## Dessau

Last summer, when the mark was high, we'd been able to have something of a reunion in Rügen. Our four met Kaspar and Irmi at Berlin's Friedrichstrasse Station, then we trained to the Baltic Coast and ferried to the island. Visiting Pomerania had been Walter's idea; he wanted to see the cliffs as Caspar David Friedrich had done. Though Charlotte sniffed at the Romantic idea, we were all happy enough to spend a week on the beaches of Rügen.

At night the dead drop of the white cliffs gave an eerie feel to the place, but in the days the place took your breath away: the Baltic as clear as anything you'd find at Obersee. It was a hot summer and we all turned dark. We drank a lot and ate a lot that holiday: Riesling, bread and salty butter; baked fish and greens. In the days Charlotte and Jenö would bob about in the chalky sea, her blonde hair scraped and shaved on either side, so that she resembled a Fitzgerald hero, and the cast of the cliffs made her paler than she was. In Dessau, they were circumspect, but in Rügen they couldn't stop touching each other.

One afternoon, and though we were in nothing but our swimsuits, Walter wanted to pose me and him and Irmi like the characters in Friedrich's painting *Chalk Cliffs on Rügen*. Walter had borrowed Josef Albers' camera, and put it on a timer, and then threw himself into the picture. He was playing Friedrich, who, in the painting, is on his knees, as if scrambling around for loose change. We held our pose – I was looking out to the waves while Irmi made a sorrowful half-gesture to the painter – as we waited for the flash. Finally it caught us when Walter was just about to see if it was working – hence he is so blurred – and then we disbanded once we'd heard the pop. (In the Dessau dark room we watched the picture's development: Irmi cocking a hip, offering a fading smile; Walter, slightly blurred; while I looked like I simply wanted to put on more clothes. In the distance there was a deathly sailboat, which fitted the original completely. It was only then did I realise that the framing of the tree had caught Irmi and me in a love heart.)

After the shot, Walter fiddled with the camera while Irmi and I stood watching the view, with the warm pine needles under our feet, and the sailboat already gone, as if it had never been there. I was conscious that she had spent a good deal of the holiday in observation of us both. 'You should come to Berlin,' she said. 'It'd do you good.'

'My life's at the Bauhaus.'

'Is it?' she asked.

On the train home the weather turned. Irmi and Kaspar said goodbye to us at Friedrichstrasse Station. Jenö and Charlotte weren't speaking to each other after an argument outside the spa in Binz. Once we reached the Bauhaus, they went to their separate rooms without a word.

While Walter was in Weimar that weekend I thought about Irmi's Berlin idea. Maybe she was right, and a change of scene might do me good. I thought about how I had felt yesterday in the mausoleum: that our home wasn't a school but an asylum. Since collecting her diploma, Irmi often said the Bauhaus was a hotel. All I did here anyway was shadow Josef, whose abilities were so wide-ranging – in stained glass, wood, metal, stone, anything he put his hand to – that he didn't really need a Journeyman to assist him.

And so I wrote to Irmi, saying I had thought about her advice in Rügen, and Berlin appealed. I asked her if she knew of any rooms or boarding houses close by, or whether she had one of those permissive Berliner landladies who might let me stay on her floor. I looked at my letter, not really sure whether I should send it. I signed it off: *Pauli*, and decided there was no harm in at least telling her how I felt.

I found Charlotte on the walk from the post office, hunched in her man's coat in the snow-spooked city. I wondered where she'd been; I so rarely saw her without her twin that at first I had assumed it was someone else altogether. Then I felt guilty about writing to Irmi. Ridiculous; I know I owed her nothing.

'Where did you go yesterday? You left us in the mausoleum without a goodbye.'

'Walter needed to catch his train.'

But then, I thought, it didn't make sense that they would both leave; it was only Walter who needed to rush off. And in any case, why leave both me and Jenö quite literally in the dark? I bought her a coffee at the station cafe and myself a newspaper, and let it go. We talked about other things instead: the Metal Ball was soon, and we'd have to plan our costumes. She'd given up on trying to make an openwork weave and told me about a wall hanging she was planning, inspired by the movies, and made from real film. The Director was pushing us all toward utilitarian products that could be mass-produced, and available in every department store in Berlin, and Bonn, and Britain. Charlotte had won her diploma with a weave made with cellophane and chenille, which was hung now in a theatre at Jena, where it stopped dead the room's acoustic reverberation. She had invented a type of soundproofing. This was how she had made weaving interesting; she had made it functional.

I told her about Kaspar's latest exploits in Berlin; he was in love, apparently, with a Roma woman a foot taller than him.

'Do you ever wish Kaspar and Irmi were here?' she asked as she finished her coffee.

'A lot of the time, yes.'

'I miss them. Kaspar the most. I always think those two kept us from the worst versions of ourselves. Irmi doesn't work any more? Not at all? Not even in paint?'

I shrugged. 'She says she's happy at the Kaiserhof.' Irmi couldn't afford a loom, but she said that not making art didn't bother her. Kaspar, meanwhile, lived like a sultan in his mother's grand apartment on Wilhelmstrasse, though he didn't actually have two pfennigs to rub together.

'She's lucky,' said Charlotte. 'You know what Irmi said to me once? She said you'll never give up on all of this, because as long as you have the Bauhaus, you'll always love the drama. I've always thought that Irmi thinks she's better than us.'

I stood to go. 'That might be true.'

'Do you really think that?' Charlotte said; shocked, maybe, that I disagreed.

'Yes. Irmi might be better than all of us put together.'

'Then what does that make us?'

'Idiots. No. Worse. Idiots in alignment.'

As she gathered her things for the walk back, I watched as a train left its platform. Destination: Berlin.

When Walter returned a few days later, Charlotte was reading a romantic novel lying on the casement bed, while Jenö studied a Picasso monograph at my desk. We had been like this all evening, in silent companionship, getting slowly drunk on a bottle of brandy.

When I opened the door to Walter the first thing I noticed was the shimmer in his eyes. I had assumed he would return as he always did with wet boots and misery, but this time he was feverish and excitable. He kissed me and said hello to the others. 'Is there anything good to drink?'

Jenö looked up. Like me, he did not much like Walter in the aftermath of Weimar. 'Brandy.'

I poured Walter a drink. I had no idea where we'd found such an expensive bottle, but sometimes things showed up like this.

'What are you reading?'

Charlotte turned the book over. 'I've nearly finished it and I don't even remember the title. I found it in the market.'

'*Schund und Schmutz?*' Walter said – which translates roughly to 'trash and filth'. 'Franz is a fan too, you know.' He picked up the mail on my desk: a scantily clad woman framed by the illuminated advertisement of a cabaret. 'Is everyone at it?' Walter said. 'Who's this from?'

'Take a guess.'

Kaspar found it hilarious to send anonymous postcards to the communal postbox. 'Paul Beckermann' was always spelt very legibly, but he then signed it with an 'X', as if he was still worried about getting in trouble with the Director. There was also, in the pile, Irmi's reply from Berlin a few days ago. *Paul, Thrilled about your move to Berlin. When can I expect you? Of course you must stay with me!* Walter looked at that one too, but didn't comment. I hadn't yet had the chance to reply.

I took our drinks outside. The balconies were cantilevered downward, so that sometimes it felt a touch perilous to be out there. Walter launched himself against the rail, as if trying to gather momentum for a leap off it. He took a wildly big drink then tugged at his nose.

'How was it?'

'Haven't slept a wink. Ernst worked me hard.' He smiled. His still-present handsomeness made me remember how alluring he'd once been. Listening to him now, however, I could hear his breath after his climb up the stairs. 'Did you hear,' said Walter, 'a student once climbed the facade of the building? Swinging like an ape from balcony to balcony?'

'That's not true,' I said. 'We would have seen it.'

'It was Christmas. Everyone was gone. He found the first bit so easy he went all the way up.'

'To the roof? But that's fifteen metres! He couldn't have done it without ropes.'

'I don't know. I look at the school and think I could do that. Scale it to the top.'

A slow number came on the gramophone and Jenö pulled Charlotte up to dance. Though they were both garbed like stable boys, they had that shine that people of talent give off. There was always this sense that they were two people on the ascendant, but since the mausoleum I wondered whether there wasn't something shallow about the show.

There were other parties going on other balconies. We spent most of our nights here, getting drunk in my room (I don't know how my bedroom had become the centre for our socialising, but it had). Sometimes we'd invite others: Josef and Anni, Otti, my students, but most often it was just us four – Jenö and Walter, me and Charlotte – dancing, drinking, dressing up in crazy costumes, painting our bodies in signs and totems. Often Charlotte would think up some weird game (even now she still wanted things to escalate) and one night we used a Ouija board, calling up the spirits of the dead, until someone spelled out all of Kaspar's ex-girlfriends, and we'd given up.

'Where's Franz?'

'Ah, Franz.' Walter's tongue swept his lip. 'Honestly,' he said, smiling at his own joke – since *Ehrlich*, Franz's surname, translates to that very word – 'the man's flighty. Jumping from party to party without a care in the world. Plus his appetite is worse than mine. I can't afford to keep him.'

'He's young. We were like that too.'

'But one might expect more loyalty. I don't know. He took offence. He's gone off me.'

Walter tugged again at his nose. 'It was nothing.'

'What did you do, Walter?'

But Walter wouldn't answer.

'What did you and Charlotte talk about?'

'When?'

'When Jenö and I were in the mausoleum.'

'Sniffing around dead bodies.'

'Sniffing around dead bodies,' I repeated.

'Oh, nothing much.' Walter picked up a torch and swung it across the settled snow. 'What did *you* two talk about?'

'Me and Jenö? It was rather a frank conversation, actually. He said he'd told her about the Bath-house in Rügen. I hadn't realised that's what their argument had been about.'

'You hadn't? Oh, Paul, Paul: all roads lead back to Rügen.'

'Yes. I see that now.' I changed tack again. 'What shall I wear to the Metal Ball?'

'Any thoughts?'

'A skyscraper? An automaton? I don't know,' I said, 'I can't think of anything original.'

'Don't you worry,' he said, 'I'll think of something.'

'For me?'

'For us. We'll go together. We'll be a pair. As always.' He turned the torch beam on the swaying couple. 'Ah, but aren't they majestic!'

As the song closed I saw black light begin to pool around his nose. 'Walter!'

'Oh.' He pinched his bridge but this only made the nosebleed worse. It started dripping onto the balcony until he collected it in his glass and the brandy turned scarlet. Though I tried not to look, a warmth spread over me. I heard someone say *Paul, Paul!* but the world had furred. I grasped at the rail and tried to stay upright. Through a keyhole of sight I saw the glass drop from the balcony down to the snow.

Walter's eyes slowly met mine. The look I saw was gone so quickly there was a chance I might have mistaken it, especially with my impaired sight, but what I saw there was pleasure. 'Whoops,' he said, 'hand must have slipped.'

Quickly, the vertigo stopped, the fur receded, and the world went back to normal. 'Walter! You could have killed someone!'

'It was an accident. I haven't slept.'

Jenö came out to the balcony and looked down to the snow.

'The blood made my hands slippery. Stupid of me.'

'There could have been someone down there,' Jenö said.

'Get a tissue for your nose. It's made my head wonky.'

'I'll get the glass,' said Jenö. 'Paul, you direct the beam.'

'I'll go,' said Walter.

'No,' said Jenö, more definitively. 'We don't want you in more trouble.'

Walter went inside as I waited for Jenö then I directed the torch below.

A voice sailed out of the dark. 'Hey! What's happened?'

'It's fine!' Jenö shouted to the building. 'A mistake. Walter dropped something.' Very carefully, using his shirt as a basket, Jenö picked up what he could of the shattered glass.

I had done well not to faint, but I felt a fluttering in my ears, faintly suggestive of a migraine. Maybe seeing Walter's blood like that had set something off inside me. I wouldn't drink any more; I hardly needed a migraine.

'Done!' shouted Jenö, and I flicked off the torch. 'Tell Charlotte,' he said to the dark, 'I'm going to bed.'

Behind me I heard the scratch of the gramophone needle. I went back inside and the atmosphere had hardened. Walter was on the bed reading through Charlotte's trashy book, his legs girlishly flicked to the ceiling, and Charlotte leapt up to greet me. 'Pauli!'

On my desk there were two lines of powder under the anglepoise light. Instantly I realised that this was where Walter's nosebleed had come from: he must have spent the journey shoving coke up his nose. There was a wrap of newspaper next to the lines, springing open like a pastry.

'It's good,' said Charlotte. 'Really strong. Where's Jenö?'

'Gone to bed.'

'That's where Jenö Fiedler will meet his maker, you know: in bed! Do you want some?'

'No,' I said, but it was as if she hadn't even asked. Instead she tipped more out on the table. I heard the razor blade's secretive hammering, and then she took a thin line up her nose. Weeks ago, in Walter's room in my pyjamas, I had wondered how much Franz and Walter had had to drink; but they hadn't been drunk: they'd been high. That's why they had been so bright and ready; so opinionated and combative.

That evening Charlotte was very talkative, as they had been. It was also out of character because she rarely talked about Czechoslovakia. 'Our nanny was such a walkover,' Charlotte was saying. 'Poor girl, a Slovak, I forget her name: Lara, or Larna, or Laura, or Leila, something like that. One day we tied her to the dining-room table and threw burrs into her hair and she cried when my mother brushed them out. We'd collected them all day to do this. She died of the Spanish flu when I was eight. I cried for days. My brother wailed for weeks. My parents didn't talk about it: she was the nanny. Odd, that I can't even remember her name.' Charlotte lay on the floor, her eyes tranquillised and inert. 'Where's Jenö?'

'Gone to bed.'

'Oh yes. You told me that already.'

'Are you all right?' I asked.

Walter was grinning as he watched us, the dried black blood flaking on his nose.

'I'm perfect,' she said, stretching into a long line, 'just perfect.'

# 30
## England

That I could have become a painter, in fact become the most famous of my group, makes no sense to me. Even now I feel I am the one making trickster pieces, as if I operate with a gang of painters out in the woods. Still, I am only relatively famous, and even in the art world I'm not always known.

I am of course known enough for Walter to have found me. His letters – I call them his Berlin Wall letters – are in my studio. I don't know why I have kept them. After the news of his stroke, I reread them. Part of me thinks I should have dignified them with a response; that I was wrong to answer his disregard for Charlotte with my own for him. And, anyway, the fact that Walter is dead should mean my hatred is moot. Not getting him out of East Berlin and he not getting her out of Buchenwald; well, they are hardly comparable. A few whispered words to Ernst Steiner and he could have got her out. In those woods, he betrayed her twice.

Irmi has not called again. She knew not to bother. After

the funeral, she would have gone back to Teddy and to her side of the Wall. Jenö would have flown home to England. Walter, now, is in the ground. That gives me a pang of something. Remorse; regret; I don't know.

I have set up my self-portrait by Charlotte's damaged weave, the last one she worked on before the raid. For a while I've painted nothing but the threads she wove, and it has helped me understand her work better: its ribbons of infinite sunlight. In the foreground my face is at a three-quarters profile. The stubble is there, the creased brow, the bald scalp that puts me in mind of Itten. (And Itten. Is he dead now, too?) The nose is smart. I've always thought I had a good nose.

I wonder, though, if figurative work is the right thing to be doing, given what I'm asking it to express. Maybe that's why I've lost myself in abstraction all these years. My gallerist won't like it: it interrupts the narrative of the exile: the abstractionist Bauhäusler. That's the story that sells: not this portraiture with the heavy oil and tight brushwork.

But the exercise at least occupies me, and every day it gives me a little respite from my story. As I peep around the canvas corner, trying to find the right way to see myself, I think this too is the hiding game – what to show of myself, what not to show; what three words might describe the man in the mirror.

The eyes, most importantly, are waiting to be done.

# 31
## Dessau

For Paul Klee's fiftieth birthday, Charlotte, Anni and Otti made a life-sized papier-mâché angel. Marianne Brandt made a metal bowl; Kandinsky, a painting; and the three women made a weave. They packed all of this inside the angel's abdomen. Jenö made brass shavings for the angel's hair, and Walter painted her delicate features. To work all together again was wonderful: a reunion. This was before the holiday in Rügen.

Otti, Anni and Charlotte then convinced a Junkers pilot to take them up in his plane. They must have paid him from Anni's private fortune; her family owned several Berlin newspapers. Charlotte had never been on a plane before and neither had Otti. The pilot's twists and turns made the women laugh and scream, but Charlotte said she hadn't been frightened. After the floodplains of Anhalt county, she said it was as if someone had dipped all that time and space into coloured dye.

The women asked the pilot to fly low over Klee's lawn, then they tipped the angel from the plane, watching it break on the grass. Gift upon gift had been delivered from the air, because, as Otti had said, Paul Klee was not of the earth, but of the cosmos. Klee stood, astonished, tears streaming. 'Thank you! Thank you!' After the flight Charlotte's eyes had been so bright: as if she too were one of the firmament; one of the sky.

After Walter brought his cocaine to Dessau, this was how she looked almost all of the time. Her eyes always gave her away; their moving glitter, their liquid brightness. It didn't matter whether it was night or day: Charlotte wasn't awake, that February, without something in her system.

Had I not been high myself I might have intervened, but when Walter brought back an even bigger stash from the post office I decided to help myself, just as she did, to Mr Steiner's pavilions of cocaine. It was done before I had much time to think about it – and it would happen again and again as the nights grew colder – that I'd snort several lines up my nose. I had learnt my lesson from Weimar: one had to be part of the trouble or else be left out. There was no other way.

In the time before the Metal Ball the cocaine was never-ending. Mr Steiner, it turned out, had a connection to a Weimar dealer who supplied the entire corps of the National Theatre, the staff at Schiller and Goethe's houses, and the classical art school that was now housed in the old Bauhaus building. Walter said that around the studio cocaine could be had in abundance; it was the way Ernst got his men to work later and more efficiently. I wondered how long Walter had had access to it: whether, when I'd seen him at the river in January, it hadn't been rocks in his pockets to sink himself, but all these parcels to lift him into ascendancy. Maybe that's why he and Franz had become friends in the first place.

Because there was no new snow Walter's bloody-brandy bowl stayed like that for a while. After a heavy night I'd regard the rubied snow, and I knew it meant something more than I could construe, but what, I didn't know, and soon enough the early light would send me clasping my roaring head, a hangover dawning. It was the memory of Walter's eyes before the thrown glass. What was it? A sense of pleasure, maybe, or prophecy? But that look was gone just as soon as it had appeared; and in any case it had been moments away from my vision shutting down, and I couldn't safely say what I had seen; at least, not with any certainty.

Now we had enough cocaine to feed a battalion. Those parties in my bedroom were always me, Charlotte and Walter; Jenö wanted nothing to do with the coke. Out on my balcony I'd often catch Jenö walking into Dessau in the evenings. He came back late; late enough that he would have had to have been in the Metropol. He never joined us in my room, though he must have heard the party from the field below, or his room above.

Anni and Otti didn't want to get involved either, and Franz was still squabbling with Walter. Walter and I talked well into the nights, while Charlotte coasted around the room: a medieval maiden in a Pre-Raphaelite painting.

The best thing about Walter's parcels was that joy had returned to the Bauhaus; or at least real fun. Those nights, we committed ourselves to our pleasures. It was like we were fasting again, as if we were all part of a new communal purpose that our group – or at least our trio – shared once more. There was a sense of striving for something, or at least living through something bigger than ourselves.

Around this time I spied Jenö in the Metal Workshop, working on one of Marianne's designs. Some time ago she had delivered a brilliant lecture about how she was getting rid of the frosted lampshade in an electric light: she would let the bulb, in all its nakedness, shine without a shade. 'I am investigating,' she had declared, 'the ontology of the lamp.'

The Metal Workshop was a different place to the rest of the school. The air was full of metal filings. The stink from the room was like blood – raw and staunchly mineral – and its sounds – the moulding, boring, pressing, grinding – were foreign. I had no idea how to work its machines. That day I caught Jenö standing there, lost in thought, doing nothing, the stick of the lamp in front of him. When he saw me I knew he wanted me to talk to him, to tell him what to do about Charlotte, and the cocaine, and the private interment to which, in her narcotic fugue, she was becoming devoted. *Tu was*, I might have said to him. *Do something*. But I didn't take a step more. He tried to talk to me but I didn't give much ground. Somehow, this felt like punishment from an old hurt. I was blocking him out, as he had blocked me out.

I knew why Jenö was concerned about Charlotte; so were Otti and Anni, although to herself Charlotte's pathology was probably invisible. The fast, the coke: both were a means of erasure. Whereas everyone else's personalities, high, were both vastly elaborated and also comically dishevelled, Charlotte was to be found on these nights semi-tranquillised, looking out to the benign world which could not touch her. She liked not to feel anything. She liked remoteness. Had it been naturally induced it might have been called enlightenment, but instead it was a system of neglect. She grew thinner.

After so much of this business, Otti, with a look of concern that turned her face mournful, told Charlotte she had to get back to work, but Charlotte wasn't interested. For days the loom had gone untouched. Anni, too, said she was worried.

'She won't be able to stop herself,' said Otti, in my bedroom, a rolled-up cigarette behind her ear, and one in her mouth. She wore round black beads and her outfit didn't look warm enough for the weather. Perhaps, at home in Zmajevac, this was more like spring. 'You know she gets into these things,' Otti said. 'She likes being emptied out.'

'Otti's right,' said Anni, who sat under Charlotte's weave, a blackened window. 'It's no good for her.'

'What am I meant to do?'

'You have to persuade her to stop.' Anni picked up a newspapered wrapper from my table. 'Or at least set an example.'

'Charlotte can do what she likes. She's old enough to decide.'

'Of course she is,' Otti said, 'but that doesn't mean she'll make the right decision.'

I looked at the two women. Both were small, both thin, and their dark hair offset their paleness. Neither smiled as Anni pressed home her point. 'The Director wants us to be productive. Charlotte's not been in the Weaving Work-shop for a week or so. People will start to notice. Gossip will get around. The Director won't look warmly on it.'

Teaching high was something of a rollercoaster. Some-times I ran out of things to say or do. At other moments I went way over time, and the students would look at me perplexed, wondering, I think, what had happened to the man who had so surely told them to eradicate the past.

After Otti and Anni's dire warnings that morning, I taught in the afternoon. I had three objects assembled before me: a lamp, a chair and a tea glass. I wanted to show the students the will to form; that good design might be made from a few simple shapes, or maybe even just one. I went off for a while on my theme – the criminality of ornament – then I remembered what we had come to do. I tried to temper my excitement because I thought maybe it was obvious that I wasn't all there. 'Each design,' I said to the babies, 'should consist of no more than a few simple parts.'

Michiko and Howard exchanged looks, and the rest of the class was silent. Maybe I'd already said all of this.

'The gramophone needles,' said one, a woman whose name I frequently forgot, and who knew I frequently forgot her name. 'You said we were going to present our findings today. Because we ran out of time last session.'

'Oh, yes,' I said, having clean forgotten I'd set them that task. 'Use them for your Metal Ball costumes,' I said, bungling it. 'I've no idea what I intended us to do with them.'

I could tell she was unhappy with my sloppiness, but I ignored her. I felt adrenal. I was a powerful teacher, and I had more important things to communicate. 'Look at this lamp,' I said, quite loudly, and pointing to the Wagenfeld and Jucker lamp. 'Spherical shade, cylindrical shaft, and a circular base to mirror its top. It's perfect. Three variations of the circle. And yet all its parts are visible; even the cord and switch. It shows its functions. It hides nothing.'

Here, as Marianne had said, was the ontology of the lamp.

I moved on to Josef's tea glass. It was a triumph of design, though it had not sold well: the story, really, of the Bauhaus. 'Heat-resistant glass, brushed chrome, but what about this cup makes it special?'

Michiko raised her hand. 'The handles.'

'Exactly. One handle for the server to give: horizontal. But it's much easier for a human hand to receive on the vertical. Two handles, two directions, one tea glass. It's a wonder no one's ever thought of this before. This happens when you *will* simplicity.'

I passed the tea glass to Michiko using the vertical disc, and she took it with the horizontal, and smiled. My teaching leapt with brilliance. 'It's wonderful, isn't it?'

Nods all round.

'You said it was the other way around,' the nameless woman said.

'What? Did I?'

'You said horizontal for the server, vertical for the receiver. Then you did the opposite.'

I looked at the tea glass. She was right. 'Well spotted. Yes. See how adaptable it is!' I turned to Breuer's slat-chair to distract them. 'And finally, regard the angular construction, and the elastic belts to promote posture. Look at the spaces in between; they're all squares and rectangles. The shapes are additive: they don't blend. Ockham's Razor: the simplest design is always the best.'

I set the students a task to make a stool with as few shapes as possible using rolled-up newspaper. While they worked, I settled myself into Breuer's chair. I knew I shouldn't have shown them the objects first; now they wouldn't be as free to do their preparatory designs and to draw ugly things. In Josef's classes he insisted draughtsmanship should be without goal, and he was right, pedagogically: ask students to produce something, rather than explore the material, and the results would be conservative.

I knew, too, I should leave, but the chair was comfortable, I felt relaxed, and I let myself wander off. From here I could see the field below our balconies. In the summers the grass would be burnt yellow, but in the winters it was covered in snow for the best part of Christmas to Easter. The thaw usually uncovered all manner of hidden things: cigarette ends, mostly, but also textbooks gone missing, used contraceptives, paints which coloured the melting snow in rainbows; once, a couple of puppets, fallen from the roof after a particularly energetic performance from the theatre department.

I don't know how I managed to fall asleep, but I did. Michiko woke me later. The room had acquired twenty new stools; all of them depressingly identical. The students looked at me with worried expressions. 'Is everything all right?' the woman said, and I remembered that her name was Viktoria.

'Fine, fine.'

'There's the design flaw,' Michiko said, staying a little longer by my side; 'in Japan we would call this chair too comfortable.'

# 32
## Dessau

It was fairly unusual to find civilians at the Bauhaus. I don't know where Walter had picked up the green-eyed Nazi, but it was certainly a surprise when, on the evening after my botched class, I saw him, hands behind his back, observing the scalding light of the painting now hung above Walter's bed. I felt so groggy from the classroom doze that I almost wondered whether he was real.

'Beautiful, isn't it?' the Nazi said. He stood at ease, as if his uniform meant nothing in here.

'I don't know. I prefer my art with a little more *Kulturbolschewik.*'

I looked at Walter, who was refusing to meet my eye.

He offered his hand. 'Oskar.'

'Paul Beckermann,' I said, thinking my formality would outdo him. 'How do you know Walter?'

'I met him at the Metropol.' A warming of his cheeks. 'I've never been inside the Bauhaus. It's less impressive than the outside.'

'Do you think so? Most people say the opposite.'

He blushed again. I don't think he had meant to be aggressive, and in that moment he reminded me of my father, who, despite his dominance, was more confused about the world than he would admit. 'I thought there'd be more of everything. Everything's rather spare, and I thought it'd be opulent. That's what everyone thinks in town.'

'I saw you once at the Lamb.'

'I remember.'

But as soon as I'd mentioned it Oskar excused himself to the bathroom. Perhaps I'd embarrassed him; I hadn't banked on him being bashful.

'Are you in the habit of picking up Nazis in the city?' I asked Walter once the door was shut.

'Wrong way round.'

'How's it going with Ernst?'

'Very well.' Walter smiled. 'I'm surprised by how much I like him.'

'And this young man?'

'Well, while the cat's away . . .'

'Ernst must like you. To send you such expensive gifts.'

Yesterday Mr Steiner had sent six more dumplings in the post, enough to keep us going for a week of weddings.

'The painting?' Walter asked, mistaking my meaning. 'Oh no, Ernst's having a clear out. They have so many customers they need every inch of space. The Americans *love* his stuff.'

'I meant the coke.'

'Ah no: that's an indulgence just for me and my friends.'

'Friends like Franz?'

'Franz got a little too demanding. I had to cut him off.'

I noticed then the scribbling on his arms: blue inked marks. The lettering looked a good deal like the 'Expressionist shit' Franz had derided, but the type was slightly straighter, which made it more legible. 'Did you run out of paper? What's that?' I twisted his wrist so I could better see the alphabet: an *L, C, A.*

I felt the tension in his arm, wanting to withdraw it.

'It's my new type.'

The tattooed letters were thin, without a serif. 'It's nice,' I said. 'Have you christened it yet?'

'I was thinking of calling it the Lotti-line.' And I saw then what word these letters would make: Charlotte.

'Why?'

'I don't know. I like the sound of it. *Lotti-line, Lotti-line, Lotti-line.*'

Oskar's polite knocking interrupted us. He looked at us as I held Walter's arm. 'Funny who you bump into, at the Bauhaus.'

On the table there was a scrap of Weimar newspaper, springing open like one of those Japanese miniature temples dropped into water. Walter chopped a line onto his desk and Oskar eyed it enviously.

'Don't worry, dear,' Walter said, 'all this is for you.'

Oskar put it up his nose at once. It was rather glorious that he was so unhindered; that he didn't separate the fat bar and have less, or snort it slowly. His green eyes dazzled. Walter looked thrilled at the young man's appetite.

Later we tried on our Metal Ball costumes. Walter insisted that he and I were to go as a pair: we'd wear chains around our necks; as hats, the inner wheel of a bicycle, held around our chins by rope. We had raided the school's chicken coop for feathers and Walter glued them onto the wheels. We were roadkill, and we thought ourselves very clever.

'What's Charlotte going as?'

'The Statue of Liberty.'

'Excellent choice, excellent choice!' He looked at the feathers. 'Maybe we could use them for her torch? I wonder if we could somehow get it to burn. Wouldn't it be great if the torch could be on fire! And Jenö?'

'Jenö's not really into it. The theme.'

'It's *his* theme! Metal! Can't Marianne fashion him something?'

I shrugged. It was entirely up to Jenö what he did. I thought of Marianne and Jenö jointly humped over a desk lamp, and I wondered if anything might be going on there.

'I wish I could come,' said Oskar.

'Maybe we could smuggle you in,' said Walter. 'You'd have to ditch the uniform, though. It's not quite Bauhaus, though it's a smart design.' Walter moved me to the mirror so that he could fix the wheel to my head. It was lighter than it looked. 'A touch of beetroot juice here, here and here' – he touched my cheeks; it felt nice – 'and we'll be on the road, so to speak.'

'Nothing too realistic.'

He pecked me on the cheek. 'Ah yes. The famous *haemophobia*. Can't have you walking around half blind, can we? Don't worry. We shan't exploit you.'

As I smoked on the balcony I looked in on the men. The room was in disarray: chicken feathers, bike parts and the residue of our lines. Walter lay on the bed, and Oskar was on the floor, a book on his knees. He actually seemed a sweet man, as much as a Nazi could be.

As I watched them Walter's finger idly traced the young man's neck: his Adam's apple, his jaw, his collarbone. I felt a shiver of excitement, knowing that I couldn't be seen, though I could see in the reflection my gaze hardening. After a while, Oskar tipped his head onto the bed. Walter's hand paused, then he propped himself up and kissed him.

Something about the way Walter's lips touched Oskar's so sensually – soon I saw the dart of tongue, the meeting of bristle and moustache, and Oskar moved himself to the mattress – made me touch my own mouth. I felt the familiar stirring to touch someone and to have them touch me: just as I had felt outside the Metropol. The men kissed more urgently, and I wondered what it would feel like to have another man against you. Then Oskar looked over, wildly, invitingly, and I swivelled around, concentrating my gaze on the snow below.

And then I had the distinct feeling, as one does, that I was not the only one doing the watching out here. A scan of the balconies below revealed no one, but then I found Charlotte on Jenö's balcony above. She waved and went inside. All alone on the balcony, she had looked sad. To my surprise I thought: I hope they don't break up. I hope they are all right.

Charlotte showed up at my room later. I'd been reading, trying to forget the image of the men together, and

233

what they were now doing. I had excused myself to their smiles, which weren't as sheepish as you might think.

'Where's Walter?' she asked.

'Entertaining a young man in his room.'

'I thought you said he had a boyfriend. Your old boss?'

'Don't ask.'

Charlotte fell like a dead man onto the bed. Maybe from the coke before, I felt good. I put my hand on her neck, trying to find her pulse, thinking how Walter had done that to Oskar earlier. Though my desire for her was all but dormant, the fact of her body – here, like this – was a maddening idea. But Charlotte pulled away, and so I did too. She said something to herself, which I didn't catch. Outside, I heard rain.

'Do you think Walter's happy?' she asked.

'I think he wants to be, and that's what's made him so unhappy, in the past.'

'After Rügen, I tried to apologise. There was no reason for Walter to accept, I suppose.'

'Only tonight he said he's forgiven you entirely,' I said, though I had no idea why I was making this up. Our lives were so complicated it was never a good idea to introduce more complexity. 'He's even invented a new alphabet. It's called the Lotti-line. It's true!' I said, when her face changed to one of disbelief. 'He's practically tattooed it on his arm. It's rather Expressionistic. Barely decipherable. But I think it's a compliment. Some kind of gesture of forgiveness.' I changed tack. 'Up on the balcony, you looked sad. Is everything all right?'

She looked toward the wall.

'Sorry. I don't mean to pry. Let's not talk about it.'

'Jenö doesn't like other people having fun.'

'Jenö was in tonight?'

'He said he wanted to spend some time together. He doesn't like all these nights in your room. He said I turn into a different person. Do you think I do?' She didn't give me time to answer. 'I saw him once, watching Franz and Walter. He looked at them as if they were little boys, when really they were just enjoying themselves. Sometimes he's so grown-up it's boring as hell. I just want to have a little fun, and he makes me feel bad about it.'

Charlotte went out onto the balcony and I followed. We watched the rain brightening the night, settling to freeze on the snow. 'Jenö has a theory that Walter threw that glass on purpose.'

'Why would he do that?'

'To get Jenö out of the room. So that he could give me the cocaine.'

'Again, why would he do that?'

Charlotte craned her neck to see where it had landed, then she looked up to Walter's balcony and shook her head. 'Did you see whether Walter checked the ground first?'

'Why?'

'Because if he checked that means he threw it on purpose. That would mean it was part of a plan, rather than an accident.'

'I'd gone all faint. The blood, remember?'

'Ah yes,' she said, 'it's always the faint.'

'Look, Jenö's getting fretful over nothing.'

'Sometimes I think that. Other times I think he might be right; Walter knew the cocaine would separate us.'

'Otti and Anni are worried,' I said. 'They say we should stop, that the Director will start to notice our whereabouts.'

'They're probably right. It just helps. Things with Jenö aren't so good.' Charlotte rubbed her face. 'I don't know. Walter's always been a mystery to me. I've never known how to be around him. Even when Jenö and I weren't together.'

Below us two men walked out from the Bauhaus gates. Under the umbrella you could see Oskar's uniform. I wondered where they were headed. Nowhere would be open.

'Paul, you didn't tell me the man was a Nazi!'

'No one's not a Nazi in Dessau these days.'

When the rain started to drive in we went back into my room. Charlotte looked around, wondering what to do. It must have been very late; it was after midnight when I'd left Walter's room. I picked up my book. It wasn't unusual for us to ignore each other like this, when we wanted company but didn't want to talk. These nights could be hard on my heart. They were like nights spent between an old married couple.

In the corner of my eye I watched as Charlotte picked out scraps of newspaper from the inkwell of my desk. I thought that maybe she was looking for a crumb or two of the leftover coke, but instead she laid the newspaper scraps out flat. She looked at them, puzzled, thinking them over. Then she began fitting them together again, reassembling the torn-up pieces. Once done, she withdrew her hand, as if scalded, and held it to her mouth.

'Charlotte?'

She looked over, her eyes glassed up.

'What's wrong?'

'Oh, Paul,' she said, but didn't elaborate. 'Oh goodness, no!' She took the scraps of the newspaper and held them in her fist.

I didn't know what on earth she meant by this, and moments later, I can only say that she fled. Upstairs, I heard Walter's door clicking, and a rumbling on the ceiling above. I was too tired to work out what she was doing – that she must, in hindsight, have pulled out Mr Steiner's padlocked crate, swivelled the numbers to *1919*, and gone through each and every notebook until she had found what she knew was there. Instead, I let her get on with whatever new escalation had gripped her, and, as I was falling asleep, I thought for some reason of the paper lantern she had made years ago, how I had loved to watch it sway above my bed in Weimar, and I wondered where it had gone, or whether I had jettisoned it, as I had other things, in yet another fit of heartbroken pique for my still beloved Charlotte.

# 33

## Dessau

There is a photograph of us from the Metal Ball which I have pinned above my desk. It must have been from early in the evening, because we look happier than we did for the rest of the night. We are on the stage, our joy lit in the magnesium flare of the camera flash, our wheels still on our heads, Charlotte's torch still plumed with orange feathers. The reflection from our costumes means there is too much light in the picture, but you can still see our faces: Charlotte and Jenö, and me and Walter, two birds who'd met their death along the way. In early books on the Bauhaus it is subtitled *Four Bauhäuslers, identity unknown*, before I rose unexpectedly to fame. (Now, they always use my German name; never Brickman, as if they know something about me of which they think I am ashamed.)

Walter and I staged our entrance at the Metal Ball so that we arrived on the metal slides at exactly the same time and we were twin birds hurtling toward our deaths. As well as the two massive slides, the theatre department had made huge skyscrapers and moons which hung from the cafeteria ceiling. Marianne's overhead lamps were draped in foil, and there were cobwebs made from silks and threads. Everything shone.

Every time someone new arrived the trumpeter from the Bauhaus band played a *toot!* and everyone laughed to see the Director, Klee and Kandinsky land on their rear ends. The staff were dressed in tin hats and steel glasses; their wives' hair arranged with picture-rail wire, and iron wool around their shoulders like wings. But it was the students who'd really gone to town. Automata, tin men, automobiles, and most of New York City shot down the slides and then began to dance.

By the time Charlotte arrived at the party, I'd already had several goes at Ernst's coke. She overshot the slide and landed sharply. In that moment I caught her expression unguarded: she looked around the room jealously. Jenö, big child, slid down with both legs thrust forward looking like a tin soldier in a spooned jacket. But she did not wait for him. He had to amble after her, and his boxy costume slowed him down. As the Statue of Liberty she had wrapped a green sheet around her and pinned it with a brooch. She had a torch in one hand, in the other her statute book. Her eyes were terribly unblinking, and her pupils were big. I wondered how much coke she'd already had. I don't know why she was in such a vicious mood, but, admittedly, she could get like that sometimes.

Walter, dreamy bird, was also quite gone. He was everywhere that night, dancing with me, big Franz (who had evidently been forgiven), even Jenö, and when Walter wasn't dancing, he was stroking his chicken feathers as if he were his own gentle pet, and the blue letters – the Lotti-line – marked his arms.

That night, I resolved not to have much to do with Charlotte. I danced instead, yanking people around the dance floor: darling Viktoria, shy Michiko. I didn't really care. I was that kind of drunk that convinces you of your own inalienable goodwill toward others, and an astonishment that you have ever in your life bothered being unhappy. I even played on someone's trumpet, though many people tried to make me stop. I insisted, thinking I was really good, until Walter drew me away for another line on the steps with the school sign looming over us and we shouted the word as loudly as we could: 'BAUHAUS BAUHAUS BAUHAUS!'

Otti danced with me for a time and I wondered at how beautiful she was: with her perfectly round face and dark eyes and that Slavic complexion the other girls were jealous of. Yes, I thought, as we danced: I was in love with Otti Berger – a beautiful weaver whose work streamed with colour.

Later the theatre department performed a dance. All flashing knives and forks and sexy spoons, champagne bottles exploding, kettles boiling, and one woman with an elaborate candelabra on her head with lit candles, which was surely very dangerous, and Masha with metal wheels painted on her uncovered breasts. I drank more while I watched and I distinctly remember thinking – *I should stop* – and then thinking – *ah, fuck it, let's carry on*.

Soon, the party started to bust out of itself. Things were falling apart, coming off the ceiling; the foiled decorations were torn and shredded; the atmosphere, too, was souring – women crying flumes of mascara, men getting aggressive with other men, or disappearing off with the wrong woman. I had no idea of the time. Hairpieces had come undone; skyscrapers had bent in two. A new punch was on the go and more cocaine was passed around. People lay about in disrepair, one unconscious woman's breast bared to the world like a cream bun.

But to all the world, I felt unthwartable.

At some time in the morning someone started to play an accordion quite badly, though the song was sweet. Walter had a long glass of clear liquid, suspiciously neat. Most of his feathers had gone and he'd lost the wheel. Only the bicycle chain was left as he leant into a young Bauhäusler. Really, in the past month, he'd almost become a cad.

It was then that I saw Charlotte, in her green bedsheet and without a coat, walking in the snow toward the Georgium Park. I went through the last of the ruined city and took the steps two by two. Behind me I heard Walter call my name, but I didn't stop.

Outside, the sun was nearly up. I was too drunk to feel the frozen air. Charlotte was ahead at the crossroads, and I shouted to her but she didn't stop. I heard someone come up behind me: it was Walter, still holding his drink. 'Where's she going?'

'No idea.'

She moved quickly, and kept on appearing and disappearing, like something supernatural. We hurried into the park, the trees so black the bark seemed burnt. We went past the mausoleum and the Ducal House, and though we kept on shouting her name, Charlotte didn't answer. We passed armless Flora fleeing a stag, and several leering statues. Walter said at one point it felt as if we were walking into a trap, but I think he was just enjoying the melodrama.

'Charlotte!' I shouted, hearing my voice ring out amongst the frozen trees. We went further in, trying to find her where she was hiding from us. 'Come on! This isn't a game!'

My voice spooked the birds from the branches. With the trees crowding in and each part of the park looking identical to the last, we had to admit we were lost – or, more precisely, that we had lost Charlotte. Impossibly, Flora appeared again. I knew the Georgium like the back of my hand; we both must have been incredibly drunk, because I couldn't for the life of me work out where she'd gone.

It was then I noticed Walter's pink freezing feet. 'Walter! Where are your shoes?'

He looked at his bare feet, perplexed. 'Oh, I must have lost them.' He laughed. 'I can't really feel my feet.'

'She's going to freeze to death without a coat. And you're going to get frostbite!'

We turned back to the mausoleum; stone bears growling, thorny-crowned Christ beckoning. At last at the river we saw a shape up on the bridge: Charlotte's Liberty robes falling over the railings. She looked as if she was about to do something stupid, or that the river would catch the fabric and drag her down by the brooch at her neck.

'Charlotte!'

We both ran toward the bridge, but she made no movement to acknowledge we were there. She kept her eyes on the quick dark river below, the dirty snow collecting at its banks. 'Charlotte!' Closer to, her skin was lavender. Her mouth was grim; her eyes, dead. 'You're going to freeze! Let's get back.'

I heard Walter's laboured breath behind me. When she saw us, she looked only at Walter. She still held her Liberty tablet. She brandished it at him, and I saw at once it was one of his navy ledgers.

'What's going on?' I said.

'You tell him!'

'Where did you find this?' he said, very pale.

'How could you?' she said, and it was almost a wail. 'Oh, how could you!'

'Please, can someone tell me what's going on?'

But Walter was dumbstruck and would not speak. All the dreamy melodrama had gone.

Charlotte's skin was goose-fleshed, her lips tinged blue. 'Why don't I explain? Here!' She flicked to the back of the notebook and thrust it at me. There was a table, with numbers on one side, names in the middle column, and nationalities on the right. I saw her name, *Charlotte Feldekova*, and her nationality, *Czechoslovak*, to the right. The list continued: other foreigners' names, and Jewish names in there, and probably some Communists too. I saw Masha's name, and Stefan's.

It was Walter's handwriting. Slowly I realised what was happening; what it was that she was showing me. That September, in 1923, he had given all these names to the newspaper. It had published the story based on Walter's information. He'd betrayed her.

He'd betrayed the whole school.

Charlotte's eyes were hard on him. 'I saw what Ernst Steiner wraps your coke in. The *Republik*. That was the paper, wasn't it? All this time I've wondered who sold our names to them. Who sold our numbers. Because it had to have been someone inside, didn't it? And to think all this time I thought you'd disappeared that month because of some Jewish bloodline! I thought that's what you were hiding. Not that you'd shopped us in!'

She pushed Walter into the railing. One could see in her tense small body that, high as she was, she had a preternatural strength. I realised it wasn't Charlotte who might go into the freezing water, but Walter.

'Why would you do this to me?'

Tears pricked in his eyes. 'You got Jenö.'

'So you gave my name to the papers!' Her face was close to his; her mouth a snarl. 'You gave all our names to the papers! They could have arrested us! Deported us! All because you loved a man who didn't love you back. If I pushed you off here at least I'd never have to deal with you ever again!'

The black river moved fast. How easily he might fall into the undefended water below; how easily the current would sweep him away. 'Charlotte,' I said, calmly but with warning: 'Walter can't swim.'

'So much the better!' Her body swayed. She moved the spit off her lips with her hand. 'I could skin you alive, Walter König!'

I felt suddenly very sober and unwell. 'Charlotte, please. Let him go.'

'How long did it take you? To get all the names and count the numbers. A week? A month? Did you do it while you were picnicking with us in the woods? You know, I begged Jenö not to bring you along with us. I told him, please! Not snivelling Walter, not fawning Walter. But he insisted. I have no idea why, seeing as he never loved you. Never even liked you!'

'It was Ernst's idea. Don't think I haven't regretted it ever since. That summer with you both, it was unbearable.'

'Oh. *Ernst* persuaded you to do it.'

'I shouldn't have. I shouldn't have done it. Please believe me. Not a day goes by without me regretting what I did.'

She picked up his arm, tattooed with blue letters. 'Get this dirty writing off your arm. Do you hear me? It is my name! It is not yours! It is my name!' Charlotte gave Walter a final shove but her energy was gone. 'You've ruined everything, Walter. It's done! It's done! Everything's gone!'

# 34

## Dessau

The day after the Ball the cafeteria was a battlefield of limbs and skyscrapers. There was an awful drilling noise, made worse by its intermittence, as the theatre department dismantled the slides that had brought everyone inside so fast. Inside the mood was apocalyptic, and disintegrating.

Walter wasn't here; neither was Jenö. Charlotte was in dungarees and a shirt. Though she looked exhausted, I also knew she wasn't high. No more the rampant sparkle in her eyes. No more the tranquillity to meet any situation. In fact, she looked anguished.

We hadn't spoken yet. Not about what had happened at the bridge. Not about what had happened in Weimar. Not about Walter's betrayal. I didn't know how to broach it with her; nor whether she wanted consoling, or to be left alone.

No one had had much more than a few hours' sleep. Everyone looked exhausted and a little sheepish at the night's excesses. I guess we were all wondering how much trouble we were in, and it was safest to be seen industriously cleaning; it was rumoured the Director was on the warpath. I hoped both Walter and Jenö were hidden away in their bedrooms.

As I packed away skyscrapers and cars, every time I thought of what Walter had done I was newly shocked. He had betrayed not just his friends, but the whole school. Whether or not it had been Ernst's poison dripped into his ear, Walter had still seen fit to do it: gather the numbers, gather the names, then pass them on to the *Republik*.

I wondered whether Ernst Steiner knew that that notebook was included in the shipped crate. Maybe he'd hoped one of Walter's friends would find it. Probably, it had just been a mistake. Everything tipped into a box, and the courier had turned up in the middle of the night, and the padlock had been slipped to the old numbers.

Now I wondered whether Walter's future at the Bauhaus was viable. How would he exist in this school with our knowledge of him plain? All summer he had written me those polite letters while his own morality had been crude and slippery. Love had set him so sour. Though I had thought of it – how I should like to push my knife against Jenö's face – I knew I would never execute my revenge. And if it did get around the school, via Charlotte, Jenö or me, then surely it would leave Walter ostracised for ever. Not to mention if the Director himself heard of it, or any other member of staff.

I was too shocked, and too hungover, to feel much grief that my friend had been a traitor. I hadn't yet worked out the consequences for me as well as Charlotte: that this, too, would be the end for us. I thought of Walter last night in the snowy park and his ridiculous feet, bright as boiled ham. There was something disgusting and revelatory about those pink naked feet.

As I heaped metal scrap into sacks I began to feel the bitterness that had so gripped Charlotte last night. What a foul thing this school was! How absurd was everything we did here, how hotel-like our existence! Irmi was right; we had overstayed ourselves. Walter's treachery was only part of how rank it had all become: the groping after one another, the shallow performances, these costumes of useless junk. It all had to go.

On a ladder Josef began to pull down the metal moons. He looked better than the rest of us, his hair scraped back, his white shirt clean against his slacks. Anni didn't look like she was suffering too badly either; they'd probably had twice as much sleep as the rest of us.

'What happened last night?' she said, a miniature skyscraper in her hands. 'Josef met Charlotte near the showers. He said she was raving about Walter betraying her.'

'It's some old Weimar business,' I said blandly. 'When things went wrong.'

Anni was pulling the skyscraper apart. 'He said she was freezing cold, like ice. He took her to Jenö's room.' Anni looked at Charlotte, who had the illusionless expression of someone newly sober. 'But Jenö wouldn't have her. In so many words, he told her to go away.'

We watched as Charlotte put on her coat and left by the main steps, just as she had done early this morning. Anni wasn't a gossip, but she also knew that her friend's reserve would make it impossible to talk to her directly. 'Are they still together?'

'I don't know,' I said. 'I don't know.'

Anni had finished flaking the building down to nothing. Michiko pulled the foil ribbons, and Otti stood waiting to collect them. As I followed Charlotte for the second time that day, Otti touched my arm. 'Is Charlotte all right?'

How carefree our dancing last night had been, when for a second I had believed I was in love with Otti Berger. I wished I still was. 'Not really.'

'You'll tell me if she wants to talk?'

I told Otti I would, and went outside, pulling the sack with me. There had been a fresh snowfall this morning: the trees were bright with it, and the brightness made my eyes sting.

A scrap man was loading his horse-drawn cart. 'What were you doing in there?' he said. 'Building an aeroplane?'

'Right,' I said, sickness rising in me, 'exactly.'

A raised voice came from around the side of the building.

'You lot!' the scrap-man said. 'Drama after drama.'

There was another person in the front of the cab; even in profile I could see that it was Oskar. 'Good party?' he said, looking at the cafeteria. They were similar enough – Oskar and the scrap man – that they might have been father and son.

'Probably the best of my life. Until things went wrong.'

The man tethered his horse. I wondered if he would spread news of our decadence around town. I heard the voices again and I wondered if one of them wasn't Jenö's. Oskar seemed to flinch.

'Let's go,' the old man said.

Just before they went, Oskar turned to face the Bauhaus, and I saw with a shock the bruise spreading from his eye. I didn't have a chance to ask him what had happened. Some skirmish with the other Nazis, probably. The scrap man moved his horse off at a gentle clip.

I followed the raised voices. By the big expanse of glass stood Charlotte and Jenö. Her cheeks were wet and red; I couldn't see Jenö's face.

'Don't,' she said. 'This is ridiculous. I'll stop.'

'It's not just the cocaine.'

'What is it then?'

'I don't know.'

I should have left them to it, but I couldn't stop myself.

'Tell me,' she said. 'You have to tell me.'

'It's just not the same any more,' Jenö said, eventually.

'What am I meant to do about that?'

'I don't know. I can't remember what it's like just to be me. What happened with Walter—'

'I don't want to hear his name.'

'What Walter did to you was unforgivable. But that's it. It's bad timing that it's all happening at once.'

'What did I do?'

'You never talk to me! Your privacy drives me crazy.'

'I'll change.'

'You said that a year ago. It's like dating half a person.'

'I'm not half a person.'

'I can't love someone turned so inward.'

'You're the one who keeps things from me,' she said. 'You're the one who kept secrets.'

'I told you. I didn't want to make things awkward.'

'They made things awkward enough.' She stood looking at her hands. 'Jenö, please. I love you. I have always loved you.'

A moment passed where neither said anything, then Jenö spoke: 'It's too late; it's too late. It's done.'

He tried to embrace her but she wouldn't do it. 'I suppose this is very ordinary, isn't it? It happens every day. I'll ask you one last time if you'll stay.'

Jenö delayed, said nothing, then finally: 'I'm sorry.'

He walked back to the cafeteria alone. Charlotte brought her hands up and her shoulders shook as she sobbed. I saw her at the bridge again last night, anger streaming from her, seeming much bigger than she was. Now she looked so sad and small.

I moved to go, but the movement must have caught her eye.

'Paul, for God's sake, stop spying on me, will you? Will everyone just leave me alone!'

And she tramped through the snow back into the school. Through the gridded glass I saw her on the staircase. I knew where she would end up. And I was right: there she was, on the long glass bridge that connected the residential quarters with the Director's office. I already knew what she was about to do to Walter. I already knew the manner of her revenge.

# 35
## Dessau

As the snow around the Bauhaus melted, there was no change to Charlotte and Jenö's separation. It was good to wear lighter clothes, not to feel the snow's crust on your boots, but I guess we all felt such a heaviness that spring came without much relief.

Even I didn't feel much to see them broken up. Everything was so withered away; our group of six down to three, and we avoided each other as best we could. There was little left to talk about; little left to say. Charlotte stuck to Anni and Otti in the Weaving Workshop. I saw lots of Josef. Jenö spent most of his time with Marianne. I often saw them in the Metal Workshop, pulling at cords; bevelling lampshades.

Charlotte didn't talk much to me that term. In fact, she said few words to anybody, and it seemed a kindness to keep away. She had long ago stopped giving me confidences, and beneath the vacant eyes I could never tell what she was thinking. Always now she was concentrated, as if trying hard to understand a pain that was private, unremitting, incomprehensible.

She existed in the school like a woman kidnapped.

She grew thinner; so thin, in fact, that I wondered whether I would find in her room signs of a Weimar fast, for Charlotte always needed her mind clear, especially in the escalation of grief. She went for long walks in the Georgium Park, and hardly spoke. And yet I thought that the moment she opened her mouth so much would stream out unbidden that it was no wonder she didn't risk it.

Hardly anything happened that term. For a while Walter's expulsion was a great mystery and all anyone ever talked about. I decided to say I didn't know what had happened to him. After all the years of involuted participations in each other's lives, this was all I wanted to say, when anyone asked me why Walter König had disappeared without saying goodbye to a soul. I don't know, I'd say: I've no idea why he left. He was popular enough that people missed him, and they didn't stop questioning me for a long time after he'd gone.

Franz, anyway, did a good job at filling in the gossip: the Director had found out about the cocaine (how he had done so was not mentioned, which was a generous gesture to Charlotte) and Walter had been expelled with no notice. Walter had left with a haversack, home to Weimar. He had been the scapegoat for the Ball. Many were thankful he'd taken all the blame.

No one had been around to see Walter go, not me, not Franz, not Jenö. Later we saw removal men (paid for by Ernst, surely) come for the rest of his things: clothes; the painting; his wheeled hat, bloody feathers still stuck to the spokes, and the crate of navy notebooks which had long kept Walter's secret.

It wasn't a cruelty to think that it was better he was gone. He'd always done well with his blowzy pastorals and, really, he had failed to thrive in the Print Workshop – or at least his typography, as Franz had said, was too outdated for the school's mandate. He had always been a little too Expressionist for the school's rationalism.

I found Franz in Walter's bedroom some time after his expulsion. The room, which had been a mess at the best of times, had been clarified back to the Bauhaus box. 'Walter's career is over,' Franz said, dressed all in black. There was a book on his lap as he sat by the desk.

'He's got all the work he wants at the studio.'

'That's not what I mean. I mean the career he actually wants. I don't think Charlotte should have reported him for the cocaine. It wasn't fair.'

I'd lost sight of what was and wasn't fair, and I said nothing. I sat down on the coverlet. There was a slight discoloration where the painting had been. I thought of Oskar and Walter lying on this bed, and myself on the balcony as I had watched them. 'Did he tell you what he did? In Weimar?'

Franz nodded. He put the penny novel on the table. It looked like one that Charlotte would have liked.

'She could've been deported. It was very grave, what he did.'

'He was in love. He was mad.'

'We were all in love. I'm afraid it's no excuse.'

It occurred to me once more that it might be time to go; that we had overstayed ourselves. There was no air in the school. No ventilation. 'What did you two argue about? You were the best of friends, then nothing.'

'Walter had started to be stingy with the coke,' said Franz.

'Really?'

'At one point he even asked me to pay. I was hardly going to pay when I knew he got it for free. It was a minor disagreement, but he seemed to go off me.'

Walter had never been anything less than generous to me and Charlotte, and I wondered, finally, whether Jenö had been right: maybe the cocaine had been administered to Charlotte in the hope that it would put distance between those two.

'He could take offence,' I said. 'But he was quick to forgive.'

Franz looked at me and smiled. We both knew this was not true. Walter could take an age to forgive. Franz snapped the novel shut.

'How'd you patch things up? I saw you dancing at the Metal Ball.'

'I started doing his homework for him.'

'Ah,' I said. 'Well, there we are. Walter was ever the strategist.'

It was tricky to know what to do with my feelings. What he'd done to Charlotte, and to all the others who'd been caught in the Survey, was reprehensible, but it didn't stop me missing him. I had no other confidant. Irmi and Kaspar were in Berlin. I couldn't talk to Jenö; nor could I talk to Charlotte.

Often that spring I thought I heard him pottering around in his room, or I'd go out onto my balcony half expecting to see his face upside down, asking me to come up for a drink, or dangling a knotted bed sheet toward me. I missed my friend. I missed having someone to talk to.

Several letters arrived. The paper was smeared with Walter's inky hand; maybe he was drunk or high when he'd written them. I wondered if he penned them in Ernst's studio. Weimar was the same, he wrote; though there were now enough Brownshirts to give Dessau a run for its money. *I know Charlotte reported me* – he wrote – *hardly a surprise, I suppose: she had just cause.*

I wanted to reply but I didn't know what to say. Slowly, anyway, I was able to put away my feelings for him, and what he had done hardened inside me. And, very soon, the betrayal felt insurmountable, and it became unthinkable that I would even consider replying.

That spring I often stopped to look inside the old gallery in Dessau. I always dreamed I'd find a Steiner painting there. And then, some time in May, I did. All the Steiner hallmarks were there: frolicking girls, trees flourishing, and then (obvious, now I knew the trick) those double loops of light which I knew now were Walter König's signature of guilt from a summer spent betraying his friends. I had finally worked out what the painting signified: his confusion, which was total, and his anguish, which was the same. After seeing it, though, I walked quickly away. I forced myself to say the words aloud, as if making a promise to myself: I would not give him back our friendship. Not for anything.

# 36
## England

I realise now how much my self-portrait is similar to Walter's double painting. How its light streams from everywhere and nowhere. I wear such a strange expression; costive and cowardly. The portrait has hardly said what I thought it would. Though it's unfinished – I have hardly a neck and the eyes are approximations – I don't want to carry on. It won't sell, and I look a clown. I play with blurring my gaze: Elaine de Kooning did this to her friend Fairfield Porter: as if, in the picture, floodwater has reached his eyes. This might be the only way around it. This might be the only way of getting it done.

I should have known figurative painting just wouldn't work, which is why I've lost myself in abstraction all these years. Figuration can't get close. Anni knew that in *Six Prayers*, the Jewish Museum commission she did a few years ago. *Six Prayers* is a woven wall hanging, but its colours suggest stone. There are six columns in cotton, linen, bast, and silver. The threadwork on the panels is uneven. I won't say one of Anni's pillars is for Charlotte in Buchenwald or Otti in Auschwitz, because I don't know if that's true. It's enough that I see them memorialised there.

I wrote to Anni after seeing it. She was in Connecticut by then, still with Josef. 'It's so beautiful,' I wrote on functional blue airmail paper I thought she'd like, 'I keep coming back to what you have expressed in the colours. Your prayers are six poems.'

Anni never replied. Maybe she couldn't remember who I was. Or I had signed off *Brickman* rather than *Beckermann*. Part of me thinks Anni just couldn't say any more. Who knows who else she'd lost; which family, which friends. The threads had said enough.

Hard dreams, this week. Charlotte is imperilled somewhere and if I could do something then I might save her, but I cannot get up, out of bed, out of the studio. Granted, I can feel the wetness of my tears but it's not enough to force me to act. Instead: bogs and trees; and Walter looms somewhere, a victim, an aggressor, in the pale dreamed forest.

When I wake I'm exhausted, and roam the house trying to make my dead friends quit talking to me. In the early mornings I go down to the beach to shake them off, so that the wind might blast them away. I wait for the sea to give me some answers. It doesn't.

I watch the fishermen bring in the lobster traps. I am intrigued about their catch; I never see them pull the lobster from the pot. I wonder where they do it, and what the bright trapped thing does in the pot overnight, hitting its claws against the tin, wondering what it has come to symbolise.

# 37

## Dessau

News from Berlin that summer was not good. Gangs were mobilising in the suburbs, a group of Communists were beaten outside a theatre. There were rumours of abductions near the Potsdam Gate. There were more Brownshirts in the Dessau beer-halls, and I saw Oskar often in town, but after Walter's departure, he no longer talked to me. Oskar wore a different uniform now, the same as Hitler's men. But otherwise, beyond the tracks, the school was still a separate zone of swarming light.

It was a hot summer. Naturally, the students who'd stayed behind sunned themselves on the roof, or wandered the Georgium Park, or swam in the Elbe. We caught Paul Klee walking in the gardens, 'communing with the snakes,' or showcasing his new Tunisian paintings, or drawing on the bridge where Charlotte had almost drowned hapless Walter. Since the Metal Ball, there was renewed moderation. No cocaine, modest drinking, niceness encouraged, nothing off; we were all well behaved. I never fell asleep in one of my classes again.

School had closed for the holidays and I decided not to make the same mistake again: Dresden did not need me. Jenö had gone home to the Munich farm. Our six was down to two.

That summer, the talkies came to town. Dessau had a cinema not far from school. This was the first time we'd ever heard a voice synchronised with the actor's moving lips and Charlotte soon became a fixture there. She was a strange sight marching into town in her trouser suit and short-cropped hair, while other women wore dresses and showed off their tanned shoulders. She had new dark hairs on her arms and had lost almost all of her visible femininity. Most people, most of the time, thought on first meeting her that she was a man.

On the day of the Nazi rally there was general consensus between whoever was left that we'd stay in the quarters of the Bauhaus, which stretched to the Georgium Park and the Masters' houses, but no further. This land was ours; we didn't think they'd come here. But when I saw Charlotte heading into Dessau I asked if I could go with her. She didn't say yes or no, but walked on.

Dessau was empty; not a jackboot or *Stahlhelm* in sight. I wondered if we had missed the rally or whether we'd hit it as we came out. Possibly, everyone was already holed up, knowing that home was the safest place to be. The theatre was still open, however, and we had the cinema to ourselves.

The film was a horror flick: a monster preying on local women, and the hero an unlikely professor type in spectacles. I began to relax. Watching Charlotte was more interesting than watching the picture: whenever anyone spoke, she moved her lips along with the actor's voice. She had dropped the watchful expression she'd worn since the Metal Ball, and instead her face tracked the actor's emotion, so that her expression cleared and changed with every cut to a new character. It was as if in the lit rays she was able to feel all the emotion she had decided to put away during the split from Jenö. It was both childish and heartbreaking. As the monster in the lake zoomed into view, the shadows and the light were the only things animating her face. Then the actress, on her knees in a torn dress, screamed, 'Help me!' and Charlotte whispered those words too.

Under Anni's guidance that spring Charlotte's weaves – she had returned to the workshop with added zeal – had developed an almost sculptural form. (Anni was an altogether different weaver to Charlotte, although they showed the same preoccupation with restraint and repetition.) Though the colours didn't change – they were still immutably dark – Charlotte started braiding in horsehair, and uncut stones, and milk glass and bones, so that her new pieces had a little colour and shape. Anni said they were beautiful, and she was right.

After the trip to the cinema we found Josef and Anni up at the Weaving Workshop, sharing a cigarette out of the window. 'Did you see the rally?' Anni shouted.

'Not a soul! Town's deserted!'

'Oh good,' said Josef. 'We might win yet!'

Otti emerged as a third head. 'Come up later?' She had her curly black hair wrapped up in an Eastern-style scarf. 'I've found some gin!'

'We will!'

Anni whispered in Otti's ear, and Otti gave us a thumbs-up. 'Hurrah for liberty, and all that. Charlotte, I want to show you my new piece when you're done with him,' she said, and then Otti, too, disappeared.

We walked over to the residential quarter. There was a flash of movement in Walter's room; perhaps it was Franz.

'Jenö got in another fight in a beer-hall in Munich,' she said. In many ways, this was the first fully formed sentence Charlotte had said to me in months. It felt good to hear her voice again. 'Silly fool hasn't learnt his lesson.'

'Is he in trouble?'

'Oh, I'm sure he'll have enough money to pay them off. They're all fascists there anyway. They probably deserved it.'

'My father's a fascist,' I said. 'Munich's his holiday destination of choice.'

'Poor you.'

'He keeps sending me articles from Paul Schultze-Naumburg. "Have a look at this from PSN," he says: with his initials, as if they're pals. And then he always frames it as a question. "Art as racial purity?" My mother says he wears a swastika on his lapel. She can't abide it.'

'What about your brother?'

'He's burying his head in the sand.'

'Right response,' she said, as we took the stairs.

My father's letters were steeped in memories of the

past. Amongst the politics, he reminisced about the summerhouse in Obersee; our shirtless lunches there; and how my mother would adjudicate when Peter and I raced with cherries in our mouths, our lips stained black. But for my father there was nothing in between the glass lake and his new fascism: there was no bridge between.

Upstairs there were no students draped across the balconies; no laughter serrating the air; the school was nearly empty. I brought out glasses of water and we sat outside. In the winter a fringe of icicles might hang from the rooftop, flying down at terrifying speeds when the thaw came. It was a wonder no one yet had been killed. Now Charlotte shielded her eyes against the summer light. 'I don't know if Jenö's coming back.'

'Why?'

'Just the tone of his letters. He's done. He calls the Bauhaus "the nest". And not in a good way.'

'I thought about that a while ago too. Leaving.'

She looked at me quickly. 'Why didn't you?'

'I don't know,' I said, with a pang: I'd never replied to Irmi's letter. 'I think I forgot,' I added, laughing it off.

'Sometimes I think Jenö might be right. Walter slept with Jenö. I stole him away. Walter told my name to the authorities. I gave his name to the Director. He did this. I did that. It's both trivial and endless.'

'Feelings were running high.'

'Feelings were always running high. There's a point at which you have to call it normal, and stop making excuses.'

'True.' I had said the same thing to Franz.

'Why did we both have to love him?'

'Bad luck?'

'Yes. Bad luck. Let's chalk it down to that. Do you miss him? Walter, I mean?'

I didn't think she'd mind me telling the truth. 'A little.'

'Me too,' she said. 'That's why it's all quite so painful. I thought we'd patched things up. I thought we were friends again.'

'Everyone has bad luck, you know. You. Me. Irmi. Even Kaspar.'

'Not Kaspar,' she said. 'Maybe if I read more Nietzsche I'd feel less confused.'

'Kaspar doesn't actually read Nietzsche. He just finds the good quotes. And he still lives with his mother. Which is another kind of luck. Do you want to go find Josef and Anni?'

'Not really. Do you?'

'No,' I said.

We idled on the balcony, talking about work, and about our plans for next year; whether either of us would make it as a junior Master. Charlotte dismissed the idea for herself. 'You will be, though,' she said, 'I'm sure of it.'

As we talked, I had the feeling that I was dipped in an old September day, back in Weimar, years ago, when I had tried, in the shadow-tossed cafeteria, to make sense of the inscrutable challenge of her gaze, and the privacy of her smile, and the intrigue of her self-possession, and I'd made not head nor tail of any of them, but felt on the brink of falling in love with someone I had only just met – and the way that sensation had already in that moment felt dreamlike and treasured – and how I had wanted to lead her away so that we could sleep it off, this feeling of inescapable lightness, of flight, and how I hadn't let myself feel that in a long time.

My heart was a scrap of cloth; still, she held it in her hand.

Soon we went inside. After a while we lay on the bed. The breeze coming in was fresh, and the light was like that which fell from the cliffs at Rügen. Moths were going berserk in the open burn of the lightbulb. I could hear the click of her eyelids as she watched them. There are a few nights in my life that stand out: some, for their abjection, others, for their beauty. All night it was enough to rest my mouth behind her ear, my hand on her hip. We did nothing; which, as Walter had said, is my favourite word; but I can safely say it was one of the best nights of my life; the very best.

# BERLIN, 1932

# 38
## Berlin

After the Bauhaus, we lived in a small apartment in Kreuzberg, on the eastern side of Berlin. Minus rent, we only had about fifty marks between us, and our life was simple. When we stayed at home and economised, fifty marks was ample; most of the time we scraped through the month with very little. But for all the frigid winters with hardly a lump of coal to see us through the days, I remember these years as ones of joy. To wake in a warm bed with Charlotte Feldekova, happy and naked in my arms, our breath parachutes in the cold air, this was enough to make me think I was one of the uncommon few tipped for happiness.

Our flat was cold in the winters, and the wind came in through the floorboards, and in the mornings the leaves of the spider plant would be frozen stiff. In the summers noise bled from one apartment to the next, so you could hear the flap of Mrs Müller's washing hanging from the windows, or her yelling at her kids, or the mass stampede of shoes down the staircase as the working day began. The noise of others' lives always made me think of the stacked balconies of the Bauhaus, but our old school was a palace compared to this. I counted twelve families at least over the four floors of our tenement, and that wasn't including the lodgers brought in for extra rent.

Next to our building there was a dubious hotel where twig-legged women brought men back from Kurfürstendamm. We could hear the taxis dropping them off, and the lamplighters, cupping the flame, would call out to the girls they knew in a friendly sort of way, and from behind the headboards, if I was still awake, I could hear the whirr of the lift as it dropped off the couple on the floor next to ours, and the laughter from the street transferred to the corridor; and I wondered what had been done in the mirrored space of the accelerating box. Then the lock clicked, the couple were gone, and I'd hold on to Charlotte in the deep feathered bed, warm, drowsy, her loveliness plain on the pillow, thinking: how lucky I am; how lucky, lucky, lucky.

Berlin was so grown-up. It was a hatched city of swaying telegraph wires and buildings, newspaper kiosks and rattling trams, omnibuses creeping along the Invalidenstrasse, neon signs for the cabaret, and everyone dressed very fashionably. We went to the Romanisches Cafe with the Russian intellectuals who'd fled the revolution. When we could afford it, we went to the Scala Casino, where tall men in garish make-up and sequinned ball-gowns provoked the audience, and we'd finish the night with beer and hot rolls at Aschinger's. Aside from money, we were rich in everything.

We had converted the small nursery room into a studio, and it was where Charlotte and I painted: she took the mornings; I, the afternoons. We were careful not to intrude on each other's time; when one was working, the other kept away. Since leaving the Bauhaus, Charlotte hadn't touched a thread; we couldn't afford a loom, nor did we have space for one. Now Charlotte painted her weaves on paper. They were just as beautiful painted as woven: these ash-coloured seas with a movement through them like a ripple in silk. I had asked her once if she hadn't thought some time about using colour. She had shrugged and said no. This summer she had quit the fabric factory where she had worked for the past few years in Neukölln. Though I knew she missed the loom, and that painting onto paper was nothing like handling thread, I thought her to be happy, working away in our studio, with its modest easels and paints and the light that came in slightly greyer from the foundry.

Happily, my days were no longer formed around the waiting catastrophe of Charlotte changing her mind. Now love lived in the habits of the day, in the things we cherished: the blanket she had quilted for us, the studio easels we painted on, our simple meals and evening rituals of books, music, wine; a sausage, if we were lucky. This wasn't the September love which had lit the month in its terrible blaze, but a love that was because of its daily repetitions, not despite them. As the days passed in churchlike slowness, our pleasures were not complex nor were they painful. Gone was Charlotte's need to empty herself: there was no fasting, no cocaine. I shouldn't have, but I put this down to me. Her peacefulness had been hard won. Jenö was a forgotten fact.

Like everyone else that winter, we had nothing. Ministers on the radio told us to live within our means, but it didn't do much good. Men like ants were everywhere doing nothing: in patched coats, the ants did nothing in the squares, nothing in the Tiergarten, nothing in the boulevards or by the Spree, with the wind that came from all corners which made it a fine kind of misery to be out all day. Other men cried *'Tssigars! Tssigarettes!'* as you walked from the cafes or came out of the cinema at the Tauentzienstrasse, but that was useless too, since no one had any money and the cocaine was only ever cooking salt and aspirin – this is, at least, what Kaspar told me. I made sure we never had any in the house.

Kaspar, who didn't have a job but always did have nice things, was always producing expensive bottles of alcohol found at various girlfriends' apartments. Irmi, too, salvaged treats from her job at the Kaiserhof. Living like this felt familiar to us: we who had lived through the antic strangeness of the Weimar years when we'd all been useless millionaires. Now that money meant something, nobody had any.

Ever since we'd left the Bauhaus I had ceased thinking much about Jenö. Indeed, I would not have thought of him at all were it not for his letter that arrived during

November's transport strike. Usually from our apartment we could hear the horns or the grinding of the streetcars rounding the corners hazardously fast. But not a bus or a tram had left the depot these last few days, and the city's quietness made the sky bigger; the tram wires idle in the windless days. As Irmi and I had walked to the Kaiserhof we'd seen buses abandoned in the streets, and the sleepers ripped up. No gusts of warm air from the U-Bahn vents, either; only footfall and bicycles on the Möckernstrasse.

Irmi was cheerful this morning. This was a ritual we kept. I'd pick up a new tube of paint, and we'd stop for coffee or even go to a museum, if Irmi's shift allowed it, and while Charlotte had the studio.

'I've met someone,' Irmi said, as we walked past stalled buses.

'That's great,' I said, though my words had an odd emphasis.

'You'll never guess what he does,' and before I had a chance to offer a suggestion, 'He's an insurance clerk!'

'But that's so glamorous!'

'That's what I said. Money's so attractive these days.' She smiled ironically. Her hair was pulled into a low pony-tail.

'What's his name?'

'Teddy. His mother was American. It's from Edward. Somehow.'

A light rain came. As we strolled down Wilhelmstrasse under a shared umbrella, Irmi explained how they'd met at Aschinger's, through a mutual friend who had introduced her, rather embarrassingly, with her full name: Irmgard Annabel Schüpfer, and he'd said 'Teddy', and that despite a number of dates, she'd still yet to learn his last name, whereas he went around using her full name as much as he could. 'He thinks I'll stick around until I know his surname. He might be right.'

Soon we reached the Kaiserhof. Very near the Reich Chancellery, the hotel was a newish building designed to look old. (*A hotel shouldn't be the Alhambra! A train station shouldn't be a Scottish castle!*) Irmi said she had met almost every politician under the sun drinking there at the end of a long day (bar the Communists, who would only come in to make deals). With the dirt she had, she'd make a good source for any journalist.

Uniformed officials were filing in through the revolving door, and Irmi looked inside with some apprehension. 'I thought it would be a quiet day. How did they all get here?'

'I'm not sure these people rely on public transportation,' I said. 'Will I get to meet him? Teddy?'

'We'll see,' she said, snapping the umbrella shut, and smiling at me like a woman in love.

Quitting the Bauhaus had been one of the best things for my work; all the time I'd spent teaching I now put into my own labours. That afternoon I came home to a blue square and pot of yellow flowers. I had spent days priming the canvas so that the paint on its surface was flat and uniform. Over the afternoon I took a palette knife and began scraping away at the different layers, so that the painting – which seemed at first concerned with the outward blossom of the petals and the stout vase – declared its surface not as decoration, but as paint. The illusion was all gone. I wasn't completely satisfied with it, but it had kept me occupied these past weeks. Surfaces and depths; I already knew my obsessions well.

Because of the strike our flat was quieter than usual. Maybe Mrs Müller and family were sleeping away the afternoon, and there were no new customers in the brothel either, since business had to be drummed up closer to home, and no one in Kreuzberg had any money. In any case I could hear with exceptional clarity Charlotte's footsteps later as she returned home, pausing on the landing to read whatever had come in the post.

I waited for her but she delayed, and I wondered what had held her up: maybe the letter was from her parents, whom no one had ever met, and who had never visited her; not in Weimar, not Dessau, not Berlin. They wrote so irregularly that I sometimes wondered if they even existed.

When Charlotte came in she handed over the letter directly. As soon as I saw the writing I understood it to be Jenö's. I dropped the palette knife and wiped my hands. I couldn't be sure, but I didn't think they had corresponded at all since we'd left Dessau, when the Director had said there was no more money to pay our salaries. I skipped to the signature: there was his name. I worked backward.

Jenö's tone was not overly personal; in fact, it was quite plain. Last month, he explained, the Bauhaus had been shut down. The Nazis had come in the middle of the day, smashing in windows, kicking in the looms, rounding up 'Communist' students and arranging for them several nights in jail. She might remember Franz Ehrlich, Walter's friend? He'd been one of those in jail. A young officer had orchestrated the whole thing. (Could it have been, I wondered, Oskar?) The Director had handled it all rather wearily, and had started looking for premises elsewhere. In passing, Jenö mentioned that he'd been made a Master. I felt pleased for him and not in the slightest envious. He deserved it. He signed off with love, but also with his surname – *Jenö Fiedler* – so things could have been worse.

'The Director's brave,' she said. 'I wonder that he has the energy to begin again.'

It was the second time the Bauhaus had been closed down; the second time uniformed men had stormed the workshops. I felt glad that we were out of it. 'Brave or foolish,' I said, picking up my palette once more.

Soon the city's noise returned again: the buses were released from the depot and the U-Bahn could be heard from the subway vents. Despite the strike a thousand men were laid off, but in better news the Nazis were down a few hundred thousand votes at the last elections. In any case I forgot about Jenö's letter, and thought no more about him, until I was suddenly faced with him once more at Irmi's Christmas party.

# 39

## Berlin

Irmi's flat was a short walk from ours, and Charlotte and I argued before setting off. She had cut her hair very short again, and continued to wear only men's clothing. I was terrified that every time she left the apartment something terrible would happen. Our street had once teemed with children, but now it was mostly men in different shades of uniform. Invulnerable to the Prussian winds they lurked on the brownstone steps and the ironwork balconies. Mannish Charlotte would be as good a target as any Jew or Red or gypsy.

A man might be beaten in daylight on a street where there were lawyers' offices and a police station, where snow dusted women's expensive hair and lavish furs. Razor blades, chair legs, glass bottles: all might be used with no provocation. There were bullet holes chipped into the local cinema and hoardings splashed with blood. Men spent workless days idling for the distraction of violence: better, anyway, than selling laces or dishrags or singing for pennies at the Alexanderplatz. Sundays, really, were the worst: since church finished at eleven, and the cinema did not start till eight, and it was a good fight that filled the long gap in between, and the newspapers sold whatever deathbed photographs they could get.

'What do you want me to do?' Charlotte said on our doorstep. 'Wear a hooped skirt and girdle? I won't, Paul. That's not me.'

'Fine. Let's just go.'

We walked quickly. The lit Advent wreaths did nothing to lift our mood. With the streetlamps giving not much more than a fizz, at least people might think she was a man, with the ironed-in creases of her trousers and her hat hiding her face. The air that night was wet and freezing. Around us people left the cinemas, blinking at the tumbling colours. People did not look us in the eye. Nobody wanted trouble. I put out my hand to Charlotte's and though she took it there was little promise of her speaking to me. She didn't like being told what to do – fine – but I just wanted her to be safe. It was not a crazy thing to want.

We arrived at the party almost silent. If Irmi noticed the chill between us, she didn't let on. Her flat was stuffed with people. Candles lit the condensation on the windows so that the world outside was nothing more than diffused light. There were bottles of colourful alcohols – ambers, emeralds, rubies, all cold and beaded (Irmi had stolen them from the Kaiserhof) – and people were drinking from jars or glasses stamped with the hotel's logo.

Charlotte went to find a drink. Irmi kissed me on either

cheek, gave me a consoling smile, and handed me someone else's glass. 'Let me find Teddy. I want to introduce
you.' And then Irmi disappeared too.

She had been stiff with me when Charlotte and I had
first arrived in Berlin; not surprisingly. I'd forgotten to
reply to her letter; I'd only just got together with Charlotte and was at the height of my obsession; in short, I'd
behaved badly. But Irmi, saint that she was, forgave me.

I looked around for someone I knew, but it was Kaspar
who found me. Since Weimar he had failed to age, but he
had got heavier. He looked sunburned. 'However did you
get that tan?'

He kissed me on both cheeks. 'Artificial light treatment.
Otherwise I look as if I'm made from paper.'

By his side was a tall woman with a big smile in not
much of a dress. 'It's Berlin. It's December. That's how
everyone looks,' she said. She had a strong Russian accent,
but then there were so many Russians in Berlin it almost
went without remark.

'Dacia, this is Paul Beckermann, an old friend of mine
from the Bauhaus.'

'How do you do?' she said, looking elsewhere.

He leant toward me. 'I'm going to marry this one, Paul.
I know it.' The warm air in the room made Kaspar's face
pulse brighter.

Vaguely I looked to see if I could find Charlotte, but
couldn't. Irmi had assembled a Christmas tree from
rolled-up newspapers, and I remembered Itten's class,
and Walter's failure, that day. I tried hard these days not
to think of Waldemar König. It only made me unhappy;

the whole business of the Survey was still a bitterness, and I knew it upset Charlotte to think of what might have happened to so many people because of what he had done that summer.

'Everyone said the Nazis would have a majority by Christmas,' said Kaspar. 'And yet here we are!'

'Where are we?'

'Hitler's a postmaster. Berlin will never do it.'

'Berlin doesn't matter. It's the rest of the country that's the problem.'

'Von Schleicher will resist.'

'He'll roll over.'

'Well. I don't know. Perhaps you're right,' Kaspar said, muttering something to himself which I didn't quite catch.

I didn't want to talk politics; it was all anyone ever talked about. A new record scratched before it settled. Near the ancient gasolier a couple shared some coke; the lines so thin we would have had them for breakfast in Dessau. I wondered what to do; where in the party to go; I couldn't see where Charlotte had ended up.

I watched as someone put an angel, folded from a champagne label, on the top of the tree. I thought again of Walter: whether he was still at his glades and waterways. Though I didn't care to admit it, it was also true that I thought of him often. Sharp-tongued, honeyed in his own selfishness and servant to his own crazy notions of Jenö's love for him; Walter had been my best friend for so many years, and, yes, I missed him.

'Do you ever hear from Walter König?' I asked Kaspar,

who had started dancing with Dacia before my question brought him back.

'Walter König? Oh, Walter was never interested in keeping in touch with *me*. He dropped me as soon as you all moved to Dessau. Last I heard he was fucking some fat Nazi.'

'A Nazi?'

'That's what Hannah said, anyway.'

Dacia pulled him away again. No surprise that Ernst – if it were still Ernst, and not someone else Walter had picked up along the way – should be a Nazi. Maybe Walter might even be one too. He'd look good in a uniform, I'd give him that.

I pushed my way through the crowd. I could hear Irmi's laughter above everyone else's, and I was cornered into the paper tree as the floor cleared for an expert couple who knew the latest dance. I saw Irmi with a handsome man who was so tall he had to stoop to talk to her.

A thudding came from the ceiling below; a broom banging.

Irmi stamped on the floor in reply. 'I don't know why she's complaining. Her brats keep me up all night.'

Someone else changed the record; it was Jewish *klezmer*, to vex the neighbour even more. 'Quit that noise!'

Irmi put her head outside the window. 'Oh shut it, you old crone!'

And everyone laughed.

Finally, with most of my drink spilled, I found the kitchen. I looked for a cloth to clean myself, but just then I heard a voice from the past. I knew it to be Jenö without even looking. I turned, and there he was: a blond block, leaning against the counter, his grey eyes observing the room, sadder than they had been. I froze. I didn't know what to do.

'Paul.' He smiled, and there were new wrinkles near his eyes.

'Jenö.'

We shook hands. Neither of us knew what to say. A woman in a lively hat pushed past us with a fresh bottle of champagne.

'How long's it been?'

'Years. I didn't know you were in Berlin.'

'They shut us down in Dessau. The Director's set us up in a telephone factory.'

'Oh. Right. Where?'

'Steglitz. It's not quite Dessau. But it'll do for now.'

Steglitz! Steglitz was no more than half an hour from here. Immediately I thought how little I wanted him close. I wondered if there had been a postmark on the envelope; whether I should have known he was in Berlin. 'Well. How are things?'

'It's been a little rough,' he said, clearing his throat. 'My father lost his farm after the Crash.'

'I heard. I'm sorry. My father too. The whole shoe factory. Gone in a puff of smoke. Well, a puff of American loans.'

He nodded. There were so many stories like ours. 'When I got back everyone was gone' – he clicked his fingers – 'Walter; you; Charlotte. I did lots of work.'

'I bet. The Director couldn't afford to keep us on.'

'He said.'

It came to me then that though the Director hadn't been able to afford us, he had been able to afford Jenö. I searched myself for how I felt, wondering if I still hated him, or whether that was over, now that I had, in some ways, won. 'Are you still working with Marianne?'

'A little. But mostly I'm doing my own work.'

'Good for you. And Anni, Josef, Otti?'

He smiled at the list of names. 'The Albers are still at the Bauhaus. Otti's set up a textile company, an adjunct to the school. You should see her. She's the same.'

'An expert on everything and nothing?'

'Exactly. Did you hear about the Weimar Bauhaus? Schultze-Naumburg's whitewashed the murals.'

'The townspeople will be happy,' I said.

'Oh, I wonder if they don't miss us. Baptising babies in the Frauenplan. Getting up to no good in the woods.'

We stood in the narrow kitchen as both of us thought of what else to say. I wished Irmi had told me she'd invited him. She hadn't mentioned he'd be coming, though she'd talked of nothing but the party for weeks on our morning walks.

'How've you been? The painting's going well?'

'Yes,' I said, not quite committing, and when I asked the same of him, he simply said the same thing too. 'Are you teaching the Metal Workshop?' I asked.

'No. They don't have one. Can't afford it. I'm teaching the preliminary course with Josef.'

Now I really had run out of things to say. 'Have you seen Charlotte?'

'Briefly. She said she was going home,' he said, slightly fumbling his delivery. 'She said she had a headache?'

I didn't say another word. I pushed past women dancing with their eyes closed, maybe even asleep; men shuffling their feet along; the couple with the cocaine on their knees having more. I imagined Charlotte's lip bleeding; her body beaten in a gutter. I grabbed my coat. As I ran down the steps I heard a drunken rendition of 'Silent Night' begin as Irmi shouted down the staircase: 'What about Teddy? I wanted to introduce you! Paul! Paul! At least say goodbye!'

# 40

## Berlin

Neither of us was in the mood to work the day after the party. Usually this meant a trip to the zoo, or the Tiergarten, or maybe a walk to the Pergamon for the busts. Instead, that morning Charlotte became without warning furiously domestic. She did all the laundry then hung the sheets from the unbarred windows, though the day was so frigid they would freeze. She fetched the coal, wound the clock in the living room (a present from my mother) and then, most implausibly, she began to darn our socks, the holes in them so large it would have been better to throw them out. With the window open to the courtyard, radios blared Berlin's bad news.

I asked if I could help but she shooed me away.

I tried to push Jenö from my mind but he kept on returning unbidden. The Bauhaus was in Steglitz. A train ride away; not much. In bed this morning I had asked Charlotte why she had left the party so abruptly. She'd said, as Jenö had said, that she'd been gripped by a sudden headache. While she was in the kitchen I scanned the

letter for any subtext I had missed, then found the Steglitz postmark on the envelope. I should have checked. I
should have known he was in Berlin.

'Come on,' I said, in the afternoon, when thoughts of
Jenö were circulating worse than ever. 'Let's go out.'

Charlotte put aside her darning. 'I thought you'd never
ask.'

We took the streetcar to the Spree and watched the
steamboats on the river. The water was a set of moving
tiles, all slates and greens and boat oil rainbowing its surface. I held her close as we walked in the bright day. We
looked out to the coffee houses and theatres on the other
side of the riverbank, then we walked to Friedrichsstrasse
Station. At the War Academy there were still glass cases
nailed to the walls so that the names of the dead wouldn't
blur in the rain. We'd had the same building in Dresden:
I remember watching women gather every Friday when
there was a list of new men dead. In Dresden, there'd
been no escape: the schools, the library, the hospital, the
assembly halls: all of the city had been turned into bar-
racks. At night you could hear the gun drills and in the
mornings you could hear the men marching, and I was
convinced as a boy that I was on my way to join them,
that very soon I'd be minced into French fields, and that
I'd return as a name to be pinned in the glass case, then
found by my mother, her eyes already dampened in the
long walk over.

I had saved up twenty marks to buy Charlotte a gift

for Christmas, and Rosenberg's windows were done extravagantly. Mannequins were dressed in silks; the men in evening suits of black velvet. In another display there were several bits of Biedermeier furniture, and a string of cut mirrors reflecting the better off, saved from the wind by mufflers and fur. All that was needed was one of Steiner's oil paintings to finish off the scene.

But it was easy to see that Rosenberg's situated its most expensive things up front. Inside, the stock was discounted, and labels were cut two or three times the original price. We went up a floor to men's outfitting. Charlotte at the best of times could pass as a boy; especially today, in her ulster and wool trousers. It was her slim neck and hands that most often gave her away.

There were several smart businessmen in the men's section, some being measured up for a new suit, others buying items off the peg. Seeing them there, looking as old-fashioned as the Kaiser, gave me a bounce in my step to know we were so different. I had that feeling, as one gets near a precipice, of baseless joy; that the world – or at least Rosenberg's department store – was ours for the taking. A hangover sometimes lent me a bigger sense of bounty than the situation gave.

We walked over to the scarves; there was a silk one I'd had my eye on. Charlotte wasn't interested, though, and decided on a shirt with an Oriental collar instead. 'Are you sure you can afford it?'

A few shoppers looked at us as I brought her closer: we were two men embracing. 'Of course.'

The shop boy coloured scarlet as he tried to work out

who it was he should be serving. 'Me,' said Charlotte, 'I want to try it on, please.'

I sat in a chair meant for waiting wives. The boy changed to a yawning salesman, but the looks from the other customers continued, and I briefly wondered if we were in some kind of trouble. But I put that thought away. Together, we were storm-proof; I knew it.

Maybe it was the curtain, closing her off, that afforded me the confidence to speak. 'Irmi said the Bauhaus has moved to Berlin. Jenö didn't mention that in his letter.'

'I heard,' she said. Her hands shot above the rail, pulling down the shirt. 'Bizarre that the Director thought Berlin safe.'

'There's probably nowhere in Germany that wants the Bauhaus right now.' A pause. I would say it: name what was between us. 'Jenö was at Irmi's. Did you see him?'

The curtain stopped moving. 'Yes.'

'He looks well.'

I wondered what she was doing, whether she was staring at her reflection in the hot lights. Whether she'd be saying to herself, *just tell him the truth. Tell him you're in love with Jenö. That you knew this fact as soon as you saw him again last night.* She came out and began tucking the shirt into her trousers. 'How do I look?'

I wanted to say: stupid. You look ridiculous.

She must have seen my face. 'What's wrong?'

'I'm fine,' I said, though in my heart there was a darkness, building into something big; sepulchral.

'Paul?' She put her cool hands on my cheeks. 'What's wrong?'

'Nothing.'

(*Nothing! nothing! All you ever do is nothing!*)

Wisely, the salesman slipped away, and Charlotte disappeared again behind the curtain. 'Irmi should have told us he'd be there,' she said. 'It wasn't nice to spring him upon us. I was as shocked as you. It doesn't mean anything; that he's in Berlin.'

'Then why did you leave so quickly?'

The curtain snapped open. Her regard was cool. 'I had a headache, I told you. Look, I didn't want to talk to everyone there. I didn't want to be there with all those people. They're your friends, Paul. Not mine.'

'I don't understand who your friends are if it's not them. Kaspar. And Irmi, and the rest.'

'It was a shock. All right? I'm allowed to be shocked. I haven't seen him in years.'

Our man returned. 'Sir. Other people are waiting.'

'We'll go,' she said. 'We'll take it.' She handed over the shirt. Then she looked at me, her light eyes focused. 'Paul. I'm warning you not to get carried away with this. Do you hear me?'

But after we had paid the journey home was almost wordless.

# 41

## Berlin

The front page of the newspaper announced that von Schleicher was planning on relocating all of Germany's unemployed to the 'thinly populated East'. Irmi frowned at the headline, the newspaper tented on her lap. 'Where are they going to live? Are there thousands of empty houses waiting for them? What if they don't want to go?'

'He just wants to appear decisive. It won't happen.'

Irmi's apartment looked bare without people. She had a red blanket drawn around her legs, and a fisherman's sweater over her slacks; in her hands she nursed a cup of tea, which she drank with the dipping motion of a bird. All wrapped up, she looked contented; all the day's light alive in her quick grey eyes.

'You look happy sat there. Are you so in love?'

'Paul!'

'What?'

'Love is for babies.' Irmi picked off a rotten leaf from one of the house plants. 'Every time I see Teddy I feel surprised that it's my turn, that finally *I* get to do all of this; not you, not Charlotte, not Jenö. It's rather wonderful.'

'I'm glad. You're right: it is your turn.'

'More tea?'

'Sure.'

From the kitchenette I heard the gas flame. The door to the galley was open, and I saw Irmi lean against the top, her expression abstracted. Maybe she was wishing it was Teddy who was here rather than me. Weeks ago on New Year's Eve I had asked her why she hadn't told me about inviting Jenö to the Christmas party. She'd said she'd forgotten she had even invited him, and Teddy had quickly moved the conversation on.

I went to the window. It had been raining all day and the potholes in the unrepaired road were full of black water. Now the day was brightening the puddles showed the sky and clouds. Kids played football against a wall with a ball many times patched. A few streets away, Charlotte would be setting out. Since New Year she had used her afternoons to walk the city. Several times I had watched her from a window, wishing I could see if she had already met the ventilated air of the station entrance. So far I had resisted the notion of following her. So far I'd resisted searching for train tickets to Steglitz. When she came home in the evenings she brought the cold in on her coat.

I could not resist, though, the idea of her and Jenö together. Since the Christmas party I had been unable to put away the image of them together in the Steglitz Bauhaus: in a locked workshop room, in a broom cupboard;

on a lunch break. How hot would be their embrace; how urgent their need.

These afternoons waiting for her to come home; how long they were.

A streetcar wobbled the puddles. Imagine if the ripples got bigger, I thought, imagine the whole road heaving; underneath the macadam a river surging up and clearing out Berlin; this warehouse, this junk-shop city, and in its wave would be carried all the useless people with nothing to do. I knew from school that Berlin had once been a glaciated plain until its retreat had left meltwater streams and lakes underground. If they ascended, these lakes and sunken rivers, would it be a baptism? Or an apocalypse?

'Is Charlotte still not painting?' Irmi said from the kitchen.

I came away from the window. 'No.'

'What does she do instead?'

'I told you. Roams Berlin.'

'Maybe she's stuck. She's been doing the same thing for a while. These monochrome pieces.'

'Don't be mean.'

'I'm just saying she might be looking for a change in direction. Does she seem unhappy?'

'No,' I said. 'Preoccupied.'

'Have you asked her? If she's unhappy?'

'She says she's fine.'

'Well. You'll have to take her at her word.'

The kettle shrieked and Irmi flicked off the gas. The metal teapot fogged as it warmed. It was a Bauhaus teapot

– simple circles and semicircles – a Brandt design. Irmi had invested her money wisely.

'Maybe she's on a binge and doesn't want to tell you.'

I looked at her, disapprovingly.

'What? I'm just saying. Maybe that's the secret with all this walking. Maybe she's procuring coke in Wittenbergplatz.'

I followed her through to the living room. I knew it wasn't a good time, but I didn't know when I could see Irmi next without Teddy, who always stopped me talking about either Jenö or Charlotte. 'Have you seen Jenö since the party?'

'Oh.' She considered what I was saying for a good while, and then said, 'Oh,' again. 'Is that where you're going with this?'

'What do you mean?'

'You think Charlotte sees Jenö at the Bauhaus?'

'Maybe.'

'Have you asked her?'

I shrugged. 'She says she walks.'

Irmi splashed the tea into the cups. 'Maybe it's good for her. They say it clears the mind. Don't for God's sake follow her.'

'That's not what I was intending.'

'I know you, Paul.'

'I just can't help thinking—'

She raised a hand. 'Charlotte is with you. You have a home together. You are both very much in love. Leave her to it.'

'What if she's seeing him? Jenö?'

'No,' Irmi said with some finality. 'I won't be your Walter

in all of this. I won't confirm your conspiracies. Jenö's in Berlin but Charlotte's with you. Don't sabotage what you have. Oh, don't look at me like that.'

'Like what?'

'You've got everything you've wanted. Now you have to live with it.'

'Thanks, Irmi.' I stood to get my coat and scarf.

'Oh, Paul, don't be so sensitive.'

'No, you're right, I shouldn't have said anything.'

We stood watching each other, wondering if either of us would stand down. Neither of us did. Something passed between us – I don't know whether it was hatred, or kindness. I took my hat, and once again I left Irmi's apartment without saying goodbye.

Even without a strike, Berlin could be quiet. You saw that in the fishermen waiting for a catch by the Spree. You could hear the wind rattling the cages of postcards for the tourists on Unter den Linden. Only in rumblings could you hear the trains come and go from Friedrichstrasse. People said, Oh, Berlin! Full of noise and traffic and so dirty. We didn't find it like that. The arcades and boulevards could lend the city an airy openness so that it had the feel of a stockyard at night. It wasn't all Kurfürstendamm; there was also restraint, a city that knew an old Field Marshal was still president of the Republic.

It wasn't like this in Kreuzberg, of course. Kreuzberg was shitty compared to the main quarter and rarely quiet. It had rats and mice and a smell coming off the canal. If you tipped Kreuzberg upside down there'd be tram wires and telegraph cables and washing lines to catch it all in a dirty great net.

I hopscotched through Kreuzberg alleys – places dear to my heart – and when I arrived at our apartment (the suspicious porter giving me his daily once-over) I went straight to our studio. Work would take my mind off things; it always did.

But Charlotte had left the typewriter on the desk. On the paper she'd typed a blueprint for a weave out of the letter P and various spaces – one, two, three spaces at a time – so that it made chevrons in the intended fabric. I smiled, remembering the notes she used to give me for lunch, all the Ps coloured red. She often made blueprints for weaves. This in itself didn't mean she was necessarily at the Bauhaus.

One of the legs was still prone, the P depressed. Perhaps this was the moment she'd left, or maybe someone had come to collect her; perhaps even Jenö. I hated the idea of him in the apartment. I held the paper so as not to disturb the leg. These black letters; what were they but little hobnails of love? (But who for? Who for?)

Next to the typewriter there was an open book where she had stickered a Paul Klee painting called *Castle and Sun*. Even though it was a black-and-white reproduction I could conjure easily the North African oranges and yellows that had so obsessed Klee in Dessau.

Ah; perhaps the P stood for Paul Klee, not Paul Beckermann.

I sacked off work. Instead I went in and out of the

Klee book on the sofa, occasionally closing my eyes to imagine the saffron warmth of the Tunis scenes, finding I had dropped off, then coming back to the grey picture of Kreuzberg at the window. Through the foundry's grime I watched men working on the scaffolding opposite, a boy-messenger come and go from an office's reception, a woman working at some books. At some point there was the machine noise of a low-flying aeroplane. I thought of Charlotte, Anni and Otti flying over Klee's house. Where was Klee now? France? Switzerland? And who lived in the Masters' houses: how many Nazis occupied those white cubes? And here was Berlin, going to the dogs, and Charlotte was somewhere in it, and I didn't know where. No matter how much Irmi might reassure me, that fact was going to drive me crazy.

Charlotte had always walked the city. When we had first arrived we walked it together, top to tail. After Weimar and Dessau, the metropolis was a gift. In the night-times we'd go to a club, and I'd be so worn out that, listening to the music, drinking wine, often I'd be overcome by a profound awareness of my own happiness. Under the table Charlotte would pull my hand into her trousers then push it away, smiling with her lovely dull teeth, and I'd go crazy with her smell on my fingers; telling her we had to go home *now*. She would say, all right, after this song, knowing the wait would twist my longing even tighter.

Surprising: how hungry she was.

We wouldn't wait for home. Instead I'd push myself

into her against the brickwork of the club's alley where so many other couples had been before, or else she'd take me in her mouth, shielded from the road by hanging laundry. The colour would rise on her cheeks, and I'd feel for her breasts, and her eyelids fluttered as the sounds of the city surrounded us: people laughing, footsteps close, an omnibus brake released.

As we rode home the tenements outside the window were proofs that all this was real and undreamt.

Our passion was a little rank. We were always a hair's breadth from being caught down alleys, behind a fairground ride, in the cinema. That first winter we were always fucking and never changing the bedsheets. At home everything had our rime on it: our hands, the kitchen counters, the bath-tub. Kaspar would call round to the apartment and even he – the man with multiple girlfriends – would scrunch his nose with faint disgust. I did wonder if she had been like that with Jenö. I liked to think, frail man that I was, that he couldn't fulfil her like I could. That, I know, is ego speaking, but there we are.

That first winter after Dessau, when our rent was in arrears, both of us knew we couldn't survive from my paintings alone. I took in some students to tutor – the Bauhaus name got us this far – and Charlotte started some shifts at a fabric factory in Neukölln. We saw much less of each other; and, because work made us tired, in the nights we fell asleep rather than made love.

Life turned a little more normal; things do. But it was those later Berlin years that I learnt who Charlotte really was, and who she was to me. She sang in the bath. It was the only time I heard her speak Czech; they were lullabies her nanny had sung to her (her old nanny – burrs in her blonde hair; dead of the Spanish flu). I learnt she had a curious habit of becoming obsessed with clubs or cafes she rated as excellent, then, just as suddenly, dismissing them as absurd. She was lively and enthusiastic, then she could be taciturn and, as Jenö had said, maddeningly private when she wanted to be. Sometimes she suffered depressions, which made her quiet for weeks, when it was all she could do to force herself to her shifts at the factory. During those times she was far away and impossible to find. We rowed, of course we did; we had arguments when sometimes we both doubted whether things would work. Then she'd pull a chestnut curl; kiss me; tell me she loved me. I was, she said, her Serious Painter.

I was dozing when Charlotte came home, shaking the sleet from her umbrella. 'Sorry,' she said, 'I lost track of time.' She put her hat on the stand, untucked her shirt. She brought in a smell of the wood glue we'd used in the carpentry workshops. Outside the trams sliced the tracks; there were car horns too; in front of me, she yawned. 'Good book?'

I put the Paul Klee back on the coffee table. 'Where've you been?'

'Walking.'

'Until now?'

'I've got a new idea.'

'Go on.'

She took a large drink of her wine. 'It's a secret. I don't want to jinx it.'

I put my nose to her neck. 'What do you smell of?' I said. 'Marzipan, is that it?'

She batted me away. 'Soap!'

'Charlotte. Do you ever think of having a baby?'

'A baby! Aren't I too old for that?'

'Of course not. My mother was forty when she had me.'

'Well, I'm hardly forty!'

'Exactly; we could try.'

She smiled. 'A girl or boy?'

'Both.'

'Shouldn't we be married first?'

'Sure,' I said. 'Let's get married.'

'We can't get married in Berlin.'

'Why not?'

'Such a bloody stage for a wedding!'

'Maybe in the summer, when things have quietened down?'

'Yes. Maybe in the summer.' And she smiled at me, and we both wondered, perhaps, how serious we were.

Attached to her shoe I noticed a woollen thread. I wondered what colour it had been; whether it had been discoloured by the dirty streets, or whether it was from her dark coat, or her black scarf; or a Bauhaus loom, where she might be making, again, her *Almost Nothings*.

'A baby,' she said, crossing her legs, so that the thread was lost. 'What a thought.'

# 42

## England

The beach today is packed: it's that moment in the English calendar when holidaymakers arrive here. I suspect they are Londoners; there's something about their delight that is metropolitan; made fresher by their remembered lives in the complex city. There's a sunny haze to the scene: with a few brushstrokes the families could just as well water down into the misrule of the sea. (*The Beach at Trouville*, is that what it reminds me of? That absurd but genteel scene of Parisians come to Normandy to bathe; a painting as far away as possible from the *Bathers at Moritzburg* that sent me into such a frenzy aged fifteen.)

I lay on my towel. There's heat on my skin, a warm breeze. Waves crash and retreat. Not far away there's a couple cuddling by a windbreak. They are scandalizing the families. The woman has auburn hair which curls to her shoulders. She is all curve; hip; breast. Her boyfriend or her husband – but I suspect her boyfriend – can't stop touching her, and it is this that is earning them the tourists' censure. One or two caresses would be fine, but it's the fact he won't stop, and the woman: she luxuriates. There's something of the Turk to her, an odalisque; you can tell her body gives her pleasure; with the breeze which she must feel playing on her pale skin.

I am happy for them. Long may they delight in each other; love each other. That's the thing about the English: sometimes they don't know how to spend their pleasures.

We too were like this when we were first together in Dessau. It's hard to recall how we passed the days, since they were spent mostly making love and drowsing. But on other days we found the pickings of late summer: blackberries, sweet and sharp in our mouths; swimming the turquoise water of the Elbe; we caught silver trout, and packed them into ferns, and kept the wine cool against the stones. In the Georgium Park the green trees doubled the green of her eyes. It was impossible to think snow should ever again freeze the ground or strip the trees to branch. And it felt strange that my heart was expanding just as it felt that it should break.

To have in your possession the person who has been the object of both your desire and your misery is an unsettling thing. I had always measured my love by the intensity of my envy. Now that envy was no longer there, it was different. It felt unusual. Here was Charlotte, here was I, and here, in between us, there was nothing in our way.

That I should never have such happiness as I had that month was a certainty I did not resist: in fact, I surrendered. I was sure what we had would only last days, and when it lasted weeks I was sure it would end in months, and when it turned into months I begged that I might get a year – which is what, to my surprise, in the end, I had. Three of them. Three whole years.

Perhaps I might even have had more.

It's my fault that I lost her in Berlin. Not Walter's. I underestimated the dangers. No one – not me, not Kaspar, not even Charlotte, I suppose – thought things would get so bad. And yet. And yet. The black wing of memory brushes against me.

I look over to the couple. They have gone, and I know where: home to bed. Good for them. There's a space where their bodies were, a dip in the sand, and two neat holes where their windbreak stood.

The day is no cooler. The waves tip and rock. Squawks of children; pinkened bodies. I wonder whether we would have stayed together: whether we would have set up that family. I act like it would have been a straight trajectory. It might not have been.

I swim. It takes some time for me to be clear of the families but when I do the water is so cold it's a brace. I kick out further then dive to where it's darker. I stay there for as long as possible until I must shoot for breath.

Later in the day I walk the cliffs. I have never thought about jumping, but today I do; I wonder what it would be like to hit the sea at such a speed. I know it's just this story, making me miserable. All this remembering. At least I'll be done soon and I'll lay all these people to rest. Winter will come; I'll burn the self-portrait and return to my painted breezeblocks. I didn't realise the force of my confession, and I want it to be over.

I stop where the view from the cliff is the best. I search

for a patch of sea where there are no swimmers, setting it up in my mind for me to dive into. When I look at my square of pure blue sea I forget the Bauhaus: my love for Charlotte; Walter's poison; my own sins. For moments I forget everything, until the blue rises up and I am tumbled back into the past by a wave so violent that it moves toward this solitary diver and overwhelms him where he stands.

# 43
## Berlin

In the last weekend of January everyone stayed off the streets. Rumours of an army putsch surrounded Berlin: reports said that von ~~Schleicher~~ had ~~kidnapped Hinden~~burg, that martial law had been proclaimed; that most of Prussia would secede. We stayed at home. The world outside was as quiet as it had been in November's strike, and a frost each morning made the streets smoke in the first sun.

We stayed in bed, our bodies warm. Such a sweetness to have Charlotte all to myself. We listened to the radio, drank tea, ate soup with rolls, held hands while we slept. We talked about who our kids would grow up to be. To have this weekend with her – well, the putsch was a blessing. I could have shaken the hand of every general staked out on the city's perimeter.

'Do you know when I fell in love with you?' she said, over lunch and a cheap bottle of red wine.

'The night after the cinema.'

She shook her head. 'It wasn't then.' Her neck was long

with her haircut. 'It was when you presented me with these sausages.'

I kissed the salt off her mouth. 'Yesterday?'

'No. It was when I saw you on Walter's balcony.' (She never mentioned Walter; never.) 'The night he spent with the Nazi. You thought I hadn't been watching you for long, but I'd been on Jenö's balcony for a while. You looked so free there; free of worry, of doubt. You looked so sure of yourself. And I thought: I can't remember feeling like that, not for a long while.' She took a drink. Her lips were a little dirty with the wine. 'And I thought: when did I lose Paul Beckermann? I knew it was no one's fault but my own; that I'd thrown away what we'd had. The truth was that in Weimar I'd been in love with the both of you. But when I watched you that night—'

'High,' I interrupted her. 'Knocked out of your brains.'

'A little high, yes, but don't spoil the story. Anyway, I had this feeling we'd be together. That we had been apart for a long time, but we hadn't been able to stay away from each other. We hadn't been able to stop being friends; we couldn't stop being in each other's rooms, or at the Workshops. Jenö put up with it, but I think he knew. I think he just saw it as a condition of us, back then. Some part of me wonders whether he didn't tell me what he did in Rügen because he wanted out of it. The triangle; the *troika*.' She reached out and touched my hand. She almost never spoke like this, so openly, and I wondered what had brought it on; maybe it was the violence outside. 'And I knew, as I watched you that night, that everything would be all right. That it was going to be hard, but you would always be there. That you weren't going away.'

I remembered how she had come to my room later that night. We had lain on the bed, and I had touched her neck, and she had moved away, knowing perhaps that it was not yet the right moment.

Now she rubbed at her eyes. 'The wine's made me mushy. This is why we can't drink in the day.'

As we finished our lunch I told her that as she had watched me I had watched Oskar and Walter, two men nearly fucking; and then how I'd had to creep past them, out of Walter's room. It must have excited her – because we quickly made love again that afternoon.

After, in the January dark, as she dozed in my arms, I thought about running to Irmi's flat to tell her I'd been wrong. She was right. She was right! Charlotte was here, she was fine, nothing was happening between her and Jenö. I wanted to tell her I was sorry we had argued. I imagined Irmi, curled up against Teddy just as Charlotte was curled up against me, watching and dreaming next to the fogged-up window, where I had days ago imagined the snapping road, the snaking river, the coming flood.

The army did not come that weekend.

Instead, on Tuesday, the unthinkable happened instead: Hitler became Chancellor. Perhaps to others, who had paid more attention, it was not as much of a surprise, but to me and Charlotte, who had spent all weekend cloistered away, it was nothing less than astonishing. We heard it first from Mrs Müller's radio before we switched on ours. By the time the bulletin ended, Charlotte had gone very pale. 'What's going on?'

'I don't know,' I said. 'It might be all right.'

We listened to more before the broadcast returned to an afternoon play. 'No other Nazis have power, do they? It's only him.'

'Göring does. And Frick. But that's it, I think.'

'Let's go into town,' she said.

'Why?'

'To see what's happening.'

'Why?' I asked again.

'Because I want to see it with my own eyes.'

She wore Rosenberg's shirt. 'Charlotte, it's a Nazi parade, not Irmi's Christmas party.'

'We must see it for ourselves.' She swung her legs off mine to find her coat and scarf. 'Besides,' she said, her voice muffled, 'I can't stand to be inside any longer.'

Ah; yes. This was what she needed: a small break, a little distance – whereas I could have had weeks more with her like this. That was always the difference between us. She was always the one to break first.

Our train was full of people with the same idea. The tunnels were dark aside from the lamps which lent passing brightness to the commuters hanging loosely from the leather straps as the train crashed along the tracks. The platforms were full, and our carriage only got fuller as we approached the city: businessmen and students and housewives and the unemployed, ready to see whatever spectacle we deserved.

After we reached the station we walked toward Unter den Linden. Everywhere illuminated advertisements sold politics and health. Around us was the helpless brickwork of the city, and khaki trucks on the road, their cargo covered. Several fireworks shot into the sky, far away enough to be Luna Park.

There were many women in the crowd when we reached the boulevard. There were men too but not as many. I asked one woman how long she'd been there and she said 'since lunch', which was when we'd heard the radio announcement. Flags snapped loudly in the quick wind. The women might have been our age, though they seemed older. They kept on looking at Charlotte. They would look once, trying to divine her; then look back again.

We shared our kirsch amongst the women and they let us closer to the rope. Victory was in her chariot at the top of the Gate, and the horses looked ready to ride out from under her. I wondered if we might see Jenö in the crowd.

It must have been an hour or so later when everyone without warning surged forward, a whisper going through the crowd – *he's coming, he's here!* The noise of drums came from the avenue, then a rattling, but most of the boulevard was dark. Then the drumming became louder, and we could hear hundreds of boots marching in time. Torches suddenly provoked from the night the Storm Troopers, grimly, steadfastly, entering Berlin. Whatever the torches burned made the air foul. Everything was quiet as the men marched toward the gates, burning rivers of light into the boulevard beyond the rope.

'Look!' one of the women exclaimed. 'Over there!'

Another surge moved the crowd and Charlotte's hand was pulled from mine. I found her man's hat quickly amongst the women's. Her face froze as a thousand arms rose in unison and a roar called up Hitler, upright in the open cab. He gave the crowd a small smile before he vanished through the gate as quickly as he had come.

The crowd was running west now but Charlotte managed to get back to the rope. Hitler's retinue followed in four more cars, black and sleek and willing.

We should have followed the women into the park. We should have run with them, under the gate, under Victory with her open skirts and reckless mouth, over to the Reichstag. There was this last moment – flaming out; already finishing – before I saw him, but the last car is already coming into view, and though Charlotte doesn't see him – might not even recognise him from our chance meeting at the Swan – Ernst Steiner was standing in one of the open-topped cabs in his brown shirt and cap, still as fat as ever, and any opportunity I had had to change the course of this sorry history – well, it was gone.

The way Steiner watched the crowd: he had given us exactly the same look from his office. Imperious. Delighted.

It was Ernst all right.

He sat down as the car passed through the gate. I looked around the crowd to see if Walter might be here. A longing stirred in me, ever so slightly romantic, definitely ancient, that I should like to see Walter König, my old friend, counsellor, and sometime traitor. Because I knew that if Ernst was in Berlin, there was a good chance Walter would be too.

# 44

## Berlin

When Kaspar had said, at Irmi's party, that Walter was still fucking some fat Nazi, I would never have thought that man would be a Nazi with so much power; a man to be included in Hitler's cavalcade. While I wanted immediately to find Walter in Berlin, I also didn't want to be found by Ernst Steiner. Easy enough to find someone in Berlin in 1933; not so easy not to be caught.

Neither Walter nor he was in the phone book, and it was too cold to stake out Ernst's government building all day. I couldn't send a telegram or even a letter to the Weimar studio, since I didn't want Mr Steiner to ever ask himself whether he had once known a Paul Beckermann.

A couple of weeks passed in February as I puzzled over the mystery. Though newspapers had been raided, Thälmann threatened, and his Communist members beaten, I'd say that, at least in the aftermath of Hitler's parade, things were almost normal. There was even a faintly festive spirit that we were allowed outside again. The cabaret reopened; kids played on the streets; in the afternoons Charlotte was once more on the move.

While I puzzled out the mystery of how to find Ernst Steiner, my father took me to tea at Lutter and Wegner's. Though I wasn't sure he could afford it, he made a show of paying for the whole thing. Despite the fact he no longer owned industrial property to speak of – in fact I think he and my brother both mooned about the house sending my mother half mad – he was ever the anxious capitalist, talking about a new factory he wanted to open, and how he knew someone high up in the Party who would help him get set up again. And then! Who knew, perhaps one day he might outfit the whole of the new German army with plimsolls. I remembered the summer I'd spent in his shoe factory, when he'd paid me not a pfennig more than the other workers. Still, as Walter had proved, it had kept me from worse misdeeds.

When my father shook my hand at the revolving gold doors he quoted Isaiah: 'Butter and honey shall he eat, that he may know to refuse the evil and choose the good.' Then he turned on his heel, mumbling the chapter numbers but explaining nothing, and off he went. Later my mother wrote me a letter of apology, saying the 'world was bent on dividing us'. I knew she liked Charlotte, and I wondered why she hadn't come with him. Usually she enjoyed trips away, but then I had written to her in such detail about the Nazi parade, she might have been simply too scared to get on the train.

●

It wasn't much longer after the bizarre meeting with my father that I managed to find Ernst Steiner. It was all thanks to Irmi, really. I was walking Charlotte out at lunchtime when I saw the porter's newspaper: on the front page was a photograph of some of the Party's top men. I asked the porter if I might have a look.

'What are you doing?' Charlotte asked quietly. She didn't like the porter – Mr Schmidt – she found him unsettling. I knew he didn't like doing anybody any special favours but he handed over the newspaper anyway. The photographed officials were smiling, war medals hung on their lapels, and the caption read *Hotel Kaiserhof, Berlin*. Ernst wasn't in the picture, but he was a politician, and he had always enjoyed a drink.

Charlotte scanned the picture. 'Who are all these people?'

'Leaders of the Fatherland,' I said, in earshot of Schmidt, who, like all Berlin porters, was a paid-up Nazi.

He asked, and not in a friendly way, whether I wanted to keep it. 'No. Thank you.' As he took his newspaper he narrowed his eyes at Charlotte's boyish haircut.

We said goodbye at the front door.

'That man gives me the creeps.'

'Just ignore him. Where are you off to?'

'Off for a walk. Everything feels crammed in my head.' She held her satchel close to her, as if she were worried someone would snatch it. I could tell she was distracted as she kissed me goodbye. I wondered, as I did every day, whether she was heading off to the Bauhaus, and, when she was there, what – if anything – she and Jenö would do together. I knew this was a killing way to think, and that my suspicions would soon send me to the madhouse. But I couldn't help it. I imagined her and Jenö in workshops. I imagined them in the ateliers. I imagined their desire after three years of being apart; its intensity, its white heat.

Some days later, I stood opposite the Kaiserhof. Party men in uniform milled at the bar and seated women waited for their return. Ernst was at the window, just as Irmi had said he would be. He was talking to a woman, her hair done in waves, her hands braced as if she had no intention of touching her drink. He looked to all the world like an officer from the age of Bismarck, and I almost felt proud of him. How high he had climbed from the studio in the woods! How well he had done from our paintings!

I wondered if Walter, too, was thriving with all this wealth. He'd always liked money; always missed it when he didn't have any. But there was the question of the woman. Ernst's wife? Mrs Steiner? In which case, maybe Walter had been left behind. What would Walter do in Weimar, and what would he be, without Ernst's patronage? I hadn't heard from him in years. He could just as well be dead from booze and cocaine in Goethe's forest.

I scooted round to the rear of the hotel and waited for a few minutes before Irmi came out with neither coat nor scarf. I realised just then that we hadn't spoken, not properly, since our argument.

'It's the man by the window, isn't it?' she said. 'The bald one?'

'That's him, yes.'

'I'd no idea he was Walter's boyfriend!'

I was surprised that she was in a good mood. Maybe she had forgiven me; again. 'You've never seen Walter here?'

'No,' she said, looking at me funny, 'I would have said. Mr Steiner was your boss in Weimar? I've served him endless times!'

'That's right.'

'Who's the woman?'

'Not sure. His wife? Of sorts?'

'He's never here without her.'

I wondered what it was I should do. I could follow the Steiners – if that's what they were – home after their drinks, or follow Ernst to wherever he went next, and hope it would lead me to Walter. But I had no idea what I'd say to my old friend should I find him. Maybe he'd ask my forgiveness. Maybe he'd beg me for my friendship. But really, I hoped he'd say: *Follow her. Search her bag.* He'd say: *Go to the Bauhaus. You're right to be worried.* I knew he'd say all this. Unlike Irmi, Walter was the kind of person who would give me permission to think all these things.

'Thanks, Irmi. I know I don't deserve it.'

She shook her head. 'It's nothing.'

A porter squeezed past and we stood awkwardly outside the kitchen basement. Irmi wore the same expression I'd seen at her flat. 'You're a nuisance, Paul. You know all this time I couldn't ever get rid of the thought of you. Not when we were in Weimar, not even when you were in

Dessau. When you wrote and said you wanted to live with me – well, I thought, this is the beginning. We are on our way. Then silence. Nothing for months. I thought: he's busy, he has other matters to sort before leaving. Then in October you turned up, and instead of moving in with me, you got me to find an apartment for you and Charlotte.'

I wanted to say sorry but she put up her hand to stop me.

'And now you talk to me about *her* and *Jenö* and honestly, I can't . . . You can't talk to me any more about all that stuff. I have run out of patience. I have run out of advice. Please spare me. Spare me any more of these stories.'

She was right: I had taken advantage of her generosity, her ability to forgive. Before I had a chance to apologise she pulled out a folded cheque from her apron: on the front, Ernst's signature for an expensive bottle of champagne; on the back, his address: Savignyplatz, no. 14, Charlottenburg.

'Irmi.'

'Just say thank you.'

'But I would never have asked you to do that. Thank you, of course; a thousand times. Are you sure no one saw you do it?'

'It's a gift. But that's it. I'm finished. If you do find Walter, don't tell me. What he did to Charlotte was reprehensible, but it was a long time ago, and I'm not interested in getting involved in any more games. Agreed?'

'Yes.' I memorised the address and returned the cheque. 'It was never my intention to hurt you. I'm sorry if I upset you.'

'I'm happy,' Irmi said. 'But seeing you makes me unhappy.'

'Will you see Teddy later?'

'Of course,' she said, 'just an hour left here.' I saw a sparkle in her eye but she pushed it away. She kissed me on the cheek and walked back inside, with Ernst's dangerous address in her apron. What we might do for love. Even love that had gone such a long while ago.

'Thank you, Irmi! Thank you!'

She didn't turn around, but put up her hand and waved.

# 45

## England

This morning there is a letter on my doormat. I know instantly that it is from a German: it's the style of handwriting I learnt in school too. For some mad moment I think it is Charlotte writing to me. My grief: I never knew it would be so wormlike, so insistent. My German name is also used: it's from someone who knew me as Beckermann.

Paul,

I hope you don't mind me writing to you. I went to Walter's funeral last week, and afterward Irmi gave me your address. (You were missed, but Irmi explained everything.) I wanted to write because I found a case of Charlotte's in Walter's apartment. Franz said her work is inside. I haven't looked at it yet – can't quite face it alone – and I thought maybe it'd be right to look at it together, after all this time. In any case, I'd like to see

you, since we are countrymen once more. I could be
with you next Wednesday. Is this possible?

My best,

Eugene Fielder

I spent so many months trying to find Jenö when I arrived
in England, but now it is he who has found me. I looked
for him in London art schools, in foundries and forges in
Camberwell and New Cross; I looked for him in Uncle
König's gallery, but he had disappeared. I don't even know
why finding him had been important. Comradeship in
horror, et cetera. And so here we were: Eugene Fielder
and Paul Brickman – two Englishmen with no pasts
whatsoever.

I write to Jenö. Though I don't really want to see him
again, and I'd rather not see inside Charlotte's case, I tell
him that Wednesday is fine.

*Franz said there's some of her work inside.* This means
it's from the camp, if it is Franz who says so. What if I
find another green-chalked portrait? The case could be
innumerable portraits of Jenö Fiedler, and I won't have
the strength to tell this narrative revoked: that she never
loved me; that it was always Jenö. That Berlin – that our
Berlin – was a sham.

# 46

## Berlin

The house at no. 14 Savignyplatz was a wedding cake: just as Ernst would have wanted it. There were lilies in the window, more in a great urn on the mantelpiece, and bright flowered wallpaper that shone even from a distance. A darkened square above the fireplace was a mirror perhaps. Mr Steiner had left earlier but had returned twenty minutes later to pick up a black briefcase. His possible wife had left for the day too.

The day was stormy: fast winds and even faster rain showers, and, out of all this in a clearance of cloud, sunlight so strong it lit every embellishment of the house. Hats were lifted off heads, children were dragged into the blasts, and women raced to tie handkerchiefs around their hair. Then the dirty clouds skittered along until the sky had turned blue once more, and the morning was very bright, and the headscarves were again removed. Even in the sunshine I heard the grind of thunder, and saw three rainbows come and go, so that if I was looking for auspices in the weather I could have found one for every eventuality.

I wondered if making contact with Walter again didn't cross some verge that my loyalty to Charlotte forbade, but I knew if he was in there, then I wanted to see him. He'd say – a princely toss of his head, maybe even cupping my cheek in his hand – that I was right to feel so troubled about Jenö and the Bauhaus; he'd feel the same. *Follow her*, he'd say. *Work out what she's up to.* Irmi's reassurances were nothing next to proof.

I felt the expense of the gravel as I walked to the door. The nameplate said Mr and Mrs Steiner, and my heart dropped. Ernst had married; Walter was not here. I knocked.

A woman answered. Her guard came up when she saw me, and it gave me the old feeling of being a Bauhäusler again. 'Yes?'

Before I answered I heard Walter's voice, plunging me back into the past. 'Who is it, Annaliese?'

A lift of excitement, a thrill. Here he was!

'Who do you require?' she said. She kept the door closed enough that I couldn't see into the house.

'Mr König, please.'

She asked me for my name and I gave it to her.

'Paul Beckermann for you,' she said. For moments nothing happened as she watched Walter's expression in the hall. 'Do you want me to send him away?'

'No, no. Let him in.'

Walter was in a dressing gown, silk and paisley, the bones of his chest visible. He had become a slender man again. His hands shook as he drew the gown to his throat. 'Paul. What a shock.'

'Hello, Walter.' Here he was: my friend and traitor. His lips were full; his hair still thick.

'I'm not yet changed.' Annaliese the maid went off to fetch coffee. A vase of lilies gave off a boozy smell. 'Gosh, I didn't think I'd ever see you again. I'd given you up for dead.'

'As I had you.'

I smiled, and in turn he smiled so warmly I knew it was the right thing to have come.

'Please,' he gestured to the first room off the hall, but at the moment he grasped the handle he hesitated, and I saw the regret in his expression before he opened the door and I could see, immediately, his mistake. Above the fireplace was the Weimar painting. I saw it now for what it was: a masterpiece. Emblazoned in light, it looked excellent here in this room of heavy furniture and tubs of lilies. It made the whole room.

He came closer, so close that I could smell his hangover. He still had that approach: animal, noiseless. 'Site of all my undoing. Ernst's never worked it out. The trick. He thinks it's to do with delicate brushwork.' He scoffed. 'He's always been a philistine. So's his wife.' In the bottom right-hand corner it read: *Steiner Studio: Weimar, 1923.*

'It's double, isn't it? The light.'

'Most people don't see it,' he said. 'Of course, I was very confused that summer.'

A Japanese shade concealed half the room; there was a woman with a fan on the screen and a black bird with tipped wings. Nearby there was the photograph of us all at the Metal Ball with our paint wearing off and wheeled hats askew. Charlotte looked high, but it was Walter's expression that surprised me the most. I'd seen this photograph before, but I hadn't realised how happy he had looked. It must have been at the beginning of the night when we'd all been together. 'This to me is the Bauhaus.' He nodded at his painting. 'Not that.'

The maid brought in the coffee and I sat on the chesterfield. The density of the room reminded me of Walter's Weimar apartment; a man adrift in treasure. I wondered where Mr Steiner worked. Whether it was the Chamber of Culture, or whether he had worked his way into a more powerful department. Maybe he had traded his paintings with some bigwig Nazi – they would have liked his *Völkisch* style – and been offered a job. He was ambitious. I knew that. He would have loved the power.

'So many visitors this week, Mr König.'

'Paul is an old friend.'

'Yes, they all are.' The maid fussed with the cups and saucers before she finally left.

In the shaky pouring of the milk one could see how Walter's years had been used. 'How did you find me, Paul?'

'Irmi works where Ernst drinks.'

'The Kaiserhof?'

'That's right. You don't go there yourself?'

'No. That's Mrs Steiner's job. Sugar?'

I shook my head.

'I'm his nephew. It works out nicely for everyone.' Walter supressed a smile and handed over the coffee with two hands. 'Including Mrs Steiner. Irmi: how is she?'

'She has a new boyfriend. She's happy.'

'I'd like to see her. Irmi always was very kind to me.'

'She lives in Kreuzberg.'

We were warming up; we were remembering what it was to be friends. I wondered how we might conceivably operate; how I would have to lie to Charlotte about where I'd been this afternoon. I'd never thought of Berlin as a city Walter and I would share, but it might be fun to set it alight together. Maybe even Charlotte, given time, would be able to forgive him.

'Do you see anyone from school?' I asked.

'Franz visits sometimes. No one else, really. What about you?'

'Just Kaspar and Irmi. Did you see the victory parade?'

He shook his head.

'It was a surprise to see Ernst there,' I said. 'I hadn't even wanted to go. But Charlotte wanted to see history unfold.' I wondered what he would say to this: whether he might congratulate me; tell me he was happy at least one of us had got what we wanted. 'She lives with me now,' I added, without any sophistication.

But there; nothing. As if I'd told him the day's weather. Outside, the sounds of a rake against gravel. A big gull flew from the villa opposite. I looked back to Walter. He seemed self-conscious, but so was I. He took some of his coffee then looked at the painting. 'Oh, Pauli,' he said, 'you make me feel very aware of how much time has passed.'

'Do I look so old?'

He didn't answer. 'How is Charlotte?'

'She's fine. Doing lots of painting. We can't afford a loom.'

'Painting? That's nice. She's a good painter, as I remember.'

For moments he closed his eyes, like a person at prayer. They were wet when he opened them. Even for Walter this was odd behaviour.

It occurred to me that maybe coming here was a mistake. 'Did you hear the Bauhaus has set up in Berlin?' I said.

'Yes. Jenö told me.'

'Oh.' I had always assumed Walter had been cut off from all of us. 'I didn't know you'd stayed in touch.'

Walter shrugged. His dressing gown fell off one shoulder and he pushed it up. There had been something there. Old burned skin. 'When Jenö was in Dessau, and I was in Weimar, we were both quite alone. I don't know if I was his friend, but he answered my letters when I wrote to him.'

'Do you still love him?'

He smiled drily. 'What's love after a decade? A dried-up old thing. I have no use for it.' A tongue darted out; he licked his lips. I felt he was buying time. Eyes back to the painting again, as if trying to chase something down. 'Jenö came to see me last week.'

'Oh.'

In all the multiplicities of this conversation, I hadn't imagined Jenö had got here first. 'Was that nice? To see him again?'

'It was.'

'I saw him at Irmi's Christmas party. It was quite awkward.'

'He said.'

'Well, it looks like Jenö has pipped me to the post again!'

'He wanted help actually.'

327

'Help? Help with what?'

Walter's face was tight, his expression hard.

'Walter. What did Jenö want help with?' I said, feeling that inexpressible vertigo, as I had done at the Obersee lake, that everything was about to invert and veer.

'Don't be angry.'

'Just say it.'

'He asked if I could help him.'

'Yes, yes, help him how?'

'He wants to leave Germany. I've arranged a job for him at my uncle's gallery in London.' His uncle; the one who would pay *valuta*. He ballooned his cheeks and let them go. 'Jenö wants Charlotte to go with him.'

'What do you mean?'

'He wants Charlotte to leave Germany.'

'What? Why?'

'It's too dangerous for her here.'

I laughed; this was absurd. 'We're fine.'

'Paul,' he said, 'you must listen.'

A key turned in the door. Walter looked up, frightened. 'Please, come away from the window.' He pulled me behind the Japanese screen as we heard the maid's footsteps, and I wondered what I would say if I saw Ernst again in the flesh. But it was women's voices which filled the corridor: Mrs Steiner had come home; the Kaiserhof woman with her pressed curls.

Behind the screen was Ernst's desk: on top of it were papers and pens. A blueprint from an office building caught my eye, with unreadable words in blue ink.

I had no desire to be here; to hear what could only

have been confected by a man as mad as Walter König. To have visited in the first place had been a mistake. 'This is stupid. I'm sorry. It's my fault. I should go. I shouldn't have come.'

He laid a hand on my arm, waiting for Mrs Steiner to leave the hall.

'What do you want?' I asked, shrugging off his touch.

'Listen, won't you. Charlotte won't go.'

'Of course she won't. Look, this is ridiculous. This is the maddest thing you've made up so far!'

'No. Ernst has made it perfectly clear. Foreigners. Artists. Jews. They won't belong in Germany soon. And neither will the Bauhaus. You do know she's working at the Bauhaus?'

'Of course.' I levelled his gaze with my own. 'We'll be careful. Thank you for your concern, Walter, but it's preposterous. Who would Charlotte go with?'

'Paul, listen to me! You're not listening. Jenö has a ticket for her to leave with him. It leaves in two weeks.'

From the pinched seriousness of his mouth, it occurred to me that this was not a game. 'No.'

'Pauli—'

'I will not persuade Charlotte to leave with Jenö Fiedler.'

'You must. It's not safe here. You must persuade her to go with him.'

'I'll ask her to go with me.'

'You just said you don't have any money.'

'Not yet—'

'He's leaving in two weeks. Charlotte has to be on that flight.'

'Why do you want to help her? All you have done for the past decade is try and destroy her!'

He looked at me. 'You mistake me,' he said coolly. 'I couldn't care less what happens to Charlotte Feldekova. My fear is Jenö will stay if she doesn't go. I have to get him out at least.'

# 47
## Berlin

In Dresden Palace there is a porcelain menagerie. Tiny birds perch on the walls, and on the floor are hundreds of animals: peacocks; rhinoceroses; monkeys. A hen hangs from a fox's jaws; a vulture grips the heart of a cockatoo. The ruler at the time, Augustus the Strong, had suffered from what was known as a *maladie de porcelaine*. In the corridor leading from the porcelain room there are hundreds of blue-inked vases. Augustus's porcelain-sickness was so perverse that he gave the King of Prussia a whole battalion in exchange for these vases. The soldiers would have marched from Dresden to Berlin knowing they'd been swapped for some pots. A battalion for a set of vases.

My heart for Charlotte's life.

I left Charlottenburg and went directly to Steglitz. I don't remember the journey but I knew where I was going. The train took me south and when we emerged from the tunnels rain streaked the carriage windows. The buildings receded as I marched toward the Bauhaus, feeling the weight of my gloved hands swing. I walked automatically, and saw hardly a thing.

Walter's words were crazy in my mind; his request absurd. In all his morbid gentleness I had expected him to confirm my suspicions. *Yes*, he should have said: *Follow her. Go to the Bauhaus. See what she's up to.* But there had been no charitable condolences, no exhortations that all would be well, nor were there any poisoned barbs that Charlotte had been sent to devil me.

Instead, he had asked me to be Jenö's advocate.

It was outrageous. Unfair.

There had been a wildness to Walter behind the Japanese shade. Maybe the whole thing was yet another fiction. A wedge to push us apart. It was not unthinkable that Walter might meddle, even after so many years. What had I said to Franz in Dessau? That Walter was quick to forgive. How laughable that was.

I walked the invisible suburbs until the Bauhaus appeared. It was a run-down warehouse, the scrubland around it littered with rubbish. The school's sign swung lightly: 'bauhaus', it read, all in lower case. I remembered the double magnification of the Dessau sign; how big we had been back then, how grand!

A class was going on in one of the rooms. The instructor – Josef! – holding different materials one at a time: wood, stone, fabric, metal, pointing out the properties of the material. *Materialgerecht*: how we understand our own inner properties; the nature of what we are.

I waited. Charlotte would leave around now if she were

to get home at her normal time. I didn't want anyone to see me, and moved on. Around the corner, in a white room, Master Kandinsky sat at a tile stove, warming his hands, watching the fire. He was dressed in a suit with collar and tie, with his glasses halfway down his nose. It was probably the first time I had ever seen him doing nothing. I wondered who else from the staff had believed the Director's vision could win out. He leaned over and put another briquette into the stove. I left before he saw me: a watchful student of the distant past.

I climbed the earthen bank to see what I could of the top floor and suddenly there she was: a buzz-cut blonde, a man's hat in her hands. Irmi had been wrong. No walks. No city strolls. All year she had been where I had always thought she would be: the Bauhaus, of course.

And here: this is Walter's familiar magicking: the truth pulled from deceptions – she puts her coat on, pulls her hands through her hair, places the man's hat on her head. She embraces someone. Maybe it's chaste; I cannot see.

She leaves; is gone. And I am standing alone in the dark.

And, for the first time, I think that Walter might not be crazy. A new and unexpected future has opened out dangerously in this day. Maybe she will leave me. Maybe she has already decided to catch that flight. Maybe, in two weeks' time, Charlotte will no longer be with me, but with Jenö in England.

That night I gave in and went through her bag while she was in the bath. There were metro tickets to Steglitz she'd not bothered to hide, and, because of Irmi's advice, that I had not looked for. Foolishly I expected to find an air ticket to England. I found nothing. I tallied the cost of our lives: rent, bills, food. Not a pfennig left to take us from Berlin, never mind Germany. Half of my savings I'd spent on the Oriental shirt. Still, what could that have got me? A train ticket to Hanover. Nothing more.

The copper tub was in the kitchen. Inside it she was knotted up like a child, and she was singing one of her Czech nursery songs. Voices came from the apartment next to ours. I could see her breasts in the water, small spikes floating. Had it been Jenö I'd seen her kiss? In the Bauhaus this afternoon? She tipped her head; her neck open in the steam. I remembered the heavy swing of my gloved hands, and how I had felt I might do something with them.

'This couple have been arguing all evening,' she said, her voice funny with her head upside down. 'I wonder why they stay together.'

'I saw Walter König today.'

She knocked her head back. 'Walter-from-Weimar-Walter?'

'That's right.'

'Where on earth did you find *him*?'

'Charlottenburg. He's living with Ernst Steiner. They've moved to Berlin together.'

'Oh.' I could see her thinking. 'What did he say?'

'Not much. I just found out what he was up to.'

'Which is what?'

'Mostly being Ernst's boyfriend.'

She began soaping herself. 'Walter König. I'd never have thought of him as a Berliner. If you become friendly with him again, you'll tell me, won't you? I don't want to see him by surprise. Or if he starts seeing Irmi or Kaspar, you will warn me, won't you?'

'Of course.'

'I don't care what he did, but I don't want to see him again.'

I was faced with a choice; I didn't know what to do; and Walter's words were boiling in my head: *You must persuade her to go. Charlotte has to be on that flight.* 'Do you ever wish we had more money?'

'Why? No. Do you?'

'Sometimes I wonder if you might want more.'

'We're fine. Aren't we doing all right?'

A red light flew through the fogged window.

'Would you leave? If you wanted to go, would you?'

'Leave? Where would I go?' She looked at me sharply. 'What did Walter say to you, Paul?'

'Nothing.'

'You mean leave Berlin?'

'I mean leave Germany.'

'No.'

'What if things got very bad?'

'Then I don't know. Yes. Maybe.'

'You can go. If you want to go, you should go.'

Her knees rose to her chin. 'I don't know what you're talking about. Can you get me a towel? It's gone cold.'

She was wiping the water away with her palms when I came back. She wobbled on the floor as I wrapped her in the towel. 'Do you see Jenö at the Bauhaus?' I felt her body stiffen under my hands. 'I saw you there, today.'

She gave me the same cool look she had given me at Rosenberg's. 'Did you follow me?'

'No. Walter said you've been going there.'

'Good old Walter.' She smiled bitterly. 'Let go, Paul, it's too tight.' She stood away from me. 'The Director has let me use the looms, that's all.'

'Since New Year?'

'Yes,' she said, defiantly. 'Since New Year.'

She left the kitchen and I followed her into our room. Her actions were quick in the cold, pulling on her fisherman's jumper and black slacks, and towelling her hair.

'Why didn't you tell me?'

'Oh, why do you think?'

'Do you speak to him? To Jenö?'

'Please listen to yourself. I just wanted to work without suspicion. I knew you'd jump to conclusions. That's why I didn't tell you.' She lifted her face to mine. 'I haven't been able to work for years! I'm not a painter, Paul. I need a loom. I need thread.' Charlotte pulled me down to the bed with her. 'I swear nothing's happening between me and Jenö Fiedler.' She saw that I had not softened. 'Paul, what did Walter say to you?'

I was on the brink. To cross it would mean not being able to come back. I thought of Master Kandinsky: old man, sitting in his chair, doing nothing. 'Walter said Jenö wants to take you to London.'

'Ah,' she said. 'That.'

'Well?'

336

'He's offered to pay my airfare, that's all. As a friend.'

'When did he ask you?'

'Days. Weeks ago. I said no immediately.'

My body felt weak and insubstantial. 'Do you want to go?'

'No,' she said. 'I want to stay here, with you. In our home.'

'Why didn't you tell me?'

'Because I didn't want to have this argument. I thought the matter was over; it would have been, if Walter hadn't got himself involved. Please listen to me: Walter König will drop poison into your ear no matter what. It will benefit him to get me gone. He has form, don't you see? He constantly tries to outmanoeuvre me, to rob me of what I have.'

I wanted this to be true, so I let her talk and did not interrupt her.

'The Survey was meant to get rid of me. The cocaine was meant to split us all apart. Now this! Don't you see? Every time he's been in my life he's tried to ruin what I have. Getting me to England – that's just the newest stratagem. He wants to ruin what we have, and the way he'll do that is through you. He'll make everything rotten between us. He'll plant suspicion where he can. Making everything obscene. Don't you know by now, Pauli? Walter König cannot be trusted. Not with secrets; not with our lives; not with anything. Who's to say Ernst Steiner and his lackeys won't be waiting at the airport to arrest me? It's just another treachery, Paul. And that makes it number three. It's his last move.'

# 48

## Berlin

On the windows the next morning there was a pattern of scalloped ice. I kissed Charlotte, waking her; she told me she loved me, and in her eyes there was something like a promise.

All night Walter's words had roiled my brain. *You must persuade her to go with him.* In my dreams I had been again behind the Japanese screen, near the painted woman and sparrow; and there had been Walter, in his dressing gown, shaking, hectoring me for action.

'Stop worrying, Paul,' she said. 'Please. We'll be fine.'

Soon the sun fell to the bed, a gate of pale orange in which she slept, then, as it rose higher, it lit the tram wires and melted the iced windows. Between us I felt a renewal, and in the hour or so in which we drowsed, I knew it had been a bad idea to see Walter yesterday. Charlotte was right: we had no reason to trust him; his past behaviour had proved this. That this was a final flare in his perversity was entirely credible. He wouldn't want to see Charlotte happy. He'd want to see us split. When

Jenö had proposed the English plan, he'd have thought
– even if it was unconsciously – here's a way to deny her
what she has.

Like this I put Walter's proposal away.

We slept all morning, and I remembered the happiness of that frosted-up weekend, when danger was at the
periphery of Berlin, but we were safe together.

Later I brought her coffee and we watched the street.
A waiter in a bow tie and waistcoat threw a bucket of
water into the stream of a busted pipe. At the cobbler's a
mechanised doll hammered a boot. A woman passed with
flowers; a man with an Alsatian. Jets of U-bahn steam. A
boy in a sailor's outfit ran after another kid. 'He looks like
you,' Charlotte said, and she ran her mouth up my neck.
'A bit furious.'

Her smell in the morning was always a little rank.
'You need to have a wash.' I nudged her away and she
laughed.

'I'm going to the Bauhaus later,' she said. 'I hope that's
all right?'

'It's fine,' I said. The boy disappeared around the corner.
'Were you serious, Charlotte, about having a child?'

'Yes,' she said. 'If you are. It would be quite fun,
wouldn't it? A mix of me and you. Imagine. A little baby.
Ours forever.'

'Let's do it. Let's do it soon,' I said, as if to say, *and not
this, not the other thing*. Then I closed my hand into a fist.
'Let's play. One last time. For old times' sake.'

'You don't have anything in there.'

'I do. This time it's an abstraction.'

'But it has to be here. Materially here,' she said, and I wondered that she had remembered those words from the River Ilm. 'That's the rules of the hiding game.'

'You're the sleeper,' I said.

'Give me the clues, at least,' she said, with closed eyes, then opened them once more: 'Unless it's just hot air.'

'All right. Let's see. *Berlin. Family. Impossible-impending-wealth.*'

'Too many words!'

'The last one was a compound noun.'

'Is it our life?'

'Not quite.' I opened up my fist. 'Our future.'

'Impossible wealth!' she said, kissing me, laughing. 'What a notion!'

Charlotte went to find her clothes. Maybe it was not so impossible; such wealth. Now that she could use the Bauhaus looms, Charlotte could sell her weaves. Maybe she'd even be able to patent a design, invent fabrics with industrial application, just like she had done with her soundproofing. What had Jenö said, about Otti setting up an adjunct company, one over which she had control? And I could see if Josef needed an assistant. After all, Jenö would soon be gone.

I sat on the bed, wondering what to say next. 'Kaspar asked if we wanted to go skating,' I said, making something up. We would need to kill time until Jenö's flight.

'Sounds nice. And Irmi too?'

'Irmi's not really speaking to me.'

'Oh.' Charlotte didn't ask why. 'But she loves skating. She always does it with a frown. Very serious, as if she's

Field Marshal von Hindenburg with skates on. You won't see Walter again, will you?'

'No.'

'Because Irmi's not the only one who's been in love with you.'

'What are you talking about?'

'Oh, come on. Walter's always been half in love with you.'

'Nonsense. It's only ever been Jenö for him.'

'That doesn't mean he doesn't have a little reserve left for you. Why do you think he's so keen on getting me to England?' Charlotte laughed; laying out her trousers, shirt, jumper, blazer. There was a sound outside, a truck backfiring. She looked outside: she resembled Irmi, in that moment, her face watchful. 'Do *you* think we're in danger?'

'No.'

'And Jenö?'

'He's a Master at the Bauhaus. He's just more exposed than the rest of us, that's all. Whereas us: we're nobodies.'

'I'm a Czechoslovak nobody,' she said, her expression changing once more. 'There's a difference.'

She dressed and then, after breakfast or lunch or whatever it was, I watched her walk down the street in her man's hat and coat. I should have told her not to wear those clothes. I wondered if she was asking herself why I hadn't protested as I had done before Irmi's party. But to do so would have been a sop to Walter's presentiments about the dangerous city, and, as I have said, I am compromised, and selfish, and almost perverse. Grave errors happened because of me. I prized having her over her own safety. And then she slipped out of sight. This was only the first day I'd have to outwait. Every day at the Bauhaus Jenö would try and persuade her to go. Every evening in Kreuzberg I'd have to persuade her to stay. I simply loved her too much to do the right thing.

# 49
## Berlin

It's a strange feeling, waiting to see if someone will leave you. Stranger, too, to constantly question whether you should ask them to go. Every evening I waited for Charlotte to come home and tell me she had changed her mind. And every night, after she had not left, after she had not mentioned *London* or *England*, Walter's words turned the nights upside down.

*You must persuade her to go.*

For though I had managed the first day well enough, I soon learnt that the dark brought a different story. Depending on the time (three in the morning was the worst; my hour of lead) I came to different conclusions about what I should do. Persuade her to go. Persuade her to stay. I thought often of my father's words from Isaiah: 'that he may know to refuse the evil and choose the good'.

I'd hear the couples come in from the road, and I'd wait for the noises of the elevator, imagining their reflections in the mirrored chamber dashing away from them like fish,

343

and then the laughter in the corridor dispersed them, and the tail-lights of the motorcars rowed the ceiling, and Charlotte slept soundly by my side.

But – it was odd, I knew that even then – as soon as daylight came, the dilemma would disappear. Charlotte would be fine. Nothing would happen to any of us. After a strong coffee, my mind would clear. And the days – it embarrasses me to say this – would even turn out tolerable. I just ignored the question (remarkable that I could suppress it; that this is the way the mind works). After I kissed Charlotte on her way to the Bauhaus, flinching at the man's suit which I no longer commented upon, I put myself to work and my mind went to blankness. That week I became like one of Charlotte's Dessau weaves; a *Beinahe Nichts*, an *Almost Nothing*, with the occasional streak of such vibrant anxiety at three in the morning that I wondered I didn't pull her arm from the joint and drag her to Jenö's on foot.

But there: the mind of the liar is a spotless place aside from where dreams rise.

I have called myself perverse. I am. It's my special gift: this knack I have, of lying to myself. In the days I was able to bury the part of me that knew Walter's words were true. And when it became too much I walked out into the city's snow and tried to forget.

Porcelain days; porcelain city.

New bodies were fished from the Landwehr that week. More snow came. A Star of David was painted on Rosenberg's shopfront. We saw our friends, and walked Berlin, Charlotte wove at the Bauhaus, I painted (my overabundance; it was almost pathological).

We even went to the theatre. Dacia had come across tickets to see a Russian ballerina who'd come to dance for the St Petersburg émigrés. Charlotte wore a dress, possibly the most feminine thing I'd seen her in in a long while. It gave her skin a bluish note; like a painted woman in a Sargent or a Hammershøi. Before the show we found Dacia and Kaspar, who was smoking a clove cigarette in the foyer.

Charlotte told him about Jenö's offer of London, and a seat for her on the plane. 'He's such a worrier!' Kaspar said, pushing the cigarette's spiced cloud away. 'Always overreacting!' he said. 'Think nothing of it. You stay here with us. You can't go to London. What would you do in London without us?'

'Marry an aristocrat?' Dacia said.

Kaspar shot her a look. 'That's not helpful.'

I squeezed Charlotte's hand. Still she looked worried.

The theatre inside was golden. Charlotte kept on checking the entrances, and I wondered who she thought would join us. The government box was so far empty.

'Will you come to the Bauhaus tomorrow?' she whispered as the curtains opened. 'I want to show you something.'

'What is it?'

'A secret.'

I couldn't bear the idea of any more secrets. 'Tell me now,' I whispered.

'No, you'll just have to wait.' She put her hand in mine before the applause took it away.

Charlotte concentrated hard, watching the ballerina's dance as if it were a code which would tell her what to do. Notes from the violins filled the hall, wantonly rich. Tears magnified her eyes, then they fell away. I couldn't remember the last time I'd seen her cry.

All of this; what to make of all of this.

She is wavering, I thought. She is taking Jenö's proposal seriously.

The Russian danced alone, in dance upon dance, and the spectacle looked punishing, as if she was on the very edge of falling.

The next day we walked some of the way to Steglitz through the frozen park. Because of the grit to melt the snow, there was a reddish powder on many of the roads, and it made the city look built on sand.

The Bauhaus looked different from last week: the brickwork a shade lighter. 'There's still telephone cradles and candlesticks upstairs,' she said. 'Bits of dials and Formica too. Whenever you find something it has to go straight to the foundation class. Josef's very strict.'

By the entrance the sign squeaked against the wall: the type so rational it might have been designed by Franz Ehrlich himself.

Charlotte must have sensed my hesitation. 'Don't worry,' she said. 'He's not here.'

As soon as she opened the door the smell took me back to a decade before: solvents, glue, the marzipan of the Wood Workshop, the minerality of Metal; and then there was that drilling sound, which never did seem to have a source, but was always there. Just like Dessau, there were students and Masters in white coats. 'So this is where you've been hiding yourself.'

'In amongst the looms. Come on. Upstairs.'

In the Weaving Workshop there were women working the machines, feet pumping the pedals. I recognised none of them. They were students, and to them Dessau – let alone Weimar – was nothing but long-gone history.

As we came in, other women filed out. 'Hi, Lotti.'

'Do you want lunch?' another asked.

Charlotte said no: she was hosting a private exhibition. 'Lotti?' I said.

'It's their pet name. They won't stop, though I've told them I don't like it.'

There were balls of wool on the tables, and five or six looms. I knew these were the cheaper versions. Probably the Director had struggled to acquire even these. 'Is Anni around?'

'I think she's teaching.'

Just then Otti Berger, dressed in all black, appeared in the doorway. She hardly blinked; it was as if I'd seen her days ago rather than years. 'Paul Beckermann. I wondered when you'd grace us with your presence.'

'I heard you were still lurking around,' I said.

She looked the same. Like Charlotte, she was dressed in trousers and a shirt. I kissed her on the cheek. Her hair was streaked with grey but her eyes were lively and mocking. 'I've got my own studio. But occasionally I learn something new at the Bauhaus. Or they learn something from me.'

Otti pulled me over to her loom. She talked about her new work using the language of photography – lights, shades, exposures. One might have thought it was typical Otti, inflating her understanding of the world, but it was also clever: dress the feminine form in masculine language, and people started to listen.

'And what are your plans for the great exodus?' she said, as if all talk always returned to this. She rolled another cigarette, forgetting about the one she had tucked behind her ear.

'We're staying,' I said, the words coming out unevenly. I took the cigarette from her ear to show her. 'At least for now.'

Otti smoked the new one instead. I pocketed the old one, and she showed me all her teeth. 'Good for you. I'm off to England.'

'With who?' said Charlotte, surprise in her voice.

'Myself. I'm saving up. The hard of hearing are all the rage in England. Lilly's put me in touch with a Weavers' Guild in Norwich. I'll be like an exiled Walloon.'

Perhaps the thing about Otti was that she did actually know an awful lot. I had no idea who the Walloons were, but maybe they had been Master Weavers in Norwich.

Otti said she had to go – she had a meeting with the Director and couldn't be late. 'He's annoyed because I've got the patents on my fabrics. *Nota bene*, Charlotte dearest. Irritate the Director and you know you've done something right.'

Otti squeezed my hand, and we arranged to meet at Aschinger's the following week. All this planning was good for us. It showed Charlotte our rootedness. The ballet with Kaspar. Ice-skating this Sunday. Aschinger's the week after. It was our life that was here. Our life.

When Otti left, Charlotte rolled her eyes. 'You just can't stop flirting with each other, can you?'

'What do you mean?'

'Otti may be hard of hearing, but I'm not.'

'Why is it you think everyone's suddenly in love with me?'

'Do you want to see what I've brought you here for? It wasn't just to have Otti Berger blowing smoke in our mugs.'

Charlotte opened a big metal cabinet. Inside, there were hessian sacks pegged to the hangers. On the rough cloth of the first she had stitched her name in yellow thread: *Charlotte F.* 'Here it is,' she said. She was watching my face for a reaction, then she unsacked the weave and laid it on the desk. 'Here it is.'

Charlotte's weave streamed with colour: cadmium, yolk, mustard, but there were reds, too, pinks and oranges. The shapes were cut as if with a razor; in its geometry it was not unlike her Dessau work, but this weave was only heat:

349

roads and roads of sunshine. 'Oh, Charlotte,' I said, 'it's beautiful.' Itten's promise had been fulfilled: Charlotte had finally seen her Jerusalem of colour.

# 50

## Berlin

Later, as I neared Steglitz station, I heard my name called. It was a man's voice and my heart dropped. I quickened my step. Inside the station I heard a train pulling in. I raced to the platform and stepped into the carriage as the door closed. An echo of my name from the concourse: 'Paul! Wait!'

The Bavarian accent had been unmistakable.

At Kreuzberg, Jenö was nowhere to be seen. But no sooner was I home than the internal telephone trilled. 'You have a visitor,' said Mr Schmidt. The porter's tone was warm, even excited, as if he hadn't realised I'd kept friends as handsome as Jenö Fiedler.

I thought about telling the porter I was busy, but I also didn't want our resident snoop to think there was any funny business. I told him to invite Jenö up.

I looked around the apartment. I had a premonition that as soon as Jenö left, the apartment would be irreversibly changed; that I was seeing it in its innocence for the last time. It was one thing to dismiss Walter's words; it was another to hear them from Jenö.

*Knock, knock.*

In the doorway Jenö's eyes were silky and the tendons in his neck stood out. 'Paul.' He looked into the apartment, though he must have known Charlotte was at the Bauhaus.

Cornered, I told him to come in.

He asked for a glass of water. I asked him if he wanted something stronger and when he said yes I realised he was as nervous as I was. I poured myself a schnapps and drank all of it.

In the living room Jenö took his drink but didn't have any. I thought he'd start with other business, or some other cooked-up politeness as to why he'd followed me, but he didn't. 'Walter says you're immovable. He says you won't do it.'

'That's right. I won't.'

Jenö looked away but didn't say anything else.

'You're panicking,' I said, sounding calmer than I felt. 'It's understandable. It's all deeply unpleasant. But soon there'll be a new election, and a new chancellor. And a month after that, there'll be more elections, and another chancellor. Money will go crazy. People will lose their jobs. Then things will go back to normal. Remember Weimar: these things even out.'

Jenö cleared his throat. 'It's different this time.'

'How do you know that?'

'It will get worse.'

'We'll go then. You'll understand why I'd rather she go with me later than with you now.'

'Nothing will happen. I promise. It will only be until you get to London.'

I forced myself to meet his eye. 'It's up to her.'

'She's scared,' he said. 'You have to persuade her to go.'

I didn't want to hear Walter's words that so tormented me at night. 'She can make up her own mind. She said she doesn't want to go.'

'She's a foreigner,' he said. 'A woman who dresses as a man! Even at the Bauhaus, she's avant-garde. Don't you see what that makes her, to them? *Persona non grata*. A foreign agitator. An enemy of the state. No better than a Kozi. She's in danger.'

Outside, rain began. We turned to watch it.

He finished his drink.

'For God's sake,' he said, 'I swear nothing will happen. And if I had all the money in the world there'd be a seat on that flight for you too. But I don't. We'll fly to London. I have a job with Uncle König. You can join us as soon as you can afford it.'

'When I saw you at the Christmas party I never expected this to be your approach,' I said, though I knew it sounded petty. 'I thought it would be more direct.'

'What approach?' he said. His hands were on his lap. I wished he'd use them. I wished he'd hit me instead of this mild, dragging diplomacy. 'This isn't a strategy; this isn't an approach. Don't you see? Everything has changed. Since Hitler, nothing can be the same.'

I went to the window. I wanted shot of him: his galling innocence, his earnest goodness. As if we were eighteen again in a Weimar attic, I thought how much I'd like to

do Jenö some violence. 'You'll live together? In London?'
There was bitterness in my voice now. 'Is that how it will
be? A cosy flat near Buckingham Palace?'

'Only by necessity, Paul!'

'Don't you see why I can't do that?' I said to the glass.
'How can you be so blind? How can you force me to make
this choice?'

'I am not the one who is blind! Why do you have such
wilful disregard for her safety?'

I turned to face him. 'Because it is our life! Because it
is the only thing I have ever wanted! Because I have never
wanted anything as much as I have wanted this, and I will
not give it up! Not for anything, Jenö, not for anything!'

Then there was silence between us. Jenö looked around
the room. He picked up the Klee book, and looked at the
bookmarked painting. 'You've seen her new work?'

'Yes.'

'Magnificent, isn't it?' he said, his voice a little resigned.
'All that yellow.'

'I thought so too.'

He returned the book to the table. 'Walter says Mr
Steiner has his sights on the Bauhaus, Paul.'

I knew, then, that he would soon go, but I also knew
that with these new words I'd be caught forever. A sickness in my stomach. A feeling of the uncanny; that from
this moment on I was trapped. 'What does that mean?'

'That's all Walter said: that Steiner has his sights on the
Bauhaus. It can't be positive, I know that much.' When
he spoke again it was as if from a distance. 'Promise you'll
at least try.'

'Why do you think Walter wants to help?'

'He just wants us to be safe.'

'You don't detect anything more underhand?'

'He's not a monster, Paul. Whatever he might have done to her in the past.'

When neither of us spoke again he made his excuses.

'I leave this Monday,' he said, by the door.

'I know,' I said. 'I know.'

And then, he embraced me. The gesture was as inexplicable as when he had done so at the mausoleum. I heard his steps go down the staircase. I wondered what I meant to him. I wondered what he meant to me. Only later did I realise Jenö was saying goodbye forever.

# 51

## Berlin

For Montaigne, there's a difference between lying and telling an untruth. We can tell an untruth without knowing it is untrue. But lying is dissembling: it's going against one's conscience. I do not know whether I told untruths or lies. Certainly, I was able to pretend I did not know what I knew. Disavowal. *Verleugnung.* It's what the people of Weimar did with Buchenwald.

*We didn't know; we did know.*

And so here is my guilt: here is my secret. Here is the reason I cannot paint my eyes – and it is not just because of my failure to do anything after the conversation with Walter or with Jenö. It is because of what I saw behind the Japanese screen. What I saw on Ernst's desk. Since Dessau I had been able to decode Walter's Lotti-line, and the title on that piece of paper was STEGLITZ.

Jenö was right. If I wanted proof, then here it was in abundance: Ernst Steiner had the blueprints for the school's warehouse.

Ever since that day I have buried this knowledge

within me. I told myself I didn't know what I had really seen. I told myself the letters were blurred; then I told myself I couldn't be sure, and then, in some magicking of consciousness, I told myself they were the Reichstag blueprints, which, with the fire, made sense. But just because something is logical doesn't mean it's true. Some part of me has always known what I've known: I just haven't been able to admit it. I should have known the raid was coming. I should have warned her. I should have got her out.

Jenö's words rotted away at nearly everything in the week before he went. I couldn't concentrate. I couldn't paint. I couldn't walk the city. I tried to read Charlotte's penny novels but the romances were too much for my own *Herz-schmerz*. Instead I nursed hangovers from the sofa. In the afternoons I drank even more, and Charlotte gave me uneasy looks. We didn't talk, we didn't make love; in the nights – which the booze at first made easier and then more wretched – we hardly touched.

I longed for one of my migraines. Then I could pass this week in illness, and by a court of law I'd be judged incapable of moral reasoning. The opportunity to act would be cancelled. I'd be let off the hook.

No migraine came; the days were left to me. I wanted to talk it out with Irmi, but she wanted nothing to do with all this mess. I remembered the image of the flood breaking though the pavement that I'd seen from her apartment.

A migraine or apocalypse; those were my last hopes.

I was so turned inward I hardly noticed what Charlotte

did. I guess she spent her days at the Bauhaus. I knew
Jenö would be there: saying the same words to her that
he'd said to me. Each evening I tried to spit out three
simple words. *Go with him. Go with Jenö.* But when I
saw her standing in the doorway, shaking the snow off her
coat, putting away her man's hat, I knew I could not live
without her here. I said nothing.

On Friday a letter from Walter arrived. She held the
envelope in the light of the window, but I couldn't really
see her face. Maybe she was close to giving up. That night
I became convinced she'd soon be gone. London would be
her new home; and in a foreign land where she knew no
one, Jenö would be her only friend.

The next day Walter's letter was gone. In the morning,
Charlotte left for a few hours. I had no idea where she
went, or what she went to do. I checked her bag for the
airline ticket. Still nothing.

On Sunday we waited for Kaspar and Irmi at the ice rink.
By now I was convinced that this was the end. That she'd
tell me, as we skated, in her wine-red jacket against the
ice, that it was time for her to go.

Charlotte stared at the skaters with spacey horror.
Under her eyes the skin was dark and sallow. 'It's getting
bad.' She gestured to the muffled people skating fast
upon the ice. 'Klee's gone to Switzerland. The Direct-
or, Kandinsky, the Alberses; all everyone talks about is
where they'll end up. Someone asked me where I was
going and I didn't know what to say!' She smiled tightly.

'I just said Kreuzberg. What a thing. What will Kreuzberg do for us?'

*Scrape, scrape,* the boots slashing the ice; people wheeling round and round; and the light – from the ice, the snow, the clouds – made it appear like that ceramic menagerie, animated at last.

A woman leapt; turned. Another fell. Kids flew past.

'It's your decision.'

'It's ours,' she said. 'A few months. Then you'd follow.'

'What about this being part of Walter's strategy?'

'Jenö said he can be trusted.'

Jenö's words ball in my mind; rip, are gone.

'Go with him, then. Go. Please.' I pushed her away. I couldn't stand to be near her any more. 'It's your choice. Please don't pretend it is mine.'

Tears fell rapidly. People watched us. They were watching this man crying, they had seen how I had held this man's hand. There were even boys daring to laugh.

'I'm scared! I don't know what to do!'

'Give me six months,' I said, talking fast, knowing if I slowed down my guilt would show itself in all its ugliness. 'I promise. Six months and we'll be gone from here together.'

'Hallo!' a voice blasted from the crowd. I had never been happier to see Kaspar. He studied us both. 'Why all the glum faces?' he said, then sotto voce: 'Is Adolf himself doing the rounds?'

She gave him a smile but it changed quickly to another sob.

Kaspar took her in his arms. 'Charlotte, Charlotte.

Please, don't worry. Are we on Jenö's suggestion again?'
Very softly he said, 'It's nothing. It's nothing. What did I
tell you at the theatre? We'll be fine, I promise.'

Charlotte shook her head, as if to let the air in.

*'In the sea hast thou lived in solitude, and it hath borne
thee up. Alas, wilt thou now go ashore?'*

Charlotte pulled away. *'Zarathustra?'*

'What else?'

She took a deep breath. 'I don't know what that's got to
do with anything.'

'Well, neither do I,' said Kaspar, grinning.

The world would turn; Kaspar would quote Nietzsche;
Charlotte would stay. As the old song went, as long as
there were linden trees, Berlin would be Berlin.

I was surprised to see Irmi heading toward us, her boots
slung around her neck. 'I thought you weren't coming.'

'I was persuaded,' she replied. 'The last hurrah, and all
that.'

I wanted to tell Irmi everything: what had happened
with Jenö, with Walter, with me and Charlotte. But she
didn't want to know; she had made that clear. And if she
did, she could ask Kaspar. And so I kept quiet. I had learnt
at least one thing.

After skating we walked past the Kaiserhof as the flag
snapped on the Chancellery behind us. Irmi ducked
down, not wanting to be seen by her boss, and Kaspar hid
her in his overcoat, so that he looked like a bloated camel,
especially with his winter tan. I scanned the bar to see if

Ernst was in there. He wasn't; neither was Mrs Steiner; and neither, of course, was Walter. Uniformed men were starting early with cocktails and smart parted hair.

'You wouldn't even be able to afford a glass of water,' said Irmi. 'Come on.'

We walked down Unter den Linden. Only weeks ago men had marched here with torches. Now, Kaspar and Charlotte were horsing about. Irmi kept on dragging them along, asking them to hurry; she wanted to see Teddy. We let her go on without us, and before Kaspar was to be re-united with Dacia (I was surprised she'd lasted so long) the three of us stopped for fried potatoes with bacon at Friedrichstrasse, and the waiter had the good grace not to shame us for only ordering two plates between three.

With my mouth full of bacon and potatoes, I heard the trains' shrieks below. They reminded me of Charlotte's screams as she and Kaspar had fallen on top of each other at the ice rink and Irmi – who was a strong enough skater but no match for them both – had tried to disentangle them but fallen over herself. As I too had fallen helplessly into the pile of bodies, I had thought, with the clarity that comes in these moments: here they are! My Berlin friends!

'Serious Painter,' says Charlotte to me. 'What are you thinking?'

'Nothing,' I say, 'nothing.'

I skewer more potato. Charlotte scoots closer. Jenö's words turn to dust. The bacon is good: so salty and hot. Charlotte laughs at one of Kaspar's dumb jokes. And, despite everything, I think how happy I am.

# 52
## Berlin

A month later, Jenö's warnings came true. Steiner did have his sights on the Bauhaus, and the school was violently raided. For the third time in the Director's career the school's looms were wrecked, its canvases ruined, and its windows smashed. The contents of drawers and files – a decade's worth of the Director's notes, all the way back to the Citizens' Survey and the Metal Ball – scattered by Storm Troopers. Rain came in at the windows and drenched the papers.

Our history, our secrets; all gone.

I imagine Charlotte on the morning of the April raid, an apron over her suit. She is working at the loom. Her expression is calm, the colours she'd finally found streaming from her; a new life ablaze. Otti is near; that's important, I want her close to hand, so that she might give Charlotte some comfort when they are both taken away. Anni and Josef are teaching in the other workshops; Franz is studying his strident type. Maybe it is only the Director who watches the uniformed men approach: he's the only one looking outward.

I wonder if their eyes met: Ernst and Charlotte, as he went his way around the Bauhaus workshop, pulling out the Jews, the foreigners, the Communists; just as he had done once before in words. I imagine she was looking instead at Jenö's desk, empty since February. She must have thought of the disappeared promise of London.

Steglitz. I had seen the word on the blueprint. I had.

# 53
## England

On Wednesday, as promised, I find Jenö outside my house. His hair is silver and his heft has gone. My gaze goes straight to his hands; I wonder if they're still made for brawling. A lift of anger that he's here, then I remember we are comrades again; we are both her widowers.

'Paul,' he says, 'I hope it's not a bad time.'

Odd that we are speaking English. I suppose our ruse is important; even to each other. That he should be here in person stupefies me. Charlotte's case is against the wall. Its blackness absorbs the afternoon's light. I wonder what's inside. I think of Jenö's green-chalked portrait revealed once more. I wonder how much of the past I will be able to rethink.

'Jenö,' I say. 'Hello.'

Inside, I take him up to my studio. Jenö looks around, appraising. He puts the case on the floor. He wraps his army coat around him, rocks the chair with his weight. I wonder if he fought for the British. I'll have to ask Irmi.

The case is a black heart between us.

'Where have you been, Jenö? I looked for you when I first arrived. Mr König, the uncle' – I cannot say Walter's name in the undefended air between us – 'he said he hadn't heard from you either.'

'I was in Newcastle for a while.' With a little devotion he touches the bulb on the lamp. 'Then I came back to London.'

Jenö Fiedler, loquacious as always.

I wonder whether he has seen Charlotte's damaged yellow weave above my desk. Instead he finds a photograph from Dessau: we are on the balcony, very happy. Charlotte is trying to smile but the light makes her frown. Franz – the typographer of the gates she will walk through – is there, as is Walter. Jenö's not in the picture; perhaps he was the one taking it.

I look out of the window. Jenö too looks elsewhere. Two men in an enclosed space, our suspicions a third in the room. Everything we cannot talk about is here.

I want to say how much I miss her.

I want to say sorry.

I want to say how I should have insisted she left with him. But he knows I did not, and nothing can change. 'You went to the funeral.'

'Irmi made a nice speech.'

'How is she?'

'The same. Very funny.'

'And Teddy?'

'Good, good. He's a chef now. He didn't think much of Dacia's vol-au-vents.'

'She never was a very good cook. She passed off a lot of

things as old Russian recipes, but I think they were just bad.'

He smiles. 'We buried Walter under a linden tree.'

'Ah. Yes. Young Werther at last.'

'You couldn't make it?' he says. 'Irmi said you were busy with an exhibition.'

'I wasn't busy. I just didn't want to be there.'

Something new passes over his expression, something I can't read.

'What's Berlin like?' I ask.

'The border crossings are distinctly unpleasant. Did you know they call the crossing at Friedrichstrasse the Palace of Tears?'

'I didn't know that.'

Friedrichstrasse. *Friedrichstrasse.*

I ask Jenö if he wants some tea. I wonder whether he'll say something about us turning English, but he doesn't. When I return he's on his haunches, looking at the self-portrait I thought I'd hidden: the axed man, the eyes a-swim. 'That's nothing,' I say too quickly, putting down the tray.

'You shouldn't be so hard on yourself.'

Now I see what it is that bothered me about my gaze: what I am hiding from isn't cowardice, it's shame. 'You warned me. You said Steiner had his sights on the Bauhaus. I ignored you.'

Jenö rises. His knees click. 'It's not your fault.' His tone is neutral, though it's not quite an acquittal. 'Do you know the painting *Not to Be Reproduced*? The Magritte?'

It is a man staring into a mirror, but the reflection shows only the back of his head. 'Yes.'

'Sometimes I think that's how I should paint myself,' he says, 'since I can't see much further either. I tried one of these too. Mine also didn't work.'

We drink our tea as Jenö makes respectful noises about some of my more familiar pieces; the tart bright blocks of colour. 'You've become famous, Paul.'

'Well; hardly.'

'Come on. You've done very well. Irmi said you're rich enough to pay her back. She said to tell you that: "A message for Paul."'

Now it's my turn to smile. 'I've sent her cheques. She's never cashed them.'

Jenö gives me a questioning look.

'Irmi paid for my train ticket to Amsterdam.'

I assumed he would have known the story of my exile. But there's no reason he would know any more of me than I knew of him. 'What happened?' he asks. 'To you?'

'I was taken in by the Gestapo after the raid. Twice. Irmi persuaded me that the third time they wouldn't just question me. I left in '34.'

'A year after me.'

I cannot help my voice cracking: 'How could I? How could I have just left her?'

'You forget. I also left. I too saved myself.'

Neither of us knows what to do. We've never had much natural affinity, and now we are uneasy as crows. We know we have to have the conversation about Charlotte, about how she ended up in the camp, but it feels as abject as it is guessable, and I wonder if either of us will be able to do this. Who can steer the other? Who can be the stronger?

But not to speak would dishonour her, to disavow – again – what happened to her.

This does not mean I know where to begin.

Jenö finally looks at the yellow weave. 'What happened to her after the raid?'

'She was tried. You know that?'

'Yes.'

'She was found guilty. An "enemy of the state". Then they sent her to Plötzensee for four years.'

Jenö nods.

'When she got out, Kaspar and Irmi tried to get her to Amsterdam. But she said she wanted to go home.'

'She always hated Prague.'

'I don't understand that part either.' I smile.

'Did you hear from her again?'

I shake my head. 'She was angry at me. Angry I'd gone. Angry I'd persuaded her not to go in the first place. Did you?'

'Hear from her? No. No, I didn't.'

'Neither did Irmi or Kaspar. I think she wanted to leave her Berlin life far behind.'

'And after that?'

'Arrested in Prague. Brought to Buchenwald on a female transport.'

'I wondered if you knew anything I didn't.'

'That's it.'

'Is there any work?' he asks. 'From Prague?'

'If there is, it's all behind the Curtain. I can't remember where the Bauhaus stands, with them.'

The case is waiting. The air is tight.

'Franz said there's some of her work inside, that it's from the camp.'

'Yes. Do you want me to open it?'

Perhaps he'll go without forcing me to see inside.

'I haven't been able to do it on my own. Pathetic, isn't it?'

'No, not really; I've been rather dreading this too.'

I put the case on the table between us. I look at him, he nods, and I click the hinges. There are papers inside, yellow with age. I put them on the floorboards: there's a river in charcoal, maybe the Ilm. There are the Dessau balconies. An unknown parkland. A beach and cliffs; possibly Rügen. The last picture is of our Buchenwald, I am sure: line upon line of beech, almost completely abstracted.

All landscapes. A genre Charlotte had never been interested in. The world as last balm, I suppose. There aren't any of him. There aren't any of me. I look at Jenö, and despite ourselves, we both smile.

'They're beautiful,' he says.

'Aren't they? I didn't expect this.'

'Neither did I.'

We sit quietly as we look at them, spread out around us.

'How did Walter get them?'

Jenö looks at me, his eyes frank. 'Walter gave her the paper.'

I sense what is coming. That's why Jenö gave me that look before. 'What do you mean?'

'Walter tried to free her. He did what he could with Steiner, then with the guards. But no money or favours could spring her. All Franz and Walter could manage were food parcels. Clothes. Paper. Pencils. Small things.'

And now I see the paper for what it is: it is Walter's last gift. 'Why did he not tell me?'

'Did you ask him?'

'He sent me letters. I didn't respond. I blamed him for not getting her out.'

'Don't worry,' Jenö says. 'So did I. Franz told me at the funeral. No one knew.'

'And me,' I say, 'did you blame me?'

'Yes. But then I blamed everyone I could. Myself, the most. I just left, came to England, got on with life.' He blinks at me; his voice astonished. 'I just saved myself.'

Jenö does not stay much longer. We talk of the others: what happened to the Director, the Alberses, Franz, who has become a town planner, funnily enough, in Dresden. I ask him if I might keep one of Charlotte's drawings, and he leaves me the one I ask for.

I wonder if he'll give me one of those unexpected hugs as he says goodbye, but he doesn't. As he gets in his taxi, I wonder if I'll ever see him again. Probably not.

Not knowing what else to do, I go to the cliffs. There aren't too many people around; the children have gone; the families are in their cottages. The tide is out, and I must walk some way down to the thin surf. My eyes: they sting. The world is blurred. I have been blind.

I always thought that Charlotte would be finally elaborated; that I would then be able to say I understood her. I don't know if I ever did. But I put that to one side, now. I realise now my story has always been about Walter rather than Charlotte. It has been the quality of Walter's morality that has obsessed me; he has troubled me more than spectral Charlotte ever has, who has only ever occupied the high arcs of lit memory. Morally, Walter was the problem. Morally, now, so am I.

The beach empties until there's no one left but me.

What will I do with Walter's letters? Burn them? Keep them? I wish I had replied to them. I could have asked him about Charlotte and the camp, then he might have offered a defence. He was never a monster. I should not have thought that.

I walk home. Jenö has been; the house has survived, and so have I.

In the studio I take Charlotte's drawing and switch on the lamp. It is the picture of the beech trees. Though it's nothing more than charcoal lines, it transports me quite completely: back to the forest's scent, with the sunshine lavish, and the sky generous, and I see my friends on our bikes between the zipping beech and the fat bars of light – Kaspar and Irmi, Jenö and Walter, me and Charlotte – shouting out to each other, and laughing, and wondering how we might best reach transcendence. And now, as if for the first time, I am at last listening; to the trees, the trees, the trees!

Thank you:

As always, to my friend and agent Cathryn Summerhayes at Curtis Brown. My superb editors Kris Doyle and Francesca Main and the whole team at Picador; but especially Paul Baggaley, Gillian Fitzgerald-Kelly and Alice Dewing. Melissa Pimentel, Luke Speed, and Irene Magrelli at Curtis Brown. Katharina Hierling and Claudia Feldmann at Hoffmann und Campe. Thank you to 'Madame Bauhaus', Magdalena Droste. Thank you to the staff at the Weimar, Dessau and Berlin Bauhaus libraries and archives, who never failed to help this Bauhaus baby. Thank you to Claudia Ballard, from WME, who encouraged me with this idea in the beginning.

Thank you to my parents, Pamela and Michael, and my sister, Katherine. To Ed and the Harknesses: Philippa and William; Fran and Henry, Gabi and Letitia. To Hannah Nixon, Alaina Wong, Eve Williams, Nicola Richmond, Nicky Blewett, Tori Flower, Jonathan

Calascione, Bridget Dalton, Eleni Lawrence, Sarah Hall, Toby Oddy, Jack Underwood, Masha Mileeva, and Mel and Ali Claxton. Thanks especially to Jonathan Beckman, Fraser McKay and Ben Pester who gave me their shrewd comments on early manuscripts.

Thank you to the *Literary Encyclopaedia* which funded a research trip to Germany; to Goldsmiths College, University of London, for a term of leave to write the first draft; and to all of my colleagues at the University of East Anglia, but specifically Andrew Cowan, who gave me invaluable edits.

The Bauhaus, which celebrates its hundredth birthday in 2019, was an art school of immeasurable productivity, creativity, and joy. Even with its final closure by the Nazis it lived on: in Chicago; in North Carolina's Black Mountain College; in Tel Aviv. Twenty-first century Bauhäuslers will know there were actually three different 'Directors' in Weimar, Dessau and Berlin: Walter Gropius, Hannes Meyer and Mies van der Rohe. For narrative purposes, I have combined their role into one. Paul's speech to his class on p177 is in part adapted from Werner David Feist's memoir '*My Years at the Bauhaus*' (*Meine Jahre am Bauhaus*) (Bauhaus-Archiv, Berlin, 2012).

To find out more about the real-life inspiration for this novel, go to my website at www.naomiwood.com to find photographs of this period and the extraordinary people – Johannes Itten, Paul Klee, Wassily Kandinsky, Anni and Josef Albers, Franz Ehrlich, and Otti Berger – who populate these pages.

Everyone else is a work of my imagination.